Dear Mystery Lover,

St. Martin's DEAD LETTER continues to bring fresh new ideas to the mystery scene. Since its creation, the DEAD LETTER line has definitely "pushed the envelope" of great titles available to mystery lovers everywhere. We're pleased with the warm reception we've received from all of you, and we hope you'll continue to enjoy our eclectic list of today's best puzzlers.

Susan Holtzer won the Malice Domestic Contest for Best First Mystery of 1994 with *Something to Kill For*. This wonderful mystery, set in the garage sale circuit of Ann Arbor, Michigan, does for antiquing what John Dunning did for book collecting. Up Pauline Boulevard and in the narrow lots on Ann Arbor's Old West Side, our antique-collecting heroine and her friend discover a Preiss statue, eight Dansk flatware place settings, and the corpse of an antique dealer. If you love regional amateur sleuths in unique settings, *Something to Kill For* is definitely worth collecting. And look for Susan Holtzer's next Anneke Haagen mystery, coming from St. Martin's hardcover in October 1995.

Keep your eye out for DEAD LETTER—and build yourself a library of paperback mysteries to die for.

Yours in crime,

Shawn Coyne
Editor
St. Martin's DEAD LETTER Paperback Mysteries

Reviewers Love *Something to Kill For*:

"The interplay among characters involved in the antique trade is tight and convincingly complex, and it takes an off-beat thought and chase to come up with the murderer and the motive. An excellent first effort and a refreshingly alternate setting."

—*Murder ad lib*

"A lot of fun for readers who enjoy bright characters, fast-moving action and a really good plot."

—*Ocala Star-Banner*

"Populated with people who rise above cliche, a protagonist to be admired and a plot that baffles."

—*Deadly Pleasures*

"Characterization is strong. The author has a knowing touch with Anneke's romance, a tight handle on the computer lore, and an unassuming, good-humored style well-suited to her exploration of a familiar facet of Americana."

—*Kirkus Reviews*

"A focused plot, abundant humor, and intriguing personality...Holtzer's hilarious portrayal of the garage sale scroungers is another definite strength. And Anneke herself is a promising mystery protagonist."

—*Murder & Mayhem*

SOMETHING TO KILL FOR

SUSAN HOLTZER

SMP

ST. MARTIN'S PAPERBACKS

SOMETHING TO KILL FOR

Copyright © 1994 by Susan Holtzer.
Excerpt from *Curly Smoke* copyright © 1995 by Susan Holtzer.

Library of Congress Catalog Card Number: 94-416

ISBN: 0-312-95589-8

Printed in the United States of America

St. Martin's Press hardcover edition/May 1994
St. Martin's Paperbacks edition/September 1995

10 9 8 7 6 5 4 3 2 1

To my mother, who introduced me to mysteries in the first place; and to Judy, because if she hadn't liked it, she'd have said so.

Ann Arbor is, of course, a real (some might say surreal) city, where even the most ordinary events are often conducted with high-octane intensity. However, the characters and events portrayed in these pages are entirely fictional, the product of my own overwrought imagination, and any resemblance to living persons is pure coincidence. (Zingerman's, however, is absolutely and marvelously a real place.)

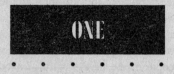

ONE

7:20 A.M.

"Anneke, would you grab those dolls?" Joyce McCarthy yanked a carton from under the rickety table and began sweeping brilliantly colored dishes into it, apparently heedless of their fragility.

"Which dolls?" Anneke Haagen peered into the gloom of the dirty garage.

"Over there." Joyce jerked her head in the general direction of a pile of rusty garden tools. She finished piling dishes into her carton, stretched to pluck a glass vase from the far end of the table, and hurried to the other side of the garage.

Although "garage" was really too polite a word for the crumbling structure, Anneke thought glumly. Doorless, barebeamed, cobweb-hung, it crouched at the back of a long, narrow lot on Ann Arbor's Old West Side. A single dirt-encrusted bulb hanging from a frayed cord provided less illumination than the gaping hole in the roof.

And it was crammed full—full of rusty kitchenware and

mismatched glasses and lamps and garden tools and books and pictures and cartons. Cartons everywhere, against the walls, on top of and underneath the three wobbly folding tables. Newspapers everywhere, littering the floor, jammed into the cartons, flapping around her ankles.

It was, in a word, filthy. Well, garage sales weren't for the fastidious. Anneke plunged forward through the chaos.

The dolls were heaped in a pink plastic laundry basket, half a dozen worn and bedraggled specimens in rags of clothing. Anneke elbowed aside a pair of chattering housewives—the only other people in the garage at this ungodly hour—and scooped up the whole batch of dolls, basket and all. Backing over a pile of baby clothes, she sidestepped a dented tricycle, just missed knocking over a pitted brass floor lamp, and emerged gasping into pale morning daylight just as Joyce shuffled her carton onto the packed-earth driveway.

Anneke dropped the basket of dolls, which landed on her foot with an impact that made her wince. Suddenly, the whole enterprise seemed so ridiculous that she began to giggle. Joyce looked at her and smiled briefly, her face cheerful but intent and somehow businesslike, and Anneke recalled that for her friend, this was not a recreational outing but the most important part of her antique business. It might be a hell of a way to make a living, but it *was* the way Joyce made her living.

"I'm going to take these things." Joyce shoved her carton and Anneke's basket of dolls under a folding card table and spoke to the woman standing next to it. "But I want to look around some more, okay?"

"Sure." The woman seemed delighted. She was young—hardly more than a girl, Anneke thought—and obviously pregnant, her "Save the Whales" T-shirt stretching over the small swelling of her stomach. "I'll keep them here for you." Joyce nodded and hurried back into the garage, motioning Anneke to follow.

If there are any antique doughnuts in there, I'll take one,

Anneke thought fretfully, her stomach growling in protest at being deprived of breakfast. Kicking aside a cardboard box, she noted the scars on her elegant suede walking shoes. Dirt plastered the legs of her Claiborne jeans and there were smears of what looked like grease on one sleeve of her Vittadini sweater. Joyce had warned her to dress casually, but she hadn't told her to dress for plowing the north forty.

Although she couldn't, in all conscience, blame Joyce, however much she wanted to; this had been her own idea, after all. After a solid month of fourteen-hour days hunched over her computer terminal, Anneke had been desperate for a break, for some activity altogether different. She'd been at the antique shop updating their accounting program as Joyce was preparing for a day on the garage-sale circuit, and she'd asked—yes, *asked*—to participate in this madness.

Which was why she now stood in this filthy garage at seven-thirty on a Saturday morning, cold, sleepy, hungry, and dirty. Especially dirty. She kicked the carton again in disgust and heard a faint click.

Probably a tasteful collection of old curtain rods, she grumbled to herself, stirring the mass of yellowed newsprint with her toe. She poked a finger gingerly into the carton and saw a glint of white, a small pink globe, a pair of upraised bronze arms . . .

She dropped to her knees, forgetting the dirt and almost forgetting to breathe. No, not possible. Ridiculous. Torn between haste and caution, she pulled away chunks of decaying newspaper; finally, reverently, she lifted the small statue from the carton, brushing away the last clinging bits of paper and staring in awe.

She looked around quickly; no one was watching her. Pushing back a small bubble of hysteria, she rose to her feet, not even brushing the dirt off her knees because to do so would mean removing one hand from the precious artifact. Casual, now. Just act normal. Above all, do not look excited.

"I think I'll take this," she told the woman at the card table, her voice cracking slightly. "How much is it?"

"Oh . . ." The woman hesitated, and Anneke's heart sank. "Three dollars?"

"F-fine." Anneke scrabbled in her purse for her wallet and extracted the bills one-handed, unwilling to relinquish the statue even for a moment. She had a moment of panic—surely the woman would see her hand shaking as she passed over the money!

"I'm done too." Joyce shoved another loaded box forward. "Can you work out prices on these things?"

"God, I don't know." The woman shoved aside long pale hair and peered into the cartons. "How about a dollar apiece for the dolls?"

"Fine," Joyce agreed. "What about the dishes?"

"There's a lot of them." The woman looked at the box dubiously. "Twenty dollars for the set?"

"Okay. And the quilts?"

The litany went on. Anneke was no expert on antiques, but even she was aware that Joyce was getting some breathtaking bargains. Not as good as this, though, she thought, hugging the statue to her.

"I guess that does it," Joyce said at last, peeling bills from her wallet.

"Are you moving?" Anneke asked curiously. Surely the woman was too young to have accumulated this garageful.

"Moving in," she answered. "This is all stuff that was in the house when we bought it. You wouldn't believe the mess; we've been practically shoveling out the basement. We can't even begin remodeling until we get rid of all this junk, so I figured we might as well have a garage sale before we ship the rest of it to the dump."

"Makes sense." Joyce smiled and picked up a floor lamp in one hand and a piecrust table in the other. "Anneke, would you get the dolls?"

"Sure." Reluctantly, Anneke laid her statue in the pink laundry basket, hoisted it carefully, and followed Joyce down the long driveway, hurrying to keep up. Only when they were safely out of sight behind the big blue van did Joyce's face explode in triumph.

"My God! Can you believe it? If I went home right now, I'd still be close to the best day I've ever had. Hell, if I didn't go to another sale all *month* I'd still be ahead. Anneke, one of those dolls may be a Jumeau!" Anneke had never heard of Jumeau and knew nothing about dolls, but she didn't get a chance to ask. Joyce dumped the lamp and the table unceremoniously at the curb. "Come on, let's go get the rest."

She raced back up the driveway; Anneke agonized over the statue, finally settled for placing it carefully on the front seat of the van and followed Joyce, casting an occasional anxious glance behind her. Between them, they wrestled the remaining cartons to the curb and set about loading.

"I didn't realize the antique trade involved so much physical labor," Anneke panted as she shoved a heavy carton into the van.

"You better believe it. That's one reason there aren't many fat antique dealers. Uh-oh, watch out."

Anneke jumped back as a Volvo station wagon bounced against the curb and a small, pale-haired woman tumbled out.

"Oh, damn." The woman made a face at Joyce. "I don't suppose you left anything for the rest of us."

"I certainly hope not." Joyce grinned. "Hi, Alice. This is Anneke Haagen, a friend of mine." Joyce made introductions. "This is Alice Cowan, one of my competitors."

"Hi." Alice smiled, but her eyes appraised Anneke closely and she smoothed the back of her gathered skirt. She was dressed in tones of dusty rose pink that did nothing for her pale complexion, and the skirt emphasized both the spread of her hips and the shortness of her legs. Why *didn't* women realize how much better they look in pants? Anneke wondered.

She herself was accustomed to that appraising look, especially from other women. She was aware that her appearance, even in its present untidy state, was far too elegant for the hypercasual Ann Arbor culture, but she was damned if she'd pig around town in baggy pants and no makeup just to satisfy other people. She was simply one of those women who looked either sloppy or elegant, no middle ground. She had made a conscious decision between the two when she'd reached forty, and refused to apologize for the result.

At least she wasn't trying to look younger than her age. Her hair, in its shaggy cut like a wayward chrysanthemum, was shot with silvery gray. There were fine lines around her eyes and elsewhere. But she'd been lucky in her ancestors, and her skin remained firm and clear over good bones.

"Are you a dealer?" Anneke asked.

"Not really. At least, not a real one. I just dabble." Alice seemed apologetic.

"You're helping out with the Show, though, aren't you?" Joyce asked.

"Yes, a little. Just pushing papers around." The other woman shrugged.

"The show?" Anneke asked.

"The Show." Joyce audibly capitalized the word. "The biggest event of the year for Ann Arbor dealers. Surely you've seen the signs around?"

"Now that you mention it, I have." Anneke recalled the brightly-colored posters sprouting in downtown store windows. "And I remember it from last year. Hell, more tourists." She made a face.

"Those tourists pay my rent for half the year." Joyce pointed out. "They really come ready to spend. Is it pretty well set?" she asked Alice.

"Oh, yes," Alice said dismissively. "I guess I'll take a look in here anyway." She moved away toward the garage.

"I'm glad we beat her here," Joyce said, stooping for another carton. "She's damn good. Oh, hi, Michael."

Anneke turned toward the newcomer and her eyes widened, as they always did when she saw Michael Rappaport. The man strolling toward the van was gorgeous, with thick dark hair and brilliant blue eyes and a wide, beautifully-shaped mouth and the kind of tall, well-muscled body that looked wonderful in clothes—or, probably, out of them, although Anneke had no direct personal knowledge of the fact. She did know that Michael was a highly successful dealer in Victoriana as well as the president of the Ann Arbor Antiques Association.

She felt a wholly uncharacteristic impulse to brush the dirt off her clothes, smooth her hair, straighten her body—the preening instinct, she thought mockingly.

"How do you do, ladies." He sketched a bow.

"Good morning, Michael. How's the computer operating?" Anneke had installed a Macintosh system for the association.

"Purring along, as far as I know. At least, the association is no more chaotic than usual. Is there anything in that squalor worth getting filthy for?"

"Not anymore, there isn't," Joyce answered gleefully. "Anyway, what are you doing here? You don't usually do the garage-sale circuit."

"There's an auction at eleven, so I thought I'd do a bit of slumming first." He smiled slightly, as if to suggest he might or might not be joking.

"Poor Michael. It's hard to be so fastidious in such a dirty business." Joyce looked down at her filthy hands and made an amused face.

"Yes, some of us *are* cursed with refinement." He rearranged the paisley scarf at his throat. "Not, unfortunately, a problem for today's auctioneer, however."

"Don't tell me—Auschlander."

"Got it in one. The word is he made a pass at the daughter, hoping to flatter her into giving him the consignment."

"You mean it *worked?*"

"Only too well. It seems she took him up on it. Made him put his gavel where his mouth was. So to speak." His look of wicked amusement was so irresistibly comic that Anneke laughed in spite of herself. Michael's eyes sparkled with pleasure.

"Ah, she laughs. Women always forgive anything to a man who is sufficiently entertaining. Only dullness is fatal."

"In which case," Anneke said drily, "a touch of Wilde-ness is therefore appropriate?"

"Wilde, perhaps, but never woolly," he retorted instantly, giving her a look of such accomplished lechery that she knew he understood the double edge to her weak pun. He pushed back an immaculate French-cuffed sleeve and Anneke saw the diamond glitter of a Rolex President, surely the most vulgar wristwatch ever designed. "Well, I must be off. Perhaps the next garage will at least have a floor."

Not until his sleek black minivan pulled away from the curb did Anneke and Joyce look at each other and burst into laughter.

"What a waste," Anneke sputtered.

"I know. All that gorgeous male splendor, so entirely self-absorbed that he's a parody of himself."

"At least if he were gay *someone* would be getting the benefit of it." With renewed laughter they stowed the last of their purchases and climbed into the van. Anneke cradled the statue in her lap.

"Still, he's right, you know. I do tend to forgive a man nearly anything if he's amusing enough."

"It does beat hell out of smoldering possessiveness, doesn't it?" Joyce glanced sidelong at her.

"Like Dennis, you mean. I know, I know. The trouble is, most women run into that type when they're younger; I'm still learning, that's all."

"Sorry, I didn't mean to rake up old messes." Joyce sounded only mildly apologetic. "We'll try the Allmendinger Park area

next." She changed the subject after consulting the five-by-seven index card taped to the dashboard. "On a day this full we'd better take them in clumps." She put the van in gear and roared away from the curb.

"How many sales are there?"

"I counted fifty-two total."

"Fifty-two!" Anneke was stunned.

"Ann Arbor in the spring. Everybody's either moving out or moving in. Don't worry, I won't try to do all of them. I'll drop you back home after twenty or so, okay? By then it'll be nearly ten o'clock and everything will've been picked clean anyway. Now," she said, eyeing the statue as she whipped the van into a right turn, "what've you got?"

"You mean you don't know?"

"I know it's Art Deco, bronze, and a pretty good piece. Is that real ivory?"

"Joyce, this is a Preiss!"

"Wow! Are you sure?" The van rocked as Joyce took the turn onto Main Street and roared south. "Of course you are; you've been collecting Art Deco for years. Is it signed?" She turned her head to peer at the statue, and the van wavered slightly.

"I never thought to look," Anneke confessed, gripping the dashboard. She turned over the statue and saw the inscription "F. Preiss" without surprise. "Yes, there's the signature." The van rocked again and she hastily rearranged her grip on the statue, but otherwise refrained from comment, believing firmly that passengers, like houseguests, had a responsibility to put up with their hosts' idiosyncracies, so long as they stopped short of life-threatening. Instead she leaned back and tried to enjoy the pastel morning, the trees feathery with pale green shoots, the sun warm through the windshield.

Ann Arbor always feels smaller than it is, Anneke thought. Too big, at 120,000 people, to be an archetypal "sleepy college town," it nevertheless had avoided the ravages of urbanization. The University of Michigan, its core and raison d'être, sprawled

throughout the city, University buildings scattered in odd pockets from downtown to the outer neighborhoods.

It's the sort of city where the kid who hands you your fries at the Burger King has an IQ of 140 (and may some day walk on the moon); the sort of place where you can use the phrase "cognitive dissonance" in casual conversation. A city with an ego. Anneke remembered with amusement a time a few years ago when the football coach of another university had accused Ann Arbor of "arrogance." Shortly thereafter, bumper stickers blossomed on cars throughout the city, stickers that read "Arrogance is bliss."

It might be a college town, but God knows there's nothing "sleepy" about it, Anneke thought; every activity in Ann Arbor seemed to be carried on at high-octane intensity, even including garage sales. She grabbed for the dashboard as Joyce's van leaped a pothole, and shifted her grip on the statue. She ran a finger lovingly along its ivory globe. Beautiful, but also valuable. At least two thousand dollars, possibly as much as four or five. Not that she had any intention of selling it, of course, but still . . .

"Do you ever feel guilty?" she asked Joyce.

"Guilty?"

"For . . . well, ripping people off."

"Is that what you think we just did?"

"Didn't we?"

"Did we lie to the woman? Did we steal anything? Didn't we pay her exactly what she asked? *She* set the prices, after all; we paid exactly what these things were worth to her."

"That feels like sophistry even if it's true. We were taking advantage of her ignorance."

"Sure we were. I don't feel any responsibility to go hurtling around town at seven A.M. on an educational mission. Besides, didn't you hear her? If you hadn't bought that statue, tomorrow it would be at the bottom of a landfill. It's not the sellers who're

the victims, it's all the wonderful things they're too stupid to appreciate. You saved that statue's life."

"I suppose you're right." Anneke considered the point. "Haven't you *ever* felt guilty?"

"No!" Joyce said explosively. "This is how I make my living. And believe me, nobody gets rich this way." She wrenched the van into a pinwheel right turn onto Pauline and gunned the accelerator. "There was once . . ."

"What?"

"Oh, hell. There was this elderly woman a couple of years ago. Poor, really dirt-poor, living in one of the public housing units. She had this batch of really pitiful stuff she was selling, and in the middle of all this junk there was a solid silver Georgian tankard. She wanted two dollars for it." The van swayed right onto Edgewood and left onto Keech.

"What did you do?"

"Gave her two hundred for it," Joyce said tightly. "And if you ever tell a living soul, I swear I'll never speak to you again as long as I live."

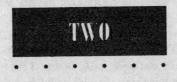

TWO

For Anneke, the next two hours were a blur of junk-filled garages punctuated by short but terrifying whips through increasingly busy traffic, as Joyce hurtled the van from sale to sale. Afterward she remembered it best as a series of vignettes linked to things she had bought or people she had spoken to.

There was the sale on Pauline Boulevard, for instance, where they'd run into Martha Penrose, a grandmotherly-looking woman with a round moon face and penetrating blue eyes under an aureole of fluffy white hair. Anneke knew her, from her work for the Antiques Association, as a retired education professor turned antique dealer, but she was chiefly memorable for her hands. They were the smallest Anneke had ever seen, and always, every single finger held a gold ring of some sort. Each of the rings was small and delicate, but on those tiny hands the total effect was preposterously flamboyant, like a Jeep encrusted with rhinestones. Today she clutched a stack of pale pink glass plates close to her substantial bosom. "Aren't they

lovely?" She beamed. "It's the Ballerina pattern—very rare in pink."

"How's it going?" Joyce asked.

"Not bad," Martha admitted. "Isn't this nice?" She held out her left hand to display a man's large square wristwatch on a worn leather strap, incongruously huge on her tiny hand.

"Very handsome," Joyce agreed. "Gold?"

"And an Omega." Martha looked with satisfaction at the enormous timepiece. "Howard will be delighted."

"He certainly should be," Joyce said. "That's not a bad teapot, by the way."

"Fairly good pewter," Martha said dismissively, looking down at the pot dangling from one small finger. "It'll go to the Treasure Mart Monday. Unless you'd like to buy it?"

"Maybe." Joyce took the teapot and turned it upside down, examining it. "How much do you want for it?"

"Oh, if I can get a quick profit I'll take ten dollars."

"Hmm." Joyce surveyed the teapot once more. "Well, it's highway robbery, but what the hell, it should sell fast at the Show." She handed Martha the money with a grin. "Wait'll I find an eight-place service of American Beauty."

Harbrooke was memorable, of course, because she'd bought a set of brand-new sheets and an unopened bottle of Bailey's Irish Cream for two dollars. And at Morningside Drive, there was an impromptu gathering as several of the regulars swarmed in for the "9 A.M. absolutely no early birds" sale. Afterward a group of them had paused at the foot of the long driveway for a few moments of shop talk.

"There's a ten o'clock on Argyle that sounds good." That was Steve Olewski, a member of Joyce's co-op, young and dark and muscular, with spiky punk-style hair, one silver earring in the form of a snake, and more black hair emerging from the neck of a T-shirt that read, "Gumby died for your sins."

"I never bother with the Crescents on a big day." That was Ellen Nakamura, another of Joyce's partners and a specialist in

Orientalia, with almond eyes and long, shiny black hair and a somehow thoroughly American face.

"There was some Oriental at Palomar," Joyce offered.

"I saw it, thanks. Just Hong Kong crap. Where the hell is Alexandria, does anyone know? It's an oh three zip."

"Off Newport just past fourteen, but don't bother." Martha Penrose shook her head. "Wall-to-wall baby clothes. I ran into Alice at Hutchins and she said Miner was a good one."

"If she's already been there I won't even bother," Joyce agreed. "She was ahead of me at Eberwhite, too, damn her."

"You should talk," Steve retorted. "Sometimes I think you must have had yourself cloned." They chatted companionably as they headed for their cars, most of them parked at odd angles to the curb or across driveways.

Oddly, Anneke remembered Westwood for what she hadn't bought. First, there had been that huge and ungainly "waterfall" dresser, a 1930s excrescence of peeling veneer and missing hardware, the sort of thing that gave Art Deco a bad name.

"Is this the only Art Deco you have?" she asked, loath to use the term for this monstrosity. But perhaps there were some smaller things tucked away. "Any jewelry, for instance?"

"Oh! I forgot all about the jewelry." The plump woman in the flowered dress looked as if confusion was her normal condition. "Hang on a minute." She scrabbled in a carton on the floor of the garage and finally unearthed a pink plastic bucket whose contents she dumped onto the card table in front of her.

Anneke peered at the conglomeration, trying to identify individual pieces. That dull glint under those pink pop-it beads was surely marcasite? She plunged her hands into the tangled pile; could that glimpse of dark red possibly be real cinnabar? But even as she worked desperately to unsnarl the disorderly mass she was aware of other hands, grasping beneath her own. The marcasite disappeared. The possibly-cinnabar, when she finally dug down to it, proved to be a chunk of red plastic. She was left

with a double handful of plastic and metal and cheap rhinestones.

"I'll take this, and these other things. What do I owe you?" The young man next to her held the marcasite-and-sterling ring in one hand. In the other he juggled a violently colored clock, an even more violently colored tray, and a large amethyst geode. He handed the woman the requested three dollars and moved away to where Joyce was rooting through a box of dishes. "Hi, Joyce. How's pickings?"

"Not bad, not bad." Joyce pulled a white ceramic teapot from the carton and tucked it under her arm. "Anneke, come and meet Peter Casaday, Ann Arbor's last remaining flower child."

"Glad to meet you," Anneke said ruefully. "I think." Her breathing was slightly ragged, as if she'd been running. The scramble in the pile of jewelry, she realized, had had the quality of confrontation, almost of combat, and she still felt a primitive adrenaline rush that was both exhilarating and almost frightening. Was this the way it always felt to the regulars, this sense of intense competitiveness?

"Peter's an artist and framer, not a dealer," Joyce was saying. "Which is just as well, considering the kinds of things he buys." She made a cheerful face at the wildly patterned clock.

"I collect the classic works of the 1960s," Peter said grandly. He was blond and good-looking, with long hair almost but not quite hippie-length. "And when the Great Wheel of Public Taste makes another revolution, the rest of you are going to owe me an apology."

"That's not exactly a sixties piece." Anneke pointed to the marcasite ring.

"Well, a guy's got to eat." He grinned again and flipped the ring into the air, catching it deftly on the downspin and slipping it onto his little finger. "It's the safest way to carry it," he said in response to her curious look. "Not much of a piece, really, but it'll bring a few bucks at the Treasure Mart. This is the stuff that makes me get up at six on a Saturday morning." He held

up the clock and the tray gleefully. "Two Peter Max pieces, would you believe it?"

Why, he's as caught up in the adrenaline rush as I was, Anneke realized suddenly. This isn't recreation to these people, it's trench warfare.

Then there was Joanna Westlake and the Chase chrome tray—on Linda Vista, wasn't it? She'd never met Joanna before, but Joyce clearly had; her introduction, and Joanna's acknowledgment, were distinctly cool.

She was a pretty woman in her thirties, wearing what Anneke thought of as a social smile, the kind that never reaches the eyes. She was dressed rather more formally than the norm for garage sales—or for Ann Arbor either, for that matter—in light gray pants, chalk-striped silk blouse, and navy blazer. As she spoke, her eyes moved continuously, surveying the objects scattered around the lawn. "Anything good?" she asked Joyce. "It looks pretty squalid."

"It mostly is, I think."

Joanna's eyes focused on Anneke appraisingly. Anneke felt sure the woman was efficiently calculating the cost of her clothing, but when she spoke she pointed to the tray, which Anneke had just bought for the magnificent sum of fifty cents.

"That's Art Deco, isn't it?"

"Yes, Chase chrome. Are you a fan of Deco?"

"I'm not sure yet. Chase—is that the maker?"

"Yes. The Chase Brass and Copper Company put out a line of housewares before World War II." Anneke turned the tray over and pointed to the tiny mark, a centaur poised with bow and arrow.

"Is it valuable?"

"Well, it's collectible." Anneke looked at the woman curiously. "Depends on what you mean by valuable."

"Anneke, we'd better get moving," Joyce interrupted. "See you later, Joanna."

Once they were back in the van, Joyce made a face. "You're going to be sorry you told that woman anything about Chase chrome."

"Why, for heaven's sake? Is she a dealer? I don't recall her as a member of the association."

"She's not a dealer, she's a hyena," Joyce said viciously, yanking at the steering wheel. "She'll pick your brains, and then cut the ground out from under you—one of those people who knows the price of everything and the value of nothing. What she is"—Joyce gritted her teeth and tromped on the accelerator—"is a garage-sale whore."

10 A.M.

"I'm going to take these old fountain pens, and the flatware, and the dishes," Alice Cowan told the man at the card table. "Can I just leave them here?"

"Sure." He was young and tough-looking, in blue jeans and a T-shirt bearing the logo of a local plumbing company. He took the heavy pottery plates from her arms and dumped them unceremoniously on the ground with a clatter that made her wince. She set the pens and the plastic bag of cutlery carefully on top of them and returned to the garage.

Funny how people so often undervalued stainless steel, she thought gleefully. Imagine getting eight place settings of Dansk for twenty dollars. And Ennis's high-powered friends would recognize it immediately, even though they professed to disdain material things.

Inside the garage she made a swift second circuit. She considered and rejected a battered and overpriced clarinet, but quickly snatched up a pink metal toy stove—definitely 1940s, and old toys had good resale value. She tucked the stove under one arm, noting sadly the smear of dirt it left on her new blouse, and picked up an evil-looking stuffed owl with her free hand.

That seemed to be not a bad haul, although nothing that qualified as a Big Score.

The Big Score. Since she'd first begun to do the garage-sale circuit regularly, Alice Cowan had fantasized about it, but for the life of her she'd never been able to visualize it properly. Jewelry, probably. Perhaps a Bulgari bracelet—no, a necklace—tossed heedlessly into a shoeboxful of costume jewelry, herself the only one clever enough to recognize it for what it was.

But somehow the fantasy had always failed to excite her. She could never visualize the next step. Once she had the necklace, what then? It would still only be a thing, an object, not an accomplishment. Ennis and his academic colleagues would still be unimpressed. One didn't brag about possessions, however cleverly acquired.

And she was clever on the circuit. She seemed to have a nose for the best sale and a quick eye for the few good items among the heaps of junk. Racing around town on Friday and Saturday mornings, weaving her tan Volvo station wagon in and out of traffic, feeling the buzz when she spotted a find, all gave her a sense of uncomplicated pleasure that few other things in her life seemed to provide.

Ennis, of course, considered the whole enterprise absurd. When he thought about it—or her—at all, of course, which was seldom. Between teaching and other duties in the business administration school, and consulting, and endless professional conferences all over the country, he spared little of his massive intellect for his wife's activities. He was, she assumed, relieved to have her busy with anything that did not impinge on his own life, so long as she was available as hostess, or for those increasingly rare occasions when he required a wife's presence at a business-related social event. (Those were, of course, the only social events he bothered with.)

Sighing, she carried her unwieldy purchases toward the card table.

"I guess that's— Uh, excuse me, Joanna, those are mine."

"I beg your pardon?" Joanna Westlake stood by the table smiling at her, sweetly acid, the bag of Dansk flatware held firmly in her hand.

"The silverware. I already bought it." Alice reached for the bag, but Joanna withdrew it, still smiling.

"Sorry, but I do have it, as you can see."

"But I already bought it. I told you I was buying it," Alice appealed to the man behind the table.

"Sorry, but she offered me more money for it," he said.

"You what?" Alice stared at Joanna, dumbfounded. She'd heard nasty stories about the woman, but then you heard nasty stories about everyone on the circuit. And she'd never heard of any of the regulars doing this. Bidding up the price at a sale was impossible, appalling, an offense against the unwritten rules so profound it was literally unheard-of. "You can't do that," she stuttered, whether at Joanna or the man she wasn't sure.

"Sure I can." The man's expression hardened. "It's still mine until someone pays me for it." His look was oddly expectant; of course, Alice realized, he's waiting for me to ask how much Joanna offered, to see if I'll outbid her.

She couldn't do it, not if her very life depended on it; the mere idea of confrontation terrified her. And yet she knew, quite suddenly, that she must do something. If she let this pass, she would never be able to go to another garage sale. She would lose it all—the anticipation, the excitement, the sense of accomplishment and competence she found here that she had never found anywhere else.

It was preposterous to take it so seriously, of course; it was a ridiculous way to spend one's time anyway, as Ennis had pointed out more than once. Even sillier than her other crazes. Like the flute lessons—she'd been determined to master the difficult instrument, even visualized herself playing with a local Renaissance-music group. But her enthusiasm, as Ennis predicted, had lasted barely six months. And then there'd been

what Ennis called her ceramics period. And even that time when she'd determined to get a master's degree in archaeology. Ennis had put his foot down over that one.

"My dear Alice, a university is not a recreational center. Putter about with your hobbies by all means, but it would be unfair of you to waste the time of busy academics for your own amusement. Besides," he continued reasonably, "you are, after all, the wife of a well-known faculty member. When you lose interest this time, it could be quite embarrassing to both of us."

He'd been right, of course. And anyway, she'd been busy enough, with two daughters and the big modern house overlooking the river and being hostess to Ennis's colleagues. Only now the girls were off at college and the house seemed to run itself as Ennis's activities more and more often took place out of town or on campus.

She'd gone to her first garage sale by accident, because it was at the home of a neighbor. There, to her amazement, she'd recognized a pre-Columbian Peruvian bowl, nearly identical to a photograph in one of her archaeology books. It was tossed carelessly on a card table and priced at fifty cents, and Alice bought it at once without even the smallest flicker of guilt. The next time, it was a Bennington bowl, which she recognized from her brief interest in pottery. In fact, she discovered that all her hobbies seemed to have been leading her to this, providing her with specialized knowledge that contributed to her success on the circuit. Out here, rooting through grubby garages, it had somehow all come together.

She didn't talk about her activities much to Ennis, or to the neighbors and academic colleagues who were all she had as friends. In their world of high-powered intellectual accomplishment, it would have been an embarrassment, equivalent to being a rag-picker. In a room full of movers and shakers, how could she refer to herself as a professional shopper?

Still, that's what she was. That really is what I've become, Alice realized with surprise. And I'm good at it, she thought

defiantly. She saw Joanna reach into her purse, her face calmly triumphant, and thought, I've got to stop her.

Honestly, the woman was too frumpy to believe. Joanna wrinkled her nose slightly at Alice's soiled and rumpled clothing. "We did agree on thirty dollars, I believe?" she asked, sparing Alice the briefest of glances as she withdrew bills from her wallet. Dansk would be perfect at the fall cocktail party she always gave for Ronald's department colleagues.

"Thirty, that's right," the man nodded.

"That's still a steal for real Dansk," Alice blurted.

"What do you mean?" The man had been reaching for Joanna's money. Now, to her dismay, he put his hand back down on the table.

"Well, it's fifty dollars a place setting at Leidy's," Alice said. Her eyes were fixed somewhere in the middle distance; Joanna glared at her, radiating fury, but the stupid woman refused to meet her eye.

"Fifty dollars a place setting?" the man repeated, sounding incredulous. "Then this batch is worth, what, four hundred bucks?"

"Well, you could only get about half that second-hand," Alice said.

"Are you going to sell it to me or not?" Joanna demanded. "We did have an agreement, after all."

"Forget it, lady." He snatched the bag of silverware from her hand, his face hard. "You really thought you had a live one, didn't you?" He turned to Alice. "You want it? You can have it for a hundred fifty."

"Too much for me, I'm afraid, but I'll take these other things." Alice was still keeping her eyes averted, her shoulders hunched. You'll have to face me some time, Joanna thought viciously. She reached out a hand toward Alice and then dropped it, forcing herself back to her normal equanimity.

It was really just jealousy, after all, Joanna told herself, look-

ing at the other woman's sagging skirt, scuffed shoes and lank, unbecoming hairdo. She'd put up with the envy of lesser people most of her life without letting it bother her, and she wouldn't let it bother her now. She was secure enough, wasn't she, to allow others their petty hostilities?

Besides, she'd done all right so far this morning. There was that cut glass decanter that might be what people called "brilliant-cut glass," or possibly even Waterford; she'd have to find someone to ask. And that chrome teapot she'd bought after Joyce's friend told her about Chase chrome. No, there was no reason to let this egregious woman bother her. She smiled forgivingly at Alice's uncommunicative back before walking down the driveway with her head held high.

"That's eighteen dollars." The man held out his hand for Alice's money. "And thanks."

"That's okay." Alice let out a long shuddering breath, her hands shaking from tension. The man seemed to have forgotten that she herself had intended to buy the Dansk for only twenty dollars. Thank God for that, anyway; she didn't think she'd survive another confrontation.

Still, she had prevented Joanna from getting away with it. She felt a surge of glee as she piled her purchases into a carton, and a sudden bubble of amusement that surprised her—this was hardly something she could brag about to Ennis's dressed-for-success friends.

And suddenly the notion of the Big Score presented itself to her once more, fully formed at last. The Big Score wasn't merely an object, an acquired thing. It was freedom.

THREE

10:20 A.M.

The last two sales had been busts. "Where to now?" Anneke asked as she and Joyce climbed into the van.

"Well . . ." Joyce examined her card and wrinkled her forehead in thought. "There's a ten o'clock on Provincetown, up off Maple Road, that sounds pretty good, and it's far enough out that it may not have been picked clean." She turned the ignition key decisively and rocketed away from the curb.

"Damn. It's not sterling." Anneke was examining an intricate bracelet she'd bought at Morningside.

"Oh, isn't it?" Joyce glanced at the offending item. "That's a shame. Well, you're only out two dollars."

"I know, but it's the principle of the thing. A professional would have examined it more closely before she bought it."

"Oh no she wouldn't. Just the opposite, in fact. Haven't you been watching us? This is a smash-and-grab operation. The only way to operate is to grab everything that looks like a possible, and sort it out afterward. Otherwise, while you're thinking it over someone else is buying."

"But don't you wind up with a lot of mistakes that way?"

"Sure I do. A margin for error is built into my calculations. At the end of every weekend I throw away a few dollars' worth of fakes and rejects. You have to cut yourself some slack, that's all. Oh, hell, there she is again."

"Who?" Anneke peered forward through the windshield. Maple Road looked surprisingly rural, although she knew that modern subdivisions lurked behind the narrow strip of woods lining the two-lane blacktop.

"Joanna. That's her car." Joyce motioned at the silver-gray station wagon parked on the narrow shoulder. "Wonder why she's stopped here? Well, since she's aimed north I assume she hasn't been to Provincetown yet, so at least we'll beat her there." Determinedly Joyce trod on the accelerator and the van shot past the parked wagon.

"Joyce, wait."

"What is it?"

"We'd better go back. I think she's sick."

"Are you sure? She's probably just checking her map or something."

"I don't think so. She was . . . There's something wrong." Anneke twisted around and looked back along the road, trying to confirm what she'd seen, but the Taurus was already too far behind. Still, she had been for a long moment right alongside, had seen Joanna's sleek blond head lolling sideways along the edge of the half-open window, eyes closed and mouth slackly open. "There's something really wrong," she repeated.

"Oh, hell. All right." Joyce hurled the van into a vicious turn, reversed and turned again with an angry clash of gears and roared back down Maple, coming to a halt opposite the Taurus with a screech of brakes and a jolt that set Anneke's teeth rattling. And both knowing immediately that Anneke had been right.

"Joanna?" Joyce jumped out of the van and plunged across the road. Anneke, negotiating the weed-filled ditch on the pas-

senger side, was slower. By the time she too reached the other car Joyce's eyes were wide with shock. "She's . . . I think she's dead." Joyce pointed unnecessarily to the dreadful bruise on Joanna's forehead, from which blood oozed slowly down her neck, matting her carefully arranged hair and ruining forever her elegant silk shirt.

"Are you sure?" Anneke reached gingerly forward, her fingers searching the unbloodied side of the neck for a pulse. Joanna's skin felt cold and clammy. "I can't tell."

And then Joanna's eyes opened suddenly, so suddenly that Anneke jerked back her hand in fright. The woman stared at Anneke intently, without blinking, her eyes wide and dark, her brow furrowed slightly.

"The Jap?" Joanna said wonderingly.

"What?" Anneke leaned forward. "Joanna? What happened?" But her eyes had closed, and this time Anneke felt sure they wouldn't open again.

"We'd better get help." Joyce's voice shook. "Flag down a car?" She looked up and down the empty road helplessly.

"Over there." Anneke pointed to a driveway half hidden by shrubbery. "I'll go." She plowed through the underbrush toward the nearby house, glad to leave the Taurus behind.

10:35 A.M.

There were already three police cars squashed against the bushes lining Newport Road when the big black Thunderbird crested the hill, wearing its flashing blue light incongruously, like a clown hat on a bishop. Already, a small army of blue-uniformed figures swarmed around the Taurus, leaving Anneke and Joyce standing next to the van, alone and apparently forgotten.

Now, as the Thunderbird approached the police barricades, there was a small, almost imperceptible pause in the activity.

Anneke, who had recently done some computer work for the police department, recognized the man who emerged from the passenger side as Brad Weinmann, a young officer who had only recently been promoted to sergeant. But it was the driver of the car, uncoiling more slowly from its confines, who captured her attention.

She had never seen him before, but she knew at once who he must be, for he was quite possibly the biggest man she had ever seen. Brad Weinmann was no pygmy, but this man was huge, towering over Brad by a full head, besides seeming nearly twice as wide. He was dressed impeccably in a dark gray suit and maroon tie, the suit so perfectly tailored to his enormous frame that Anneke knew even from a distance that it had to be custom-made. She could make out a strong-featured face under iron-gray hair cut fashionably long, but was too far away to judge his expression, or to get any sense of his personality. Still, the occasional swift glances from other officers telegraphed importance.

Brad saw her and smiled in recognition, the brief half-smile appropriate to solemn occasions. He and the big man went first to the Taurus, where they huddled for several minutes with a group of other police before heading in her direction.

Anneke and Brad handled the four-cornered introductions. The big man, Brad announced with something like a flourish, was Lieutenant Karl Genesko.

"Brad tells me you're the police department's computer consultant," he said to Anneke. His voice suited him, low and strong.

"Only on an occasional basis, now that the system's in place. Mostly administrative systems, although we've been working on some applications for investigative procedures."

So this was, as she had surmised, the great Karl Genesko. She looked with interest at the ex-Michigan All-American, ex–Pittsburgh Steelers linebacker, and newest member of the Ann Arbor Police Department. His arrival had been the subject of

intense speculation, gossip, and even a certain amount of acrimony within the department—there were line officers, she knew, who felt they had been passed over for promotion in favor of a gridiron hotshot.

Close to, he seemed even bigger than before. He looked to be somewhere in his late forties, with a craggy, offbeat face and an expression of calm assurance. He was, Anneke decided, extremely attractive without being in the least handsome.

"I take it you were one of the people who found the body?" he asked.

"Yes." Anneke forced her attention guiltily back to the matter at hand, uncomfortably aware that she'd been staring like an adolescent fan. "Only, she was still alive when we found her," she added.

"Oh?" Genesko was instantly alert. "Did she say anything?"

"Yes." Anneke paused, remembering carefully. "She said, 'the Jap?'" She mimicked Joanna's last words as closely as possible.

"She said it that way?" Genesko picked up the rising inflection immediately. "As a question?"

"That's the way it seemed to me. She sounded . . . surprised, I think is the best way to describe it."

"You knew her?"

"I did," Joyce volunteered. "Her name is—was—Joanna Westlake."

"She was a friend of yours?" Genesko asked.

"Not exactly. An acquaintance, really. She was one of the regulars on the garage-sale circuit." Genesko's expression remained politely inquisitive. "There's a group of us, mostly dealers. Antique dealers. We go around to garage sales every weekend to buy things we can sell later."

"So she'd been going to garage sales this morning," he said, more to himself than to them. "That explains the things in the back of her car." Anneke had a mad vision of solemn police officers trying to understand the significance of a chrome teapot, a crystal decanter, two throw rugs, and a frying pan. "And you

were doing the same?" Joyce nodded. "I take it you're antique dealers?"

"I am," Joyce said. "Anneke just came along this morning for fun." The last word hung unhappily in the air.

"And Joanna Westlake was also a dealer?" Genesko continued.

"Well, no, not really. That is, she didn't have a shop or anything like that. She bought mostly for herself, but of course she'd buy for resale also when she came across anything valuable."

"By 'valuable,' you mean salable?"

"I mean valuable," Joyce retorted. "Don't assume we're trash pickers because we buy at garage sales instead of overpriced and overhyped auction houses."

"Still," Genesko pressed her, "she wasn't likely to buy anything at a garage sale worth killing for."

"My God, I never thought of that." Joyce's pale complexion turned even whiter, and in the silence Anneke thought suddenly: But we do look like trash pickers. She looked down at her smudged clothes and dirty hands, and then across at her friend. Joyce had a long streak of dirt down one side of her face, and her clothes were even grubbier than Anneke's own.

She was suddenly and painfully aware of the contrast between her disheveled appearance and Genesko's immaculate attire. She was overcome by the urge, which she recognized as idiotic, to justify herself; besides, she rationalized, he needs to know how valuable some garage-sale finds can be.

"I'd better show you something." She reached into the van. "I bought this at a sale earlier this morning for three dollars." She brought out her statue carefully. "It's by a sculptor named Preiss, in ivory and bronze, and it's worth at least two thousand dollars."

"And at the same sale," Joyce interjected, "I bought a doll that may be worth seven or eight thousand dollars. I think it's a Jumeau, and none of them go for less than a thousand."

"My God, are you sure?" Anneke stared at her, momentarily diverted.

"Not positive, no." Joyce shook her head. "I'm not a doll expert, but I'm pretty sure it's French, at least. I won't know for sure until I look it up."

"But if you're right . . ." Anneke turned to Genesko. "Anyway, you see what I mean. Because whatever it was, this wasn't a random assault and robbery." He looked at her curiously, waiting for her to continue. "Her purse was on the seat next to her, and her diamond wedding ring was still on her finger."

"You're quite right." Genesko nodded, in his eyes a flicker of appreciation that Anneke noted with pleasure. At least, she thought, he's not the stay-off-my-turf kind. "And I do see your point," he added, looking at the statue with respect but no apparent favor. "There's more at stake here than a morning's recreation."

"A great deal more," Joyce said soberly. "This is our bread and butter."

"So you buy things at garage sales that you sell in your shop," Genesko said. "You must go to a lot of sales."

"On a big day, I can do around fifty of them."

"Fifty!" For the first time, Genesko seemed nonplussed. "Tell me, do you map out your itinerary in advance?"

"Not really. You can't, because you can't tell for sure which ones will open early, and you have to get to them before they're open, if you know what I mean."

"I'm afraid I don't, quite," he said patiently.

"Well, look." Joyce waved her hands. "The ads usually give an opening time, but it's not like a store. I mean, people don't wait for the exact time on the clock, they mostly just start the sale whenever they're ready. That means a ten o'clock sale will usually start anywhere from 9:30 on, and if you don't get there until it's actually ten, it'll already be picked clean. The real break is getting there just as the garage doors open; hell, sometimes you can even help them unpack things and lay them out."

"I see. So nobody could know where you were going to be at any given time of the morning," Genesko said.

"In other words," Anneke said, following his reasoning, "Joanna's killing couldn't have been premeditated."

"It could, you know," Genesko contradicted her. "If someone knew she was likely to attend a sale near here, they could have waited for her." He returned to Joyce. "Was there a sale nearby?"

"Yes, that's why we found her. We were on our way to a sale on Provincetown. She must have been on her way there, too; there's nothing else up this way."

"What attracted you to this sale?"

"Good neighborhood and good ad," Joyce replied. "There's a lot of money up here, it was a big ad, and they said they had antiques and jewelry."

"Would the ad be likely to attract Joanna Westlake also?"

"I don't know about the ad, but the neighborhood certainly would have, I'd have thought, because it's all very expensive contemporary houses. Joanna mostly bought contemporary stuff."

"So someone who knew her might have guessed she'd be driving this stretch of Newport Road some time this morning," Anneke commented.

"I suppose it's possible," Joyce agreed.

"You say there's a group of people going to these sales every weekend?" Genesko asked her.

"Yes. Not a fixed group—I mean, it's not a club or anything like that. Just certain dealers who like to buy at sales instead of auctions."

"But you all know each other."

"Well, sort of. I mean, I know some of the other dealers personally, but some of them are just faces I recognize."

"But you knew Joanna Westlake," he persisted.

"Only to chat with at sales. She was . . . she liked to talk to the other regulars. She was just sort of one of the group."

"Who are the others in the group?"

"Hell, I don't know." Joyce dragged a hand across her face, adding another smudge. "I told you, it's not a group, at least not like that."

"All right," Genesko said patiently, "can you tell me who else you saw this morning that you recognized, who might have known Joanna Westlake?"

"This morning." Joyce frowned. "There was Martha Penrose, and Alice Cowan, and . . . let's see, Steve Olewski, and Ellen Nakamura." She said the last name reluctantly, but Genesko gave no visible reaction. "Peter Casaday was around, and . . . oh, and Michael Rappaport. He doesn't usually do the garage-sale circuit anymore, but he was out today." She paused. "There were a couple of guys I've seen around buying books, and there's a woman who buys nothing but baby clothes and things, but I've never actually spoken to them."

"These are all antique dealers?"

"Not all of them. Peter Casaday is an artist who just buys for himself mostly and only occasional resale. And Alice Cowan isn't really a dealer either, at least not professionally."

"If they aren't dealers"—Genesko glanced back toward the Taurus—"how do they sell things?"

"It depends. There are a number of ways to deal things besides through a retail outlet. To other dealers, for instance. To consignment or resale shops. Or big-ticket items can go to auction houses. Even to private buyers, if you know who's looking for what."

"Did you see Joanna Westlake this morning before you found her here?" Genesko did seem to jump around, Anneke thought.

"A couple of times, I think. Once on Harbrooke, and then later on Catalina."

"What time was this?"

"Well, I got to Harbrooke a little after eight, I think. And I know I got to Catalina a bit late—say, around nine-fifteen."

"Can you tell me what she bought at these sales?"

"God, no." Joyce shook her head wearily. "I don't think she bought anything at Harbrooke—it was pretty much a bust. I think I remember her buying a pair of silver earrings at Catalina."

"She got a little chrome-and-glass table there, too," Anneke interjected. "I remember because I was thinking about buying it myself."

"Anything else?" Genesko asked.

Both women shook their heads helplessly. Anneke was aware of a sudden weariness, compounded of fatigue, depression, and hunger. She glanced at her watch, and was amazed to see its hands had not yet reached eleven o'clock. Joyce's face had the pale, drawn look of three A.M. in a hospital waiting room, and Anneke assumed unhappily that she herself looked no better. And why on earth should it matter? she thought, mentally shaking herself.

"Just one more thing." Genesko held up a sheet of lined yellow paper encased in plastic wrapping. "This was on the dashboard. I assume it was the list of sales she planned to attend?"

The list of addresses, carefully printed in a small, neat hand, was arranged in staggered groups, each entry followed by a series of letters or marks. The list, Anneke saw, was shorter than Joyce's.

"It seems to be." Joyce examined the paper without touching it.

"Wouldn't she normally have crossed out sales as she finished with them?" he asked.

"Not necessarily; I never do." Joyce reached into the van and withdrew her index card. "See? Once you've been doing this for a while, you never forget where you've been. Crossing things out would only waste time."

"So there's no way to tell from this list where she'd been this morning."

"Not exactly, no, but . . ." Joyce studied the list once more,

frowning. "I think you can assume she did all the eight o'clocks; there were only six of them. And then she probably did most of this group here"—she pointed to a cluster of addresses—"because we saw her at Catalina and these others are all in the same neighborhood. Besides, that's all good turf. She probably did most of these, too." She pointed again. "And she probably didn't get up here; that's up in the northeast corner of town. Most of the regulars save that area for last."

"Thank you; that's very helpful," Genesko said with respect in his voice. And deservedly, Anneke thought; Joyce was a professional, with a professional's expertise. Still, not every policeman would appreciate that, she knew. "Do you have any questions?" Genesko asked Brad.

"Addresses?" he asked, looking up from the notebook in which he'd been scribbling.

"Can you give us addresses for the people you've named?" Genesko asked Joyce.

"Not really, no. Certainly not home addresses." She stared at the ground for a moment. "Steve Olewski is in my own antique co-op, and Peter Casaday has a framing studio on Main Street. The others all just work out of their homes."

"Never mind." His voice sharpened as he turned back to Brad. "Okay, let's get moving. First, get a couple of pictures of her and start circulating to the garage sales she was seen at. Then do the others—" he handed Brad Joyce's index card "—and as quickly as possible, please, while the sales are still going on. The sooner we get to them, the more likely they are to remember her. I want to know if she was there, what time, and most important, what she bought. Oh yes, and send women officers if possible." He turned to Joyce. "Am I right in assuming most of these sales are run by women?" Barely waiting for her nod, he plowed ahead.

"Next, locate addresses for each of these other dealers who were at sales this morning. If possible, have someone waiting for them when they get home. You know the drill—if they saw her,

where and when, what did she buy. Besides that, an itinerary from each of them and a list of what they bought, with visual corroboration. If they'll permit it, of course. Except here"—he pointed to Mike's notebook, out of Anneke's line of vision— "we'll do this interrogation ourselves."

"One more thing." Genesko returned to Anneke and Joyce as Mike trotted across the road. "Do you have any objection to our examining the contents of your van? And also to get your fingerprints, if we may, so we can eliminate them when we examine her car."

"Sure, I guess," Joyce said tiredly.

"Thank you. I'll send someone over immediately. I know you're tired and shocked, and we'll get you out of here as quickly as we can. We're extremely grateful for all your help." He started to turn away, then stopped and turned back. "One last thing, if I may."

That's the third time he's used that phrase, Anneke thought with amusement. I imagine he finds it a very effective way to keep people from objecting. Like getting a recalcitrant child to eat "just one more bite."

"I can't order you not to talk to anyone," he said seriously, "but I must ask you as earnestly as possible not to say anything, to anyone, about those two words she spoke before she died. If they became public it could cause incalculable damage."

"I don't know if I can promise that," Joyce said, looking stubborn for the first time. "Not if you're going to try to trap Ellen Nakamura with it. Oh, look," she burst out, "I know it sounds like Joanna was accusing Ellen—she is Japanese, after all—but it's ridiculous and impossible. I know Ellen too well for that; I won't believe she could do something like this."

"I haven't met the lady, so I can't comment on that, Ms. McCarthy," Genesko said soberly. "But if you're right, and she is innocent, then allowing public knowledge of those two words is the most damaging thing you could do to her." He stared at

Joyce until her stricken expression revealed that she understood what he meant, then thanked her again and strode away.

"I didn't know you worked for the police," Joyce said when they were finally allowed to climb back into the van.

"I don't 'work for' them," Anneke responded. "I did a couple of major installations for them a while ago, but now I just do occasional updates and the odd special request."

"So you never met this Genesko before today?"

"No, but I'd heard about him before he came here, and I recognized the name when I heard it, of course."

"Recognized the name? From where?"

"The Pittsburgh Steelers. You mean you never heard of him?" Anneke asked in surprise, and then laughed at herself. Not everyone was a football fan, after all. "He was part of the original Steel Curtain, with Joe Greene, and Jack Ham, Jack Lambert—the greatest defensive machine the NFL ever had."

"A football player?" Joyce stared at her in disbelief. "What's he doing in Ann Arbor playing cop?"

"Well, he started out here; he played his college football at Michigan." Anneke searched her memory for what she could recall. "As I understand it, he finished a master's degree during off-seasons, and after he retired from football he got a job with the Pittsburgh police department. I've no idea why he came back to Ann Arbor, though."

"He's not bad-looking, I'll say that for him," Joyce commented drily. "If there were only about half as much of him, that is."

"He seems to know what he's doing, at least." Anneke's voice was sharper than she'd intended.

"Yes, he does, I'll give him that." Joyce looked at her briefly out of the corner of her eye but to Anneke's relief made no further comment. "Here we are," she said with a sigh. She turned the van onto Baldwin and wheeled up the long driveway, which led to a tiny house almost invisible from the street, surrounded by towering evergreens. She came to a halt under

an enormous blue spruce, cut the ignition, and looked at her watch. "And it's still just barely noon." Her laugh had a touch of hysteria to it. "I told you I'd have you home in time for lunch."

FOUR

1:45 P.M.

She ought to have taken the vase straight home, Ellen
Nakamura worried. For the tenth time she turned her head to
reassure herself that it was all right, wrapped in half a dozen
layers of newspaper, tucked into a carton, the carton itself
further stuffed with paper and wedged carefully on the floor of
the car behind the front seat. It's perfectly all right, Ellen reassured herself. Still, every time the tiny Ford Escort hit one of
Ann Arbor's carnivorous chuckholes, she gritted her teeth.

She couldn't have gone straight home. Ted would have asked
questions if she quit so much earlier than usual, and what could
she tell him? That she'd acquired a piece so valuable she was
afraid even to drive around with it? And that, even though it
might be worth close to fifty thousand dollars, and even though
they were dead broke, she didn't dare sell it?

As it turned out, she might as well have saved herself the
worry; the northeast area, as usual, had been a dead loss. Sighing, she turned the Escort east on Plymouth Road, swerving to

avoid a chuckhole and casting another anxious glance at the vase. She wanted to look at it, hold it, gloat over it. It was both maddening and preposterous—here she was, with the Big Score everyone dreamed of, and she couldn't say a word about it.

She pulled into the driveway of the shabby duplex near campus, not noticing the black Thunderbird at the curb until two men emerged from it and approached her.

"Yes?" she said, mildly wary although the street swarmed with activity, students sunning themselves or playing Frisbee or carrying cases of beer for the regular Saturday-night parties. For once she was glad of the bustle; this guy was just too damn big, she decided.

"Are you Ellen Nakamura?" the larger of the two men asked.

"That's right. Do I know you?"

"I'm Lieutenant Karl Genesko, Ann Arbor police." He proffered his badge. "This is Sergeant Bradley Weinmann. May we speak to you, please?"

"Sure. What's it about?" She examined the badge carefully, more from a habit of precision than distrust. It didn't occur to her to be concerned on her own account; authority never intimidated her. But Ted was so antipolice. Only then did she register the absence of his old blue bike from its customary spot chained to the porch rail.

"Is it Ted?" She wasn't sure if she meant "Has something happened to him?" or "Has he done something?" She could hardly credit either one; she was not by nature a worrier, but his absence bothered her more than the presence of the police.

"Your husband? No, this has nothing to do with him," Genesko reassured her quickly. "I believe you've spent the morning going to garage sales?"

"That's right."

"Do you know a woman named Joanna Westlake?"

"Sure," she responded promptly. "She's one of the garage-sale regulars."

"Did you see her this morning?"

"Yeah, a couple of different times. What's this all about?"

"Can you tell me where and when you saw her?" Genesko ignored her question, and she was convinced he would ignore others. Her best course, she concluded, was to cooperate quietly.

"Not really. I just ran into her at a couple of sales."

"Can you remember which sales?"

"I don't think so. Wait, I think I saw her at Keech."

"What time was that?"

"Mid-morning, maybe nine-thirty. I did the Greenview area first. Oh, right, I saw her at Chaucer, too. That was earlier, about ten of nine."

"Do you remember what she bought at those sales?"

"Not a clue. Both times I was just leaving when she arrived."

"What did she say to you when you met?"

"She didn't say anything," Ellen said sharply, permitting her impatience to show. "We just sort of exchanged hellos. She isn't really a friend of mine, she's just someone I know."

"But you did talk to her occasionally at sales? Chatted about things you'd bought, that sort of thing?"

"I suppose so. Look, isn't it time you told me what the hell this is all about?" She was feeling real tension now, preternaturally conscious of the vase tucked away in the back of the car. She braced herself for the next question, but before Genesko could speak, a bicycle turned into the driveway, scattering gravel.

"What's going on?" Ted Burns propped the rusty bike against the porch and removed his briefcase from the basket. Ellen felt a chill; much as she loved Ted, his presence was going to make this even more difficult. He was so neurotic about authority figures, so locked into his childhood memories of strange, tight-lipped women who called themselves social workers but seemed to a child—and even to the grown man Ted had become—more like a kind of Thought Police. He had described it to her more than once, trying to exorcise the memo-

ries—how they came, unannounced and at odd hours, to search his mother's run-down cottage outside Alpena for signs of male habitation, or to catechize him endlessly: What did you have for breakfast this morning, Teddy? How did you get that bruise on your arm, Teddy? Does your mother ever have men stay overnight?

Funny, Ellen thought irrelevantly, according to the conventional wisdom I suppose I should be the wary one; I should feel like an ethnic outsider. Only she didn't, and in fact never had; she'd grown up instead happy and secure, in the big Ives Woods house her parents still occupied, just another faculty brat in a faculty neighborhood. It was Ted who was the hostile, prickly one in the family.

"This is Lieutenant Genesko, and Sergeant Weinmann, from the police department," she said. "This is my husband, Professor Edward Burns." The title sounded oddly in her ears; it was used rarely in Ann Arbor, and never in social situations, but she wanted to make them aware at once of Ted's status. At twenty-six, he was still often taken for an undergraduate, and he was sensitive of his dignity.

"How do you do, Professor Burns." Genesko extended his hand; he seemed to have taken the point, Ellen thought with relief. Ted paused for a moment before he accepted the handshake; his serious, youthful face seemed to close up, all expression wiped clean.

"What's this about?" he asked, moving closer to Ellen and putting a hand protectively on her arm.

"We're just asking your wife a few questions," Genesko said pleasantly.

"About what?" Ted persisted.

"About what she saw this morning while she was going to garage sales."

"Why?" Ted asked bluntly, gripping Ellen's arm more tightly.

"Because a woman was killed this morning," Genesko an-

swered with equal bluntness, "and we're hoping your wife can help us trace her movements."

We look like a tableau, Ellen thought: the big policeman, calm and pleasant but somehow immensely threatening; Ted, his face pinched with suppressed tension and hostility; she herself between them, like a hostage to opposing forces. Ted's thick brown hair was tangled from the bike ride home from campus, and Ellen resisted the urge to reach up and smooth it.

"Joanna was murdered?" she said finally.

"What does that have to do with Ellen?" Ted demanded, overriding her question.

"Your wife was one of the people who knew her." Genesko chose to answer Ted, seeming to accept Ellen's question as rhetorical. "We hoped she could help us determine the victim's movements up to the time she was killed."

"And that's all?" Ted's voice poured suspicion and hostility.

"Not entirely." Genesko turned away from Ted and looked at Ellen thoughtfully. "When Joanna Westlake was found, she was not yet dead. She was able to say something." He paused, as if waiting for her to ask the question, but when Ellen remained silent he continued. "She said just two words—'the Jap.'"

"Okay, that tears it." Ted pushed Ellen aside and confronted Genesko, his face twisted with rage. "Nobody uses that word to my wife, cop or no cop. I want you to get the hell out of here. And don't think you're going to get away with this. I'm not some street kid you can hustle and harass because he's afraid of the Man. I'm a university professor, and as soon as you get your ass out of here I'm going straight to City Hall to file a complaint charging you with racism."

Oh shit, he's just making it worse, Ellen thought angrily. Genesko had neither moved nor spoken during Ted's tirade. She looked from her husband's flushed face to the detective's expressionless one; he doesn't give anything at all away, she noted with a kind of admiration.

"Professor Burns, I entirely agree with you that the term 'Jap' is racist and offensive," Genesko said when Ted finally ran down. He spoke with the same massive calm as before. "However, I didn't use it; the victim did."

"So you rushed right over here to bust the first Japanese-American you could find," Ted jeered. "And after this I suppose you're going to round up all the others, and probably throw in a few Chinese and Koreans for good measure. After all, you can't tell them apart anyway, can you?"

"We intend to question everyone who saw Joanna Westlake today, regardless of race, creed, or national origin," Genesko said with a flash of humor, or sarcasm; his voice was so level Ellen couldn't tell which. "That includes your wife. Ms. Nakamura"—he turned to her—"do you have any idea why Joanna Westlake would have said those words as she was dying?"

"You don't have to answer that!" Ted said hotly.

"I know I don't," she snapped at him, maddened beyond endurance and beginning to be frightened as well. "I'm not a street kid either, you know, and I'm also not one of your culture-shocked foreign students. I'm a fourth-generation American, remember?" She turned her back on him, facing Genesko. "No. I don't know what she meant. I know she didn't mean that I killed her, if that's what you're thinking. Because I didn't."

"It's much too early to begin forming hypotheses," Genesko replied. "I just have one more question. I realize this may be difficult, but can you give us a list of all the sales you went to today, and what you bought at each?"

"Christ, you don't want much, do you?" Her stomach lurched, but she remained outwardly composed. "I doubt it very much. It's the 'each' that's the problem, of course."

"Of course. But your list will tell you which sales you went to, and all your purchases are still in your car. I assume it's connecting them that will be the problem." She nodded. "May

we examine the list and the contents of your car? Oh, and get your fingerprints," he said as an apparent afterthought.

"Not without a warrant," Ted interjected.

"Oh, Ted, knock it off," she said tiredly. "Let's just get it over with."

The task took nearly an hour. Ellen checked off the sales she'd gone to, and then pulled her purchases from the car item by item, reciting, as well as her memory allowed, where she'd bought each of them. She was surprised at how easy it turned out to be; she was unsure of only two or three items. The sergeant examined everything she removed from the car and made careful notes on each, including the Chinese vase. Neither the police nor Ted, watching the proceedings with sullen intensity, commented on the vase or questioned its value.

Only when they had finished, and the police had gone, did Ellen allow herself to relax, slumping wearily against the car.

"We'd better get these things inside," she said to Ted, picking up the vase with what she hoped was an expression of nonchalance.

"Yeah. Now that the cops are done pawing over them," he said bitterly. When she didn't respond he grasped her by the shoulder. "How could you let those damn racist pigs push you around like that?"

"Oh, shit, let it alone, will you?" For once she was too disturbed to be protective of his feelings. "Sometimes I think you married me because I'm Japanese, so you could have visual proof to show the world how goddamn liberal you are." His face turned white and she thought: I've gone too far.

But all he said was: "Here, let's start unloading the car. Looks like you had a pretty good day."

"Mediocre, really." She shook her head, still holding the vase. "One piece of Chinese export, a couple of Japanese plates, a vase—everything else goes to the Treasure Mart."

"Still, the Mart stuff brings in money, too," Ted said practically. "And God knows we can use it." He hauled the last of her

purchases out of the car and examined a heavy cast-iron floor lamp critically. "Aren't old lamps valuable?"

"Not extravagantly. It'll bring fifty or sixty dollars, I suppose."

"And I'll bet you only paid ten," he said fondly.

"Six, actually," she said with an answering smile, relieved that her ugly words seemed forgotten. "But remember, money is only part of what this is all about."

"Money is what everything is about right now," he retorted. "Poor people can't afford art for art's sake."

"We are not poor." She spoke with asperity. "Maybe you grew up poor, but you're not anymore." It was an old and somehow comfortable argument, distancing her from the tensions of the day's events. "We're only broke, that's all."

"We are too poor," he insisted. "An assistant professor of sociology makes less money than a bus driver. And when you factor in the student loans I'm paying off, we practically fall below the official poverty level. What difference does it make whether you call it broke or poor?"

"For God's sake, you're a trained sociologist. You should know the difference. Poor is permanent; poor is hopelessness; poor is unemployed, and welfare. We're only temporarily broke, like every other grad student and first-year faculty member. We are not, thank God, victims of the social-work establishment, and we're never going to be."

She was quite sure of that fact. Eventually, she felt confident, when Ted was a tenured professor, and she had her degree and her own gallery, there'd be plenty of money. In the meantime, there was always enough for day-to-day life. Except, for Ted, there had been all those years when there hadn't been enough for day-to-day life, when the two hot meals he got in school were his only food for the day.

"Well, let's get these things inside," she said pacifically.

"Why don't I just put the lamp in the garage?" Ted suggested.

"Since it's going right to the Mart anyway? It's awfully heavy for you to haul around."

"That's a good idea. Thanks." His customary solicitude cheered as well as amused her; she forbore to point out that she spent a good deal of her time wrestling large, sullen objects from point A to point B. Picking up a large pottery platter at random from the pile on the lawn, she carried it and the precious vase toward the house.

She wished she could tell him about the vase; she'd never kept an important secret from him before. But even if she did, she comforted herself, he wouldn't actually think much of the vase. Try as he might—and he had tried, Ellen conceded—Ted simply had no feel for Oriental art. And the vase was a difficult piece, deceptively simple in line and color. Which, Ellen supposed, was why the stupid woman hadn't realized what she had.

No, he'd never see it her way, and she didn't dare sell it, at least not right away. How much better to say nothing, but to set the vase quietly on the bedroom dresser, where she could enjoy it for itself. Some day, when they really needed the money— say, when they had children to put through college—she would "discover" its value. By then, she assumed, it would be safe to put it on the market.

FIVE

• • • • • •

Sundays were for regrouping, Anneke told herself firmly, not for working. Honestly, she was turning into a computer nerd. She poured herself a second cup of coffee, looked longingly toward the Compaq in the den, and marched herself back to the newspaper-strewn sofa. She made a mental list: housecleaning, laundry, definitely a quick supermarket run. No football to watch on television this time of year, dammit. Sunday, bloody Sunday.

Maybe a drive out to one of the local flea markets? No, she'd had enough of that yesterday. She set her coffee cup down next to the Preiss statue and turned the small figure around, trying to recapture her original pleasure, but it was no use. The piece was still beautiful, but now there were too many other associations; it would be a while before she could view it with unalloyed pleasure. If yesterday's excursion was meant to be rejuvenating, she thought with grim amusement, it had been an abject failure.

She drained the coffee cup, stood, and gathered up the Sunday papers. Joanna Westlake's murder had made the front page, but only the lower half, beneath an announcement of the latest downtown demolition-followed-by-high-rise project. The story, which said a good deal less than she already knew about the murder, was filled with platitudes of outrage and journalistic clichés that told the reader nothing, either about the killing or about the victim herself. Joanna, she saw, had been thirty-seven years old, the wife of a professor in the Residential College and the mother of a fourteen-year-old daughter. Anneke was relieved that her name and Joyce's had not been mentioned.

She folded and stowed the newspapers in the white Lucite magazine rack, armed herself with a bottle of spray cleaner and a roll of paper towels, and set to work on the first task on her list. Housecleaning was good therapy, anyway, she thought, and the notion brought her up short—therapy for what? Well, for too much self-absorption, if nothing else. She shrugged off the question and attacked the dust on the coffee table.

In any case, she derived a certain amount of gratification from housework nowadays, because the house was a continuing joy, as satisfying a part of her current life as her work, both attained late but by her own efforts. As she dusted the shelves flanking the fireplace, Anneke felt immense pleasure that she had come, finally, to this place that was irrefutably hers.

It was small, of course, but open and airy and beautifully proportioned. The living-dining area was a broad, front-to-back sweep washed in light from windows at both ends. The tiny kitchen, separated only by a white ceramic-tile counter, was sufficient for someone who had quit cooking, cold turkey, as soon as she no longer had a family to feed. The master bedroom held an extravagant wall of closets and a queen-size bed big enough for the rare overnight guest—rarer than ever lately, Anneke conceded to herself. And the second, smaller bedroom was ideal for her computers and electronic equipment.

Certainly it was light-years away from the hulking, pseudo-

colonial split level where she'd raised two daughters, when she'd been Anneke Mortenson. That house had always been Tim's—not that he'd been all that fond of it; she doubted he'd ever really looked at it—but it was one of his "investments," visible proof of his financial abilities. Then, when the girls had gone off to college, and Tim had gone off with his twenty-two-year-old teaching assistant, she'd taken the smart-money advice and bought a neat, antiseptic condo. And hadn't even realized how much she hated its suffocating sterility until she'd seen this house.

It had needed everything—new wiring, plumbing, furnace, even a new roof. But under the ugly flowered wallpaper and stained acoustic ceilings she had discerned the elegance of line and form that was the hallmark of classic Art Deco. The amount of work the house needed appalled and terrified her; it was a ridiculous proposition for a woman alone, struggling to establish her own business at the same time. It had scared the hell out of her, in fact. And for that reason, even if for no other, she knew it was one more risk she had to take, one more exercise to strengthen her emotional muscles.

Of course, it was still not "done"; good houses never were. And she had furnished it slowly, mainly with good Art Deco pieces, preferring to do without rather than live with something that wasn't exactly right, so that even now the effect was a spare, almost sparse whiteness. That was all right; its very simplicity pleased her.

She gave a last, satisfied look around the sunlit room. Everything was clean and bright and orderly; here she had created her own life, also orderly, self-sufficient, and self-contained. But also, she thought in a rare moment of self-analysis, perhaps also a bit sparse, not yet completed, awaiting one or two additional pieces?

She was saved from further introspection by the ring of the telephone, and Joyce's voice, sounding oddly tentative.

"Anneke, are you very busy today? Could you by any chance come by the shop?"

"I'm in the throes of housecleaning," she hedged. "What's up? Computer problems?"

"It's about yesterday. It's kind of hard to go into over the phone." Joyce's voice trailed off.

"Well, I'm just about done, and I have to go out anyway." Anneke capitulated to her friend's tone. "Give me half an hour or so. You're at the co-op?"

"Yes. It's not open, but we're all here working. Come to the back door, okay?"

"Okay." Anneke hung up and headed toward the bedroom to change clothes, wondering what on earth Joyce couldn't talk about over the phone.

The antique co-op was on the old north side of town, a block or two from the Kerrytown factory-turned-yuppie-mall. I'll just drop in for a few minutes and then have lunch at Zingerman's, Anneke promised herself, turning her chocolate-brown Alfa Romeo into the driveway of the big late-Victorian structure. It was beautifully restored, painted in sophisticated hues of charcoal, gray, and pink. Attached to the porch was a big hand-carved wooden sign that said "Remains to Be Seen." As directed, she went around to the back and through the open door, into what was still a kitchen.

"I'm sorry, we're closed." The woman at the big oak table spoke without looking up. She was tall and dark and slim, her coiled black hair shot with gray and bristling with pencils. The table in front of her was strewn with ledger sheets.

"Hi, Carmela, it's me."

"Oh, Anneke, of course, we've been waiting for you." Carmela Aguilar was the daughter of a Venezuelan professor; like so many other Ann Arborites, she'd arrived as a graduate student, gotten involved in other pursuits—in her case, collecting and selling Latin American art and antiques—and somehow never left town. Now she took off large, red-framed glasses and

stood up, scattering papers. "Ugh, I hate the paperwork of this job. Come with me, the others are around in the workroom. I'm glad you came, *somebody* has to put an end to this nonsense." She pushed through a swinging door and Anneke followed behind, wondering with not a little foreboding just what nonsense she was to put an end to.

The house had been lucky in its current tenants; they had respected it enough to adapt themselves to it rather than the other way around. Carmela led Anneke through a high-ceilinged dining room filled with an eclectic but not overpowering mix of antiques; through a small front parlor housing locked jewelry and display cases and a wonderful antique cash register; through a beautifully-proportioned room, brilliant with Latin American artifacts, that was Carmela's own operation; and finally through a red-painted door into a big, untidy space that looked like the Mad Hatter's attic.

Three people looked up as they entered. Joyce was seated at a broad, scarred oak table, her hands busy with a hairless, depressed-looking doll. At the other end of the table, Ellen Nakamura was spreading glue on unrecognizable pieces of porcelain. She wore a red cotton shirt whose defiant color warred with her gold complexion, accentuating the dark circles under her eyes. Across the room Steve Olewski, his spiky hair standing up on his head, leaned over a painting in a heavy, elaborate gilt frame. He was wearing paint-stained blue jeans, sandals over bare feet, and a T-shirt that read, "I'm not as think as you stoned I am."

"Anneke. Oh, good." Joyce put down a pair of tiny scissors and stood up to greet her. "I'm glad you could come."

"Is that one of the dolls you got yesterday?" Anneke pointed at the disreputable object.

"Yes." Joyce made a face. "It's not a Jumeau, either, just a battered old French doll in lousy condition."

"Then it's not worth a fortune?"

"I'll be lucky to get a hundred bucks for it," Joyce said.

"Funny, you don't look like cop material." Steve grinned at Anneke with an expression of cheerful lechery.

"I don't look like what? Joyce, what on earth is this all about?" she asked.

"It's about Ellen." It was Carmela who answered, her voice impatient. "Those idiots think she killed that woman, can you imagine anything so ridiculous? And Joyce says you work for the police department, so we thought you could help.

"The whole thing is preposterous." Carmela plowed ahead angrily. "Anyone could have killed her, and I'll guarantee that anyone who knew her could have wanted to."

"Carmela . . ." Joyce said uncomfortably.

"Never mind that." Carmela waved her protest away. "I don't do garage sales, and anyway I was at an auction in Bloomfield Hills all day Saturday if anyone wants to know"—she glared at Anneke—"so they know *I'm* innocent, and I can tell you the woman was a misery, you know? Nobody could stand her."

"But even if everyone did dislike her," Anneke said thoughtfully, "is the kind of animosity you're talking about really a motive for murder?"

"Nonsense," Carmela retorted, "she was killed for something she'd bought, it's obvious, isn't it?"

"Imagine hitting the Big Score and getting murdered for it." Joyce shuddered. "From now on I'm hiding all my good finds."

"The Big Score?" Anneke asked.

"That's the Holy Grail," Steve explained airily. "The ultimate find, you know? Like the Rembrandt-in-the-attic fable."

"That's not really likely, though, is it? I mean, do you really expect that sort of thing?"

"Not *expect*, no," Joyce acknowledged. "It's more of an ideal, something you fantasize about."

"Have any of the folks you know ever found something like that?"

"God, no. At least, I assume not." Joyce looked sober. "You know, there's a flip side to the Big Score fantasy, too. See, if it

isn't out there, then it isn't; you don't really expect it to be, anyway. But what you can't stand is the fear that you'll just miss it. The garage-sale nightmare is to get to a sale just as someone else is walking away with your Big Score." She sighed. "It gets very competitive out there."

"How big is Big, would you say?" Anneke asked curiously.

"Everybody has their own fantasies." Joyce said.

"But something big enough to kill for . . ." Anneke persisted. "I mean, you'd have to assume a very high intrinsic value, like jewelry, wouldn't you?"

"There are plenty of other things that would qualify," Steve interjected. "Tiffany leaded glass, for instance."

"Frank Lloyd Wright furniture."

"Oriental rugs."

"A Georgia O'Keeffe painting."

"A letter signed by Button Gwinnett."

Anneke started to laugh and then stopped. "A list of things to kill for," she said with distaste.

"People have been doing it for thousands of years," Steve said.

"I know. It's the ugly underside of humanity's lust for beauty." Anneke nodded, tightening her lips.

"Well, is it any better or worse to kill for hate, or wealth, or some kind of insane idealism?" Joyce asked reasonably.

"I suppose not," Anneke admitted.

"Anyway, you can see that anyone could have wanted to kill her," Carmela repeated, "and there is no more reason for the police to accuse Ellen than any of the rest of us."

"Except that I'm the only Jap in the crowd." Ellen spoke quietly, her hands continuing their work with porcelain and clamps and glue. "I told them what Joanna said," she responded to Anneke's look of surprise. "Why not?"

"It's nonsense, it must have been a mistake." Carmela looked at Anneke shrewdly. "You must have heard it wrong, that's all.

And if you tell the police so, they'll stop persecuting Ellen and start looking for the real killer."

"Is that what you got me down here for?" Anneke spoke directly to Joyce, and there was real anger in her voice.

"No!" Joyce was clearly angry herself. "Carmela, don't be foolish. I was there too, remember? She said what she said."

"Then she must have meant something else," Carmela retorted.

"Of course she did," Joyce agreed. "Only"—she appealed to Anneke—"will the police bother to figure out what she *did* mean, or will they just take the easy way out?"

"Lord, how would I know?" Anneke was uncomfortable under their intent gaze; only Ellen kept her eyes fixed on her work. "Why are you asking me?"

"Because you're supposed to be in tight with the cops," Steve answered her.

Damn the woman, he thought angrily, couldn't she see the fear behind Ellen's tight face? Or didn't she give a shit?

He flexed his fingers slightly, willing his muscles to relax, trying to shrug off the unaccustomed and unwelcome tension he felt. The tension made him irritable—irritability born not of nerves but of self-contempt. He didn't like the feel of emotion; he hadn't felt anxiety, certainly, since his sixteenth birthday, when he'd split from home.

Life on the streets, he'd figured, couldn't be any worse than the regular beatings he and his mother endured whenever his father came home drunk, or stoned, or just mean with rage after a day on the assembly line. Besides, if he'd stayed he'd probably have killed the son-of-a-bitch eventually.

He'd helped himself to the household money out of his mother's dresser drawer, caring only a little that its disappearance would cost her another beating—if not that, something else, and after all she'd never protected him, had she—and left the dingy downriver neighborhood for the equally dingy streets of Ypsilanti, where a couple of friends had a rundown apart-

ment. Since then he'd lived cool and nonchalant and most of all alone, totally in control of himself and his life.

At first, after leaving home, he'd paid his way by shoplifting, but quickly moved on to the less dangerous and far more lucrative breaking-and-entering, first around Ypsi and then in the more affluent environs of Ann Arbor, five miles west. He didn't overdo it; just enough to get by on, and just drifting, and it was okay for a couple of years. But by his eighteenth birthday he knew he was thoroughly bored.

In the end it was the fence who changed his life for him. He'd lifted an antique gold pocket watch, beautifully chased and decorated, but the bastard only offered him twenty percent of its melt value.

"You don't mean you're going to melt it down," Steve remonstrated, appalled.

"Sonny, if I tried to pass it I'd be inside in an hour." The fence was a fat, pasty-looking man with tired eyes and a permanent gut-ache. He belched and pushed the watch back to Steve, his expression bored. "Take it or leave it."

He took it, of course; what else could he do? But the memory of the watch nagged at him. He found himself wandering through antique shops, noting in amazement the prices you could get for straight sales. And he discovered, to his vast and continuing surprise, that he actually liked all this old stuff.

By the time an Ypsi dealer recognized and appreciated his interest—and his well-muscled body—and offered him a job, he was ready to accept.

The garage sale circuit, when she introduced him to it, delighted him. It was practically a license to steal, hardly different from a B-and-E except that he could get full value for his finds. He had a lot of learning to do, of course, but the Ypsi dealer provided that; his own intelligence, once he had found a focus of interest, did the rest.

"You do work for the police, don't you?" Joyce pressed Anneke. "Couldn't you . . . I don't know, talk to them, anyway? At

least find out if they're investigating other possibilities, or if they're just concentrating on the obvious?"

"Joyce, I don't *work for* the police, I just do some computer work for them, that's all," Anneke said uncomfortably. "I can't just waltz into City Hall and start asking questions about a murder case."

"Oh, leave her alone." Ellen stood up and spun the handle on the vise, releasing the bowl she'd been repairing. Her face was a mask, unreadable. "Anneke, I'm sorry my friends are pressuring you; please forget about it. Joyce, I need some more boxes to pack things for the Show. Are there any downstairs?"

"Ellen sometimes carries her inscrutability routine a little too far," Steve commented drily. He was applying some sort of gilt paste with his fingers to the picture frame in front of him, and when he waved his hand sunlight glinted off his fingers. "You do know the boys in blue, don't you?" he asked Anneke.

"I know some of them," she admitted, looking at Ellen's closed face. "But I've never even met the man in charge of the case."

"You met him yesterday," Joyce pointed out.

"So did you," Anneke retorted. Joyce said nothing, only shook her head, and Anneke mentally withdrew the comment. That was different, and she knew it. She herself did, despite her protests, have some standing with the police, however tenuous. True, she hadn't met Genesko before yesterday, but she wouldn't mind an opportunity to talk to him again. "Ellen, do you want me to talk to the police?"

"I don't think it will help." She spoke in tones that were flat and even; Anneke wondered what this display of self-control was costing her. "And you seem to think it would be out of line." She remained painfully polite, struggling to keep any hint of appeal out of her voice, and Anneke's respect for her jumped a notch. She had been prepared for, and appalled by the prospect of, an emotional scene; Ellen's stoicism impressed her more than tears would have.

"Do you really think the police suspect you?" she asked.

"I don't know." Ellen shook her head helplessly.

"That's really what you want to know, isn't it?" Anneke realized suddenly. "Whether they actually believe you did it?"

"Yes." Behind her stoic façade the girl's eyes held real fear. I have to go in this week to sort out that printer problem anyway, Anneke rationalized to herself.

"Look, I'll drop in tomorrow and ask, okay?"

"Thank you," Ellen said, looking her straight in the eye for the first time.

"Good." Carmela clapped her hands. As if I've solved their whole problem for them, Anneke thought with dismay. "That's settled, then. Now, would you like to see the pre-Columbian jar I bought yesterday? Only two hundred dollars for a Nazca figural, would you believe it?"

"Thanks, but I'm afraid I'm blind to primitive art." Anneke smiled. "And I've got a weekend's worth of work to cram into one afternoon."

"I'll walk you to the door." Steve surprised her by jumping to his feet, wiping his hands down the front of his jeans. The action added wide streaks of gilt to the already multicolored denim. "Professional's trick," he said, looking down at the mess with every appearance of satisfaction. "Always wipe your hands on the *front* of your pants; that way you can sit down without messing up the furniture."

Anneke said good-bye to the others and followed him back the way she'd come, but when they reached the kitchen he stopped, as she'd half expected him to.

"Has anyone ever told you you have the face of an Erté odalisque?" he asked her, and when she burst out laughing he made a mock grimace. "Gee, that line usually works a lot better."

"On whom?" Anneke asked, still laughing. "Certainly no one your own age." He really did look young, although the sharp-featured face, accentuated by the spiky hair and dangling silver-

and-turquoise earring, had a wary, worldly appearance. "You didn't come out here just to hit on a woman old enough to be your mother, did you?"

"Age is an illusion. Ellen is twenty-four, but innocent as a newborn chick. In both senses of the word." His grin died away as he considered the woman in front of him. A good-looking broad, at least for her age; plenty bright, maybe even too bright; probably stubborn and intolerant, like most of her generation. Could she really do anything? Hell, what other choice was there? "Do what you can for her, okay?" he asked.

"I'll try." Oh, damn, he's in love with her, Anneke realized with a sudden wash of empathy that left a wake of remembered pain. It had been a long time since she'd felt like that; and perhaps, she thought with something like fear, I never will again.

"Thanks." He closed the door behind her and watched her retreating form through the window, enjoying the sight of taut muscles encased in well-fitting blue pants, even as he worried at Joanna's murder. Damn the woman! Why couldn't she have died right away, silently, instead of spitting out those two lousy words?

He turned back and retraced his steps, pausing in the dining room to rearrange a shelf full of multicolored Fiesta ware. Nice stuff; bright and cheerful, full of color and life. Odd, in fact, all that color. Somehow he always thought of "back then" as pale and colorless. Like the blurry black-and-white Great Depression photos in his tenth-grade history textbook.

He had never, even in his burglary days, been afraid of the police, and their interrogation after Joanna's murder merely amused him. By the time they'd caught up with him, he had already unpacked his car and was sorting and cleaning the day's take, but he politely showed them each item, gave them his fingerprints, and answered their questions without hesitation. He was no longer a street kid, after all, but a mildly successful young businessman.

I've finally got it together, he thought, pausing in the front parlor to examine a small Orrefors bowl. Lots of action, lots of women, and the brains to recognize a Big Score when I see one. He pushed open the door of the workroom and returned to the table, avoiding Ellen's anxious eyes. He hadn't counted on falling in love.

SIX

I must be the only person in the world, Anneke thought, whose favorite day of the week is Monday. On this beautiful June morning, surrounded by burgeoning greenery and singing birds, I'm delighted because I'm on my way to work.

The offices of A/H, Inc., were in the Nickels Arcade, a glass-roofed corridor cut through the main campus business block. The Arcade was a true oddity, with tiny stores lining the ground floor on each side and a warren of offices above. A Historical Building plaque was testimony to one small victory for preservationists.

Anneke stopped briefly at the pillared entry, appreciating as always the rich decoration and wealth of detail that gave the Arcade its old-world charm, although it was in fact a twentieth-century structure. The last flowering of grand style before the Art Deco revolution, worthy of respect even if not to her own personal taste. Thank God at least the Arcade had not given way to "progress," she thought fondly, stifling an urge to pat the historic plaque as if it were a puppy.

She climbed the worn stairs to her offices and pushed open the glass-paned door, taking her customary pleasure at the chaos within. Chaos meant work going on, work that no one but she herself had ever believed would come her way.

She had started the company with the conviction that, as computers spread, small businesses and organizations would need—and would pay for—all kinds of competent help. She knew she couldn't compete with the big-time consulting companies, and she didn't try; she refused even to bid on contracts from banks, or hospitals, or national chain stores. Instead, she had carved out her own niche in the world of small users, and she had made it pay.

"Ms. Haagen!" Carol Rosenthal jumped up from her terminal, waving a sheaf of papers. "Wait'll you see what came in this morning!"

"An RFP?" A new Request for Proposal was always welcome.

"Not even an RFP! A straight offer for a project, and what a project!" The girl's face was flushed with excitement, and she shoved impatiently at the tangled black hair that fell over her face.

"I take it you're putting in for it?" Anneke laughed.

"You bet!" Carol dropped a pencil, lunged for it, knocked a pile of papers off the corner of the desk, and scrabbled at the resulting mess. Anneke cleared space on her own desk, dropped her briefcase on it, and poured a cup of coffee from the nearly empty pot.

"Ken, would you make some more coffee?" she called into the next room. "Carol, pull up a chair and tell me what you've got."

The proposal, Carol explained, was from a vaguely countercultural foundation that wanted to study the political implications of computer communications.

"They're really into the heavy stuff. They want to examine corporate control of data banks, attempts to establish counter-

culture networks, the question of who gets to put data into the data banks, the whole question of authority and control. Especially the Internet."

"Hackers, of course, qualify as true antiauthority figures," Anneke commented.

"Right! That's a major point."

"How do you operationalize it?" Anneke had her own ideas, but she wanted to see what Carol had in mind.

"That's the best part. Everything we want to study is already on-line. We can run the questionnaires right on the Internet— we won't even have to use poll-takers."

"Wow." Ken Scheede had finished filling the coffeepot and now sat on top of his desk, feet on the chair. One knee poked through a hole in his worn jeans. "Has anyone ever done that before?"

"Not true random-sample polling, as far as I know," Anneke answered. "But you're already busy with that small-press typesetting consortium, aren't you?"

"I could work on this too," Ken offered eagerly.

"Only if you want to flunk out," Anneke said firmly. "Carol, what's the timeline? And what's your class schedule for the next semester?"

"Piece of cake," the girl answered promptly. "Preliminary reports in six and twelve months, final results in eighteen. And all I've got are two programming courses, one math course, and one elective. And we're nearly done with the time-share program for those minimall shops." She looked so eager that Anneke laughed.

"Okay, you're the project director. Use . . . I think Mark and Jackie should have the time to give you; check with them. And give me the proposal so I can get the paperwork out on it."

The girl picked up her battered tote bag and departed, tripping over the sill on her way out. Anneke watched her go with

intense satisfaction. At the beginning, she'd hired student programmers because she simply couldn't afford full-time professionals; now, she wouldn't care if the professionals came free. With each new generation of students, she was getting the real best and brightest.

Besides, the students were so much more fun.

"Are those legal analyses done yet?" she asked Ken.

"Yep." He reached for a stack of printouts piled on top of a filing cabinet. "Jackie finished them last night."

"Oh, lovely," she said, skimming the synopsis page. "Marshall's going to love these numbers." Marshall Lang was her son-in-law, a radical attorney living in Colorado who'd asked her to analyze judicial sentencing patterns by race for a number of western cities. "I'll pass them on to him right now."

Swinging around to her terminal, she dialed into the computer bulletin board she and Marshall, as well as her daughter Rachel, used for electronic mail. To her delight, Marshall was on-line, even though it was only seven A.M. in Boulder. Switching to Chat Mode, she typed:

```
>How come you're up so early?
```

There was a short pause; then her terminal spelled out:

```
>Because your granddaughter just learned the word
''water,'' that's why, and she's been asking for
some every five minutes.
>How's Samantha doing?
>She's going to be a holy terror. Just like her
grandmother.
>Flattery will get you nowhere.
>Will it get me that sentencing data?
>Coming at you. Hold on; I'll upload it now.
```

She entered the commands that transferred the data into the host computer; when the upload was complete she typed:

```
>All done. You're going to love it.
>Good stuff? Terrific! Anneke, you're a wonder!
When are we going to see you?
>Maybe this summer if I can swing a week off. Give my
love to Rachel and the Holy Terror.
```

He logged off before she realized she hadn't told him about Carol's latest project, which she knew would interest him. Of course, so would the murder, but Chat Mode was no way to tell a man that his mother-in-law had spent the weekend finding a body. She'd write him and Rachel a long letter next week, when it would probably be all over.

She'd do the same for her younger daughter, she decided, although Emma was so involved in her struggling jewelry design business—that and the Santa Cruz beaches—that she'd hardly notice if she found a body herself. And after all, Anneke rationalized, it's not as if I have any real involvement in the whole thing. But even as she thought it, her promise to Ellen nagged at her mind.

She put the murder, and Ellen, firmly out of her mind and checked her E-Mail. Here she'd be dealing primarily with business messages; much easier to cope with.

Except the name Dennis Grantham leaped from the monitor screen and slammed into her like a kick to the stomach, producing the same sensation of appalled nausea.

Dammit, no. Not again, not now, not anymore, not after eight months of blessed peace. Furiously she punched up his missive, relieved to see that it was at least short. Not another angry recrimination, then. No, even worse, she thought tensely, reading.

"No!" Anneke said aloud, explosively. Dennis's software company might be nearly Fortune 500 level, but she'd run a magnet over the disks before she'd let that son-of-a-bitch get his hands on her beloved program, the only game she'd ever designed.

That was the way they'd met in the first place, at a computer fair in Detroit. She was a forty-five-year-old woman with a small, struggling business; he was a thirty-nine-year-old whiz kid heading his own multimillion-dollar operation. For a while she'd been so flattered by his adoration that she mistook her own feelings. Only when she realized her mistake did she discover that Dennis had never learned to take no for an answer.

She thought he finally had, but apparently not. Well, he would this time, Anneke thought grimly, her fingers rattling over the keyboard. And then, suddenly, she laughed aloud. No, honestly, the whole thing was too ridiculous. And anyway, anything she wrote would only encourage him; this was a case in which no response was the best response. Without reading what she'd written, she punched Delete, logged off, and turned her mind firmly toward work.

She finished testing the minimall program before lunch, treated herself to a shrimp salad at a nearby restaurant, and reluctantly headed the Alfa toward City Hall. Well, not all that

reluctantly; she was certainly curious about the progress of the case, and Genesko had seemed . . . interesting. No more than that, of course; still, she was damned if she'd go all neurotic about even casual friendships with men. That would be giving Dennis the ultimate victory over her, she told herself firmly.

She first spent an hour unscrambling the department's printer-interface problem, then sat at the terminal briefly sorting out her thoughts. She might be willing to approach Genesko on Ellen's behalf; only, now that she was here, what on earth was she to say to him? In the end, she decided simply to fall back on the truth.

His office door was closed, but he answered her knock promptly.

"Ms. Haagen, please come in." He seemed legitimately pleased to see her. "Are we having computer trouble?" He stood aside to let her into an office so small he seemed almost to fill it.

"Just a minor glitch." She smiled, uncomfortably aware of his physical presence. She'd forgotten how big he was.

"What can I do for you?" He motioned to an ugly gray chair beside an ugly gray desk which was piled high with papers but contrived nevertheless to look orderly, the piles carefully lined up in neat rows.

"It's about Saturday." She waited until they were both seated before continuing. "Look, this is undoubtedly out of line, but I was asked to speak to you and for several reasons I feel a certain sense of responsibility."

"Yes, I can see that you might." He nodded. "Because you're the one who reported the victim's last words, and at the same time you know the people involved."

"You see the position I'm in, then." Anneke was relieved to note how quickly he did see. "Yesterday I was asked by several people, friends of Ellen Nakamura, if I would just find out what her situation is."

"They want to know if the police have merely settled on her

as the easiest target, or if we're actually going to conduct a real investigation." His face lost none of its studied calm, but his voice was amused. Anneke stared at him for several seconds.

"Do you do it with mirrors," she asked at last, "or are you a closet telepath?"

"It's the way most people think about the police." He smiled gently as he riffled through one of the neat stacks of paper. "Let me ask you something," he said, withdrawing a page and handing it to her. "Is there anything on that list of items that's spectacularly valuable?"

The sheet of paper, with Ellen Nakamura's name at the top, was a list that started with "scroll, picture of cranes, Chinese lettering," and ended with "heavy frying pan, orange enamel." In between were more than two dozen equally unrevealing entries. Next to each entry was an address.

"I take it this is a list of what Ellen bought Saturday, and where she bought each item?" Genesko nodded. "Then you are focusing on her," Anneke said.

"Not necessarily. We have similar lists from each of the other names your friend gave us."

"But if Ellen can confirm where she bought each item, doesn't that prove she didn't steal anything from Joanna?"

"It might, if each purchase could be confirmed. Unfortunately, most of the saleholders don't remember who they sold what to."

"No, I suppose not." Anneke recalled some of the chaotic sales she'd been to.

"We did, of course, circulate Joanna's picture and ask people what she'd bought from them," he said, "but we didn't have much luck there either. And the few things we did get identified were in her car with her. I'm afraid the people holding the sales weren't much help."

"You want to know what?" the fat woman in the yellow sweatshirt yelped at Officer Liz Holliman.

"Do you remember if any of these items came from your sale this morning, and if so, who you sold them to?" Liz proffered the list with a mental sigh.

"You must be joking," the woman retorted, angry at having her televised baseball game interrupted. "There must have been a hundred people plowing through here. Besides, my husband and daughter were helping out, so I didn't do all the selling myself. And besides that, half the time someone would come up to me with a box of stuff, tell me it added up to three bucks, pay me and leave. I didn't care; I just wanted to get rid of the crap."

"I know it's difficult," Liz said soothingly. "Would you just take a look at this picture, and tell me if you can remember selling anything to this woman? Anything at all you can remember would be a help." She sighed, aloud this time, and mentally wrote off one more lead.

"You know," Anneke said, struck by a sudden thought, "it could be even worse than you think. The seller might not even know she'd sold it."

"What do you mean?"

"What if it were something stuck in a drawer?" she suggested. "Or left in the pocket of a coat? That sort of thing does happen, you know." She looked again at the list, which was heavy on things like "small bowl, blue pattern," then handed it back to Genesko.

"Sorry, but I don't know a thing about Oriental art. And even if I did . . ." she looked at the list again. "Listen to this: 'white carved statue, old man.' I mean, ivory? Bone? Plastic? Shiny new or four hundred years old?" She threw up her hands. "Honestly, it's hopeless."

"Don't I know it. What's more, the others are even worse." He picked up a sheaf of papers and tossed them irritably aside. "And since we couldn't legally seize everything on the spot, there was no way to get an expert appraisal."

"Anyway," she remarked, "why would this thing, whatever it

is, even be on a list? I mean, why wouldn't the murderer hide it and simply not tell the police he had it at all?"

"That would depend on circumstances," Genesko answered. "He might, certainly, if he had time, and if the item is easily concealed, and if he knew the police would arrive quickly. Several were met by an officer as they were coming home. We're simply investigating all the possibilities."

"And there's something else, too," Anneke said suddenly. "It just occurred to me—did you check out what everyone was wearing?"

"Wearing?" For the first time, Genesko seemed at a loss.

"Jewelry." Anneke chuckled, recalling her foray with Joyce. "Apparently, when someone finds a really good piece they'll put it on right there. It seems that's the safest way of carrying it."

"I see. No, I must admit we didn't think of that." He looked at her with every appearance of gratification.

"You'd think one of the other regulars might have noticed what Joanna bought," Anneke said thoughtfully. "I take it they didn't?"

There was a pause. Then he extracted another sheaf of papers from the bottom of one of the stacks.

"These are the reports on our conversations with the other dealers." He held the papers out to her and she reached for them, but then drew her hand back.

"Should you be showing them to me?"

"You have police clearance," Genesko pointed out.

"Yes, but still . . ."

"I'll take my chances." She found it impossible to analyze his expression, and before she could say anything more he dropped the stack of paper in front of her. "Would you like some coffee?" He motioned toward a coffeemaker on one of the file cabinets.

As he poured coffee she thought about her reaction to the murder. Horror, certainly, and pity, but also, she admitted to herself ruefully, a very real fascination. While one part of her mind responded to the human tragedy of Joanna's death, an-

other part had already fastened on the pure problem-solving aspect. She still didn't know why Genesko was involving her in the investigation, but her curiosity was fully engaged. Without further protest she took the stack of papers in one hand and the thick coffee mug in the other.

SEVEN

It took her nearly half an hour, reading at top speed, to plow through a mass of verbiage that told her exactly nothing. All of them had seen Joanna at some point in the morning; none of them admitted seeing her buy anything unusually valuable. In fact, most of them sneered at what she did buy. The comment by Steve Olewski was typical:

"I never paid much attention to her, because we were almost never in competition for the same things. She only bought modern crap. She wouldn't have known a valuable antique if it jumped up and bit her."

Peter Casaday seemed a better bet, because his interests overlapped Joanna's slightly, but he too had seen nothing:

"I'm not really in competition with anyone, because I collect sixties stuff. You know, bright colors, psychedelic patterns, stuff that looks really super-modern today. Well, yeah, Joanna liked contemporary, but it wasn't like she really knew shit about anything, you know? She just bought stuff she thought was

pretty." (Anneke could almost feel his scorn jump off the type-written page.) "Anyway, I only saw her at one sale today, and as far as I know all she bought there was a tablecloth and some napkins."

Only two people admitted to talking to Joanna about something she'd bought. One was Alice Cowan, who told a confused story about some Dansk stainless steel flatware. The other was Michael Rappaport:

"She asked me if I could identify a tatty crystal decanter she'd bought. When I told her it was merely contemporary Waterford, available in every department store, the silly woman seemed quite delighted. There really is no accounting for taste, is there?"

Anneke finished the last of the reports and returned them to Genesko. "If there's anything there that means anything, it went right by me. A hundred-dollar decanter or a batch of knives and forks could hardly qualify as a Big Score."

"Big Score?" he asked curiously.

"That's the ultimate find." She explained. "The kind of thing so valuable you can retire on it. I gather it's more myth than reality, like the Holy Grail."

"In any case, the decanter and the silverware were both in her car," Genesko commented. "And no one admitted that she'd made any great find."

"Of course, Joanna wouldn't necessarily know it *was* a great find." Anneke recalled the various comments she'd heard about the woman.

"Well, for the moment at least, we're assuming that someone did," he said. Someone who was willing to kill for it, Anneke thought, watching Genesko shuffle the papers into a single neat pile and return them to the appropriate stack.

But still . . . Anneke thought about the people behind the interrogation sheets. She'd met them all on Saturday; it seemed impossible to visualize any one of them as a murderer. But

before she could formulate a question there was a knock at the door.

"Got a minute?" Brad Weinmann poked his head in the door without waiting for an answer to his knock. "Oh, hi, Anneke. Sorry, Karl, I didn't know you were busy. Want me to come back?"

"No, come on in." Genesko waved him into the office. "What've you got?"

"Preliminary forensics." He held out a file folder, and Genesko opened it and read through its contents quickly. When he reached the end he returned it to Brad and stood up.

"Will you excuse me, please? I'll be right back."

"There's no reason for me to take up any more of your time." Anneke started to rise.

"No, please stay. If you don't mind, that is?" He made it a question, but before she could respond he said: "Brad, would you stay here and keep Ms. Haagen company for a few minutes? I'll be right back." He opened the door and was gone.

"Whew."

"Isn't he something?" Brad's voice held awed respect.

"I've only just met him. Is he really such a hotshot?" Anneke asked with interest. So Brad thought well of him, and Brad, she knew, was not given to hero-worship.

"The hottest," Brad declared. "When I was assigned to work with him on this case I thought I'd died and gone to heaven."

"It's an odd career choice for an ex-football player, isn't it?" She let her curiosity pursue its own course.

"I know. Of course, he made a bundle with the Steelers, so he doesn't need to worry about money." Brad's voice held the mild envy of the young father struggling to make ends meet. "I guess he just enjoys the challenge—you know, he started out on the Pittsburgh force. He was the one who broke the Depford case."

"The Morning Murders?" Anneke remembered the series of eight early-morning killings in downtown Pittsburgh by their

unofficial press designation. "That was a major case. Isn't Ann Arbor a step down from that sort of thing in a big city?"

"Apparently he didn't much like big-city living," Brad said. "I don't blame him. Ann Arbor's got enough action to be interesting without having to spend all your time in sleaze joints."

Anneke was amused by this viewpoint, not so different from others she'd heard. Ann Arbor's appeal to many different professions, apparently, was that there was just enough going on, but not too much.

"Sorry for the interruption, Ms. Haagen." Genesko reentered the room and sat down again behind the desk. "They're sure," he said to Brad.

"Well, so are our guys," Brad responded firmly with, Anneke was pleased to hear, no hint of awe in his voice. "They searched the area for a couple of hundred feet in every direction."

"Including the other side of the road?"

"Both sides of the road, inside the car, every ditch, bush, and tree—you name it. And they know their job."

"I'm sure they do." Genesko spoke reassuringly, as if responding to an inaudible defensiveness in Brad's tone. He was new here, of course, Anneke was aware; he must be trying hard to avoid stepping on local toes. But what were they searching for?

"The murder weapon?" she asked suddenly.

"Yes. We're still trying to find it."

"But can you even tell what it was, beyond the generic 'blunt instrument'?"

"Oh, yes. Actually, it's very simple. She was hit with a rock, a nice, round, anonymous rock."

"How can you tell?" Anneke asked curiously.

"Flakes left in the wound."

"But then," she considered, working it out in her mind, "he probably just picked up a rock from the side of the road, did the job, then tossed the rock back where he found it."

"Yes." Genesko spread his hands on the desk and appeared

to contemplate the large diamond-set ring on his right hand. A Super Bowl ring, Anneke realized; that was all right, then, one of the few legitimate excuses she could imagine for a man to wear diamonds. "Except," he continued finally, "the murderer didn't toss it back."

"What do you mean?"

"The area was searched. Thoroughly. The rock she was killed with would have had bloodstains on it. It wasn't there."

"But—you mean he took it away with him? Why on earth would he do that? I mean even if you found it, so what? It would only be a rock."

"I've no idea. That's exactly what makes it interesting." He turned to Brad. "Would you make sure those fragments go to Plymouth?" The state police forensics lab was in Plymouth.

When Brad had gone Anneke returned to an earlier thought. "I assume there were no helpful fingerprints on her car?"

"Only her own and her husband's. And yours, of course."

"What about the husband?" Anneke asked. "Isn't the spouse usually the prime suspect?"

"Often, certainly." He seemed amused. "But Ronald West-lake was conducting a seminar Saturday from eight A.M. until noon, in continuous view of ten people. And their fourteen-year-old daughter is away at a special school. Oh, yes"—he responded to Anneke's appalled look—"teenagers have been known to murder their parents."

"I know. It's just . . ."

"Well, that's not the case here, anyway," Genesko said briskly. "It's not an absolute, of course, but for the moment, at least, we think it's likely that Joanna Westlake was murdered out of plain, ordinary greed."

"I'm not sure that makes me feel any better," Anneke said unhappily, rising to take her leave.

Well, at least I can reassure Ellen that she's not the only suspect, Anneke thought Tuesday morning as she drove toward the

antique co-op. She had spent the first part of the morning at her office doing paperwork, which she loathed, and was glad enough for an excuse to put it aside.

This time she went in the front door, where she found Carmela removing silver bracelets from one of the glass cases at the direction of two teenage girls.

"That one over there." The one with stiff jet-black hair cut short on one side and long on the other pointed into the case.

"Ooh! What about that chain thingy?" exclaimed her friend, a blue-and-redhead done up in three or four layers of indeterminate clothing finished off with ankle-high hiking boots over black lace stockings.

"Hi, Carmela." Anneke grinned.

"Anneke!" Carmela dumped half a dozen pieces of jewelry onto the counter and left them for the girls to examine. "Tell me, what did you find out?"

"Nothing much. But nothing bad either," she added hastily as Carmela's face grew stormy. "It's really still all up in the air," she said with a warning glance at the two girls. "Is Ellen here?"

"The others are in the back getting things ready for the Show. It's my morning to work the shop."

"Can we see that red necklace?" the black-haired girl called out. Carmela rolled her eyes and Anneke retreated, laughing.

But before she broached the red door to the workroom she detoured to the side parlor, where she stood for a moment contemplating the displays of Oriental porcelain, furniture, and assorted artifacts. Ellen's area of the shop, crisply clean and organized. Not top-of-the-line antiques, of course—that was evident from the prices—but decent quality nonetheless. No Taiwan schlock, and no hype either, just the best Ellen could afford at the moment, presented honestly and lovingly. With a sigh, Anneke moved on to the workroom.

"Anneke! Did you find out anything?" Joyce jumped from her chair, scattering Styrofoam pellets, which clung to her hands and hair. She brushed them away impatiently. "Ugh, I hate this

stuff, but it's the best packing material there is. Here, sit down." She cleared three aging teddy bears off a chair. "Well?"

"What's the verdict from the cop shop?" Steve, today's T-shirt declaring "I'm your mother's worst nightmare," looked up from the table at the back, where he was arranging glass vases in a carton and pouring Styrofoam around them. "Are they ready to haul anyone away?"

"I did talk to them," Anneke said, aware of Ellen's half-averted gaze from behind the big table, where she sat surrounded by several dozen small items of softly polished brass. "But I'm not sure what to tell you, except that they really don't seem to be concentrating on Ellen any more than any of the others."

"What did he actually say?" Joyce insisted.

"Two words less than zilch, is my guess," Steve interjected. "The cops taketh, but they don't giveth away much of anything."

"I really don't think you have to feel like a target," Anneke said to Ellen.

"No more than the rest of us, anyway." Steve finished pouring Styrofoam and sealed the carton with masking tape.

"Do they really think it was one of the garage-sale people?" Joyce asked.

"Well, I'm sure they're looking at other possibilities," Anneke said uncomfortably.

"Still, they'll focus on us, won't they?" Ellen looked up from her polishing, her expression still tight and controlled, seeming to derive little comfort from Anneke's report.

"Imagine. Little me, a murder suspect," Steve chirped. "And in such august company." He sketched a bow in Ellen's direction. "Who else is in the running besides the two of us? Martha, of course, and probably Peter and Alice Cowan. Anyone else? How about the baby-clothes lady? I suppose not. She never talks to anyone, just scuttles around. Although she could have offed Joanna. Maybe she bopped her with a potty chair."

"Steve, don't be an ass," Ellen said with the ghost of a grin, the first sign of animation Anneke had seen.

"You forgot Michael," Joyce commented. "He was out doing sales Saturday."

"The great Michael Rappaport?" Steve whooped with glee. "Oh, cosmic. That'll teach him to poach on our turf. Can't you just see him being questioned by the cops, all comfy around the tea table? Anyway, it couldn't be Michael—he'd be afraid of getting blood on his clothes."

"Well, it couldn't be you, because Joanna wouldn't let you near her in one of your T-shirts." Ellen laughed. Steve was doing exactly the right thing, Anneke realized; Ellen saw herself now as merely one of a group of suspects, rather than the primary target.

"We could do a pool," Steve suggested. "Work up odds on all the suspects and sell chances." He stopped. "Nope, won't work."

"Why not?" Ellen challenged him, now thoroughly in the spirit of the thing.

"Because the only way to have a winner is for the cops to find the killer, and that's gotta be the longest odds of all. I'll bet they haven't even found the weapon yet." He looked at Anneke. "Have they?"

"She was killed with a rock," she equivocated after a brief pause. Steve eyed her sharply.

"Well, that lets me out." He leaned back in his chair, balancing on the rear legs. "I've never owned a rock in my life. How about you?" he asked Ellen.

"Never touch the stuff," she retorted.

"Never touch what stuff?" a voice asked from the doorway.

"Oh, good, someone else to join the pool." Steve waved a hand.

"Hi, Ted." Ellen turned toward the door. "What're you doing here?" It was not the most welcoming of greetings, but Ted Burns didn't seem to notice.

"I thought you'd like to grab some lunch. I know sometimes

you get so involved you forget to eat." He was carrying a large brown grocery bag, which he set down on the floor. "What pool?" he asked Steve.

"Murder suspects. Anneke's just brought us the latest scuttlebutt from the cop house."

"Oh? Have they decided who they're going to railroad?" Ted swiveled to confront Anneke, his face ugly with tension and something else she couldn't identify. She'd only met him once or twice, and she remembered him as an intense but good-natured young man; this hostility surprised her.

"They haven't decided anything, as far as I can tell," she responded mildly.

"We're all still in the running," Steve announced grandly. "Still time to place your bets."

"So far I'm the odds-on favorite," Ellen said with a hint of defiance.

"Oh, I don't know." Steve teetered farther back in his chair. "I think I'll take a flyer on the husband, myself. If I'd been married to her she wouldn't have lasted this long."

"Yes, what about the husband?" Ted challenged Anneke. "Or is he too upper-middle-class for the police to mess with?"

"As I understand it, he's got an airtight alibi." Surely there's nothing wrong with telling them that much, Anneke thought, wishing Genesko had flagged the confidential material somehow. Of course, she'd made him no specific promises, but she'd accepted the implied responsibility. "Ronald Westlake was teaching a seminar all Saturday morning."

"Ronald Westlake?" Ted's eyebrows rose. "From the Residential College?"

"I think so," Anneke replied. "Do you know him?"

"I've met him once or twice—I've been over to the RC a few times to see about teaching a course for them. I never made the connection." He shook his head. "I sure as hell know of him, though. Are they dead sure about that alibi?"

"Why?" Is this going to be one of those things Genesko wanted me to find out? Anneke wondered.

"Because Westlake's been having an affair with Carla Bridges—she teaches art at the RC—for at least two years."

"Are you sure? How do you know?"

"Hell, everyone knows." Ted made a disgusted face. "The two of them are a sleazy joke all over campus."

"Well, with a wife like that, who can blame him?" Steve drawled.

"I can," Ted snapped. "I don't mean that he should have put up with a lousy home life, but he should at least have had the guts to move out and get a divorce, instead of screwing around and making messes of everybody's lives. And not just his and his wife's, or even Bridges', although God knows this mess isn't helping her career any. Did you know that his daughter had to be sent away for treatment for anorexia?" He made pushing motions with his hands. "He was a damn good teacher, too. Still is, I guess; at least the kids all love him. But he's got his life so fucked up he can't do any decent work anymore."

He spoke so passionately that the others in the room seemed embarrassed, and for several moments after he stopped there was a strained silence.

"I take it Joanna didn't know?" Anneke asked finally.

"No idea," Ted replied. "Never met her."

"But surely they couldn't expect to keep it from her for very long, if everyone on campus knew about it."

"You don't understand," Ted burst out. "I think he wanted her to find out. He didn't have the guts to confront her and demand a divorce, so he was hoping she'd find out about his affair and take the decision out of his hands."

"If he didn't have the guts to divorce, though," Joyce offered, "would he have the guts to murder?"

"Sure." Ted nodded with the certainty of the social scientist. "Happens all the time, when a repressed personality finally snaps. That's one of the classic causes of violence."

"Too bad about the alibi, then," Steve remarked.

"Yeah, if he really has one." Ted looked skeptical. "Oh, by the way," he said to Ellen, "I brought this along. Thought you'd want it here instead of at home." He picked up the paper bag and withdrew a pale bluish-green vase.

"Oh. Where did you . . . ? Here, let me take it." Ellen jumped from her chair and grabbed the vase from her husband's grasp, cradling it in both hands. "How did you . . . did you bring it on your bike?" She sounded slightly breathless, and her voice was higher than usual.

"Sure, no problem. It fit in the basket. How about it, lunch at Kerrytown?"

"I don't think so." Ellen looked around the room, crossed to a set of shelves and placed the vase on the highest shelf, then shook her head and removed it. "I've got too much work to get ready for the Show," she said, placing the vase finally on the table in front of her. "And I've got a class at two."

"But you've got to eat," Ted insisted. "And you didn't look all that busy when I got here."

"Well, I was," Ellen snapped, all her newfound good humor seeming to evaporate at once. "I've got a show to get ready for, and two seminars to prepare for, and the police to worry about on top of it. I think that entitles me to eat what and when I damn please."

"Well, I'll do something major for dinner, then." Ted seemed entirely unoffended by his wife's outburst.

"Don't worry, I'll look after her," Steve volunteered. "If she starts to keel over I'll hold her up and spoon-feed her." He winked at Ellen, who smiled wanly.

"Good, please do." Ted also smiled, becoming once again the pleasant man Anneke remembered. "Sometimes she needs a keeper, especially when she gets involved in her work. See you later, hon."

Was that an example of unparalleled naïveté or extreme sophistication? Anneke wondered, watching him leave. Cer-

tainly Ted seemed concerned, indeed very nearly patronizing, toward Ellen; in fact his behavior reminded Anneke uncomfortably of Dennis. But unlike Dennis, Ted seemed totally devoid of jealousy. More, he seemed entirely at ease in his relationship with Ellen, at ease with her responses and her moods. Was he, Anneke wondered, simply not picking up her cues properly, as Dennis had always misread hers? Or was he reading cues that outsiders like Anneke simply couldn't see?

Sighing over the complexities of male-female relationships, she stood up to leave, only to be stopped by another voice from the doorway.

EIGHT

"Oh, good, I've caught you all together." Martha Penrose bustled into the room, her tiny fingers as always gleaming with rings. "And Anneke too, how nice. How are you, dear?" Martha's voice sounded pleased, but her pale blue eyes said otherwise.

"Hi, Martha." Joyce waved a greeting. "Ready for the Show?"

"Oh, yes, I'm always ready. I do the show circuit regularly, after all. And of course I've got Howard to help me. I do wish antiques weren't so heavy, though."

"I know what you mean." Joyce sealed a carton and wrestled it off the table onto the floor. "What a way to make a living."

"Still, of course, it is our living, isn't it? I mean, we aren't doing this as a hobby, are we?"

"I only wish," Joyce said ruefully.

"Well, then," Martha said firmly, "you're a professional, just as I am."

"What's the matter, Martha?" Steve asked. "Having trouble with the IRS?"

"Heavens, no." Martha looked positively offended. "I make quite enough to qualify above the hobby classification, thank you. That's precisely my point."

"What's precisely your point?" Joyce asked.

"Professionalism," Martha declared. "Are you aware that Michael Rappaport wants to open the Antiques Association to nondealers? Including allowing them into next year's Show?"

"I've heard him mention the idea," Joyce assented.

"We really must act together, so that Michael understands from the very beginning that the whole idea is totally unacceptable," Martha said sternly, waving one tiny hand. "I've already spoken to Frank Copley, and I'm going to see Carolyn Herbert this afternoon."

"What's the big deal?" Steve asked.

"Simply that the association is a professional organization," Martha stated. "And if we let every ordinary collector in, we're cutting our own throats."

"I don't see how," Ellen remarked. "It might be a good way to increase interest in antiques generally."

"It might look that way at first, dear, but I'm afraid that's a very shortsighted view. You must see that the interests of amateur and professional are very different, and it would mean serious alterations in the operations of the association. Besides, what we'd end up doing is giving a group of amateurs access to one of our major retail outlets. It's bad enough we have to compete with civilians when we're out buying." Martha's eyes flicked toward Anneke.

"Still," Joyce said thoughtfully, "it could increase our visibility within the community."

"Perhaps, but at what cost to the association?" Martha rejoined. "We concentrate on professional matters—tax information, reference materials, auction information, that sort of thing. Do you really want the public at large to know the current book values of everything they buy?"

"Or worse yet, of everything they sell," Steve declared. "You've got a point, Martha."

"Thank you." She beamed at him. "I imagine we've all lost out on things to these amateurs buying and selling just as a hobby, especially on the garage-sale circuit."

"Well, after all, most garage-sale buyers are civilians," Joyce pointed out.

"I'm not talking about the people who buy things for their own use," Martha insisted. "It's the ones who buy for resale who are the problem. They don't have to deal with tax forms, and overhead costs, and all our professional problems, so of course they can outbid us and then undersell us. Why, just last week Alice Cowan bought twelve pieces of Manhattan. In pink!" Her voice rose angrily.

"Well, it happens to all of us." Joyce said.

"Perhaps." Martha resumed her calm, schoolteacherish tone. "But there's no need to assist at our own execution." She smiled gently. "I'm sure you can see that Michael's idea is just dangerous nonsense."

"Besides," Ellen commented, "amateurs are likely to degrade the quality of the Show, aren't they? I mean, right now it's a top-flight antique show, and it's important to keep it that way. We don't want to turn it into a flea market."

"Exactly!" Martha exclaimed.

"Maybe you're right," Joyce said dubiously. "I'll think it over, anyway, Martha."

"I'm sure you'll come to the right decision, dear. After all, we can't let Michael Rappaport have it all his own way, can we?" She twinkled. "Well, I must be going. I'll see you all at the association meeting this afternoon?"

"This won't come up today, will it?" Joyce asked in alarm.

"I hope not," Martha said judiciously. "I certainly wouldn't upset the meeting right before the show. But it did seem best to be prepared. And I'm sure as soon as the show is behind us Michael is going to raise the issue, and I did want to be sure we

were all well-informed when it arose." She smiled gently. "And now I must get home to give Howard his lunch."

"I didn't realize there was so much hostility toward amateurs," Anneke commented after Martha had left.

"Oh, I don't think there's any real hostility," Joyce assured her. "It's just . . . well, we're in business to make a living, after all."

"It's easy for Michael," Steve remarked. "He's not on the garage-sale circuit anymore. You don't compete with housewives in flowered dresses at Sotheby's."

"And it is absolutely maddening to see some halfwit walking off with a netsuke for two dollars," Ellen added.

"Does Martha deal in anything besides Depression glass?" Anneke asked, following a troubling train of thought.

"Not much anymore," Joyce answered, "although when she had her shop she was more of a generalist. Now it's mostly Depression glass, with other Depression-era things that go along with it—kitchenwares, that kind of thing."

"Actually, that covers most of the Art Deco period," Anneke noted, half to herself. Joanna had been one of the despised amateurs, of course. And while Anneke couldn't imagine even the rarest Depression glass constituting a Big Score, there was plenty of Deco that would qualify. Besides, if Martha had a background as a general antiques dealer, she'd have the expertise to recognize any number of possible Big Scores.

". . . and Frank Copley is definitely with us, he's quite fed up with Michael's high-handedness." Martha spread fat-free mayonnaise carefully to the edges of a slice of whole-wheat bread, selected a slice of ham and a leaf of lettuce, and folded the result to make a neat half sandwich. "Oh, and I stopped in at Remains to Be Seen." Martha wrinkled her nose slightly at the preposterous name; her own business was dignified by the name Penrose Antiques.

"What did they say?" Howard Penrose asked, obedient to his cue.

"Well, I think it's all right." Martha furrowed her brow. "I'm pretty sure of Steve Olewski—he knows which side his bread is buttered on—and Ellen Nakamura is leaning our way, I think. Carmela Aguilar is a dead loss, I'm afraid, but then what could you expect? After all, those people hardly even speak the language. It's Joyce McCarthy I'm worried about—she's very influential, you know, and she seems to have some very . . . egalitarian notions."

"Well, it sounds like you've got a majority on your side even without her." Howard spread safflower-oil margarine on his bread and topped it with a piece of Swiss cheese.

"I think so. Have some salad, dear." She forked lettuce and tomato onto his plate and moved the bottle of low-fat French dressing to his side of the kitchen table. "But I want to be absolutely sure. You remember what happened last time."

"Mmm," Howard mumbled around a mouthful of salad, unwilling to be drawn into another rehash of the Great Computer Debacle.

"Imagine spending twelve thousand dollars of association money—our money—on a computer," Martha continued regardless, still smarting at the memory. It had happened more than two years ago, but she could still remember every scalding moment of the debate, every defection from her side. She had a long memory for grievance.

Of course, Michael had been very glib, very good with figures; well, those people always were. Still, she might have expected elementary loyalty; she was after all one of the founding members of the association. But instead, most of the membership had gone along with this flashy, overdressed, pushy upstart.

"And now he wants to bring in even more outsiders," she said aloud. "Well, this time I'm prepared for him." She finished a last

mouthful of sandwich and rose. "Are you done, dear? Good. I think I'll put this last bit of bread out for the squirrels."

"They probably won't want it this time of year," he commented, pouring himself another cup of Sanka. "They've been gorging themselves on my tulip bulbs."

"They are cheeky little beggars, aren't they?" she said appreciatively. "Well, if the squirrels aren't interested the birds will eat it." Most people, she knew, went to great lengths to feed birds and keep the squirrels at bay, but she'd never understood their attitude. She had a high regard for squirrels—not an emotional response to their furry cuteness but an intellectual respect for the creatures. Squirrels were copers, the only mammals who coexisted peaceably with urban mankind.

She liked to think she had a certain amount of squirrel in her, herself; she too had looked the world in the face, accepted it for what it was, and set out to coexist with it on her own terms. There were, after all, always ways to get what you wanted if, like the squirrels, you were prepared to accept the givens and go on from there.

She'd examined the world around her at an early age, decided what was and wasn't immutable, and made her choices with her eyes open. She went to college, because she concluded it would give her maximum opportunity, but she also determined to marry because she knew a single woman was inevitably handicapped in the world-as-it-was. She selected Howard Penrose over other likely candidates because the academic life he was preparing for seemed both secure and flexible, and Howard himself was easygoing and undemanding.

Once she'd seen him safely through the academic shoals to a Ph.D. and a niche in the anthropology department, she'd moved on to her own career. She knew without vanity that she had the ability to succeed at most things, but based on her twin tenets of flexibility and the art of the possible, an academic career was the obvious choice. She toyed briefly with history as her chosen discipline, but concluded that education provided the best op-

portunities—and the lowest level of competition—for a woman.

Now, after forty-one years, two children, a full professorship, and a comfortably interesting life, she was entirely satisfied with her decisions.

"I think you're right," she laughed, looking out through the screened kitchen door. "One of the squirrels just sniffed the bread and then sat up and chittered at me." She returned to the table and began stacking the pale green glass dishes—Vernon pattern—into the dishwasher. "More coffee before I wash out the pot?"

"No, thanks." Howard drained his cup and handed it to her. "Oh, by the way," he said with elaborate casualness, "I won't be able to go to the meeting with you Tuesday. They've asked me to participate in a conference on carbon dating."

"Oh, Howard, not all day?"

"I'm afraid so."

"Oh, Howard," she repeated. "That's rather unfair of you, don't you think?" She didn't raise her voice, but long experience allowed Howard to recognize the steely undertone.

"I know, dear, and I'm sorry, but four or five of my former students will be there and they specifically want me to participate with them. I don't see how I could have said no."

"I suppose not." He always had found it difficult to say no, Martha thought, sighing; well, that had its advantages, too. "Still, remember antiques are a major source of our income now that you're retired." It wouldn't hurt to remind him that her income was now the dominant one.

"I'm sorry," he repeated.

"Well, I don't think anything important will come up," she mused. There was no point in making an issue of it, after all; she was enough of an academic herself to recognize necessity when she saw it. "Can you at least pick me up at Peter Casaday's studio afterward? He's doing his open house, you know—irritating boy, but I do think I'd better attend."

"Yes, of course. Around seven?" Howard was relieved to be getting off so lightly. Not that he was afraid of his wife, exactly. Except that somewhere along the line, the balance of power in their relationship had shifted. When had he lost control of their day-to-day lives? Even before he'd retired, certainly, perhaps long before. He supposed he'd simply been too busy to notice. It didn't occur to him that perhaps there had been no change at all.

"Because," Martha continued, "after what happened Saturday I'd really rather not come home alone."

"Because of the murder, you mean?" That surprised him; she hadn't seemed particularly disturbed by Joanna Westlake's death.

"No, not exactly." She shook her head. "At least, I'm not worried about my own safety, if that's what you mean. I've got more sense than to broadcast a valuable find, believe me. But I must admit being questioned by the police was very unpleasant. I would have been much happier if you'd been there with me."

The unexpected presence of a police car in her driveway when she got home had been both a shock and an embarrassment. Guilt or innocence didn't enter into it; it was the violation of her privacy, the outrage to decorum that disturbed her most. The young policeman had been studiously polite and respectful, but she had had to stand by while he pawed through the things in her car, attempting to appear dignified and unconcerned even when she saw Mrs. Draper watching avidly from her window across the street. And then the final indignity of being fingerprinted. Of course, she'd had to laugh when she saw the list the policeman made of her purchases; he hadn't the smallest knowledge of antiques.

"Well, it can't be helped," she said briskly, removing her apron and hanging it neatly on its hook inside the pantry. "You will be here Saturday to finish preparing for the Show?"

"Yes, of course," he declared. "We're just about ready, aren't we?" He rarely went to garage sales, which he found tiring and

irritating, but he genuinely enjoyed doing shows; the constant flow of people and conversation amused and entertained him.

"Oh, yes. Most of it is still packed up from the Southfield show. There are just a few new pieces to add in. Oh, and you will wear your new wristwatch, won't you?" She smiled down at him fondly.

NINE

Honestly, the things people wear, Michael Rappaport thought to himself, allowing his mind to stray from the heated debate over Vignelli Security Service. He cast his eye toward the end of the table, where Carolyn Herbert (antique jewelry and Jensen silver) sat swathed in layers of hand-printed batik that clashed hysterically with her blotchy complexion and black-dyed hair. Even when she was the right age for it that style must have looked demonic on her, he thought cattily. She looked up at that moment, caught his eye and smiled archly. Hastily Michael returned his attention to the matter at hand.

"... and there was a lot of bitching about rent-a-cops hassling people last year," Frank Copley was saying. He was a sloppily dressed middle-aged man with Benjamin Franklin hair whose antique-cum-resale shop was heavily dependent on student trade. "We don't want to scare the kids off, after all; they're good customers."

"But they are unfortunately rather undisciplined," Martha Penrose said in her high, fluting voice.

"Anyway, it's easy for you to be tolerant," Carolyn Herbert snapped at Copley. "Your stuff's so cheap it doesn't matter if half of it gets lifted or broken. I'm selling real antiques, not handfuls of junk jewelry."

"Spare me the elitist crap," Copley retorted. "Why don't we match profit ratios at the end of the year?"

"I think we all want to minimize shoplifting and other security problems at the Show," Michael said, moving quickly to avoid a full-scale row. Joyce McCarthy, the fifth member of the Antiques Association steering committee, sighed and looked pointedly at her watch. The last steering committee meeting before the Show was always a tense one, Michael knew; still, he'd really have to maneuver that Herbert woman off the committee once the Show was over. "I'll discuss your concerns with Mario Vignelli, I promise you."

"I talked to him last week," Alice Cowan blurted. She sat off to one side, as befitted a nonmember who was merely a temporary Show assistant. Now, as heads swiveled toward her, she twisted in her chair, causing her brown skirt to ruck up under her thighs. How can anyone spend so much money on clothes to so little effect? Michael thought irritably.

"Oh? And what did he say?" he asked curiously. He hoped she hadn't gotten Vignelli angry enough to pad their bill even further.

"Well, you see, I read this article a while back," Alice said confusedly, "and I thought it would be a good thing for the Show." Oh, God, Michael groaned inwardly, what now? "It was about what they called 'informal uniforms,'" Alice continued more coherently. "Several security agencies have tried them out for public events and gotten good feedback; they're easily recognizable but project a less authoritarian image. Anyway, Mr. Vignelli was familiar with some of the reports and liked the idea of trying the uniforms out. Oh, yes," she added, "I made sure it wouldn't cost us any more."

"That's a great idea, Alice," Joyce said warmly.

"It might work, at that," Copley said grudgingly.

"Alice, if we were paying you a salary you'd have earned a raise," Michael stood and made a mock bow in her direction, feeling relieved and, indeed, thoroughly pleased with himself. He'd invited her to help with the Show on sheer impulse last month, and the decision was already paying off. Not that he was entirely surprised; he'd bought various bits of Victoriana from her over the last couple of years, and had concluded that, despite her scared-rabbit look, she actually had a good eye and a quick intelligence. Perhaps he'd adopt her as a protégée; it was always useful to have allies in the cutthroat antiques world.

"And now," he said, rising from his chair with a gust of relief, "I believe the only remaining business of this meeting is to pray for good weather."

"One more thing, Michael, please?" Joyce raised her voice over the scrape of chairs.

"Yes, Joyce?" Let it be something minor, Michael prayed; Joyce at least was rarely troublesome.

"Could the computer print out a list of my customers who bought something at last year's Show? You've got my mailing list on the computer, and that list of buyers from the charge slips."

"Doesn't sound too difficult." Michael nodded. "Lydia, can you punch that out for her?"

"Gee, not the way it's set up I can't." From her position behind the oak roll-top desk Lydia Frazier, the association's half-time secretary and only paid employee, shook her long, shaggy blond locks dubiously. "I can get you a copy of your mailing list, and a copy of the sales list, but I don't know how to put them together."

"I thought the computer would solve all our information problems," Martha said, cocking her head like a hungry bird.

"Oh, it's all there," Lydia tapped a red-polished nail on the computer. "It's just that it's in two different places." She tilted

her head delicately, sending cascades of hair billowing over her red-silk-clad shoulder.

"Well, the information hardly does us any good inside the machine if we can't get it out," Martha pointed out with a sweet, faintly malicious smile.

God, I've got to do something about that bitch, Michael thought savagely. She's just not going to give up, and I'm damned if I'll let some anti-Semitic cretin cost me the presidency of the association. Especially now, he emphasized to himself, aware of his perilous cash-flow problem; yes, the solution was in sight, but not for some time yet. Meanwhile, the extra status of the association title was worth thousands in additional customers. Wealthy, important, trusting customers. He kept his face carefully noncommittal while his mind raced, seeking a solution to this latest attack.

"Never mind," Joyce said hastily, only too well aware of the undercurrents she'd stirred up. "It's not that important."

"Maybe not, but it's a good idea," Copley declared. "That's exactly the sort of thing we paid all that money for. I'd like the same thing, assuming you can get the computer to spit it out." He glared at Michael and Lydia impartially.

"And you shall have it," Michael replied without hesitation. "Are you both going over to Peter's open house?"

"I suppose so, for a while," Joyce said.

"Yeah, sure." Copley nodded.

Of course you are, Michael thought sardonically. Trust you not to miss free booze and a roomful of young girls.

"I'll get the lists and bring them to you there. All right?"

"If you're quite sure," Martha said meaningfully.

"Oh, absolutely," Michael nodded with an elaborate show of unconcern. Mustn't, above all things, let the bitch see him hesitate or, worse, become rattled. Rule One: never let them see you bleed. He gave a quick nod and rose from the table, signaling at last the end of the meeting.

"I thought you'd been fully trained on the computer," Mi-

chael said to Lydia when the other committee members had left.

"She never taught me that," Lydia replied indifferently, standing up and reaching for her red patent-leather purse. "Look, I've gotta go. My boyfriend's taking me to the Mitch Ryder concert in Detroit tonight."

"It's only four-thirty," Michael said sharply.

"I know, but I've already worked six hours today, and I'm only supposed to be half-time. Sorry, I really gotta go."

"Did you collate and fold the Show programs?" Michael called to her retreating back.

"I did them this afternoon, Michael," Alice said quietly.

"You did? Oh good, bless you. Honestly, I know that girl has a brain somewhere under all that hair, but if she doesn't start using it soon it's going to atrophy." He went to the phone and pushed buttons rapidly. "Anneke?" he said into the receiver. "Thank God I caught you."

"Hi, Michael. I was just on my way out. Is there a problem?"

"Indeed there is. How soon can you get here?"

"Tomorrow morning," she replied with asperity.

"Anneke, dear Anneke, this is a desperate emergency. My entire reputation is at stake. No, scratch that; you don't give a Victorian damn for my reputation. It's far more important than that—the reputation of the computer itself, of computers in our lifetime, hangs in the balance. Now, will you come?"

"Good God." She laughed, and Michael knew he'd won. "As bad as that? Oh, all right." She sighed theatrically through the receiver. "But you owe me one."

"You don't have to stay," he told Alice after replacing the receiver.

"That's all right." She smiled at him dimly from amid a welter of papers. "I want to finish mailing these last press releases, and anyway Ennis is out of town."

Oh, yes, the hotshot husband, Michael thought but didn't say aloud. Honestly, how could an obviously intelligent woman let

herself become such a wet mess? She wasn't even bad-looking—those fine features and that pale blond hair could be turned into a delicately dignified style, if she only had the poise to go with it. Like Lady Marjorie on "Upstairs, Downstairs," very upper-class British. He had a sudden, antic thought.

"Do me a favor, will you?" He opened his burgundy leather attaché case and extracted a pair of earrings he'd bought earlier that day—long, graceful drops of gold filigree set with small diamonds. "Would you model these for me? I want to see how they look on someone."

"Oh, beautiful," she said appreciatively, taking the earrings in the palm of her hand. "Victorian or Edwardian?"

"What do you think?" he challenged her.

"I'd guess Edwardian," she said slowly, examining them more closely. "The delicacy of the work, for one thing. And I think the stones are a later cut, aren't they?"

"Very good," he said happily. "I tend to agree. Try them on."

"Oh, I can't," she said, looking faintly embarrassed. "I don't have pierced ears." She dropped the earrings on the table. "Besides, they'd look silly on me."

Well, you can't make a silk purse out of a sow, Michael thought nastily, retrieving the offending jewelry and replacing it in his briefcase. Although if I could make something of myself, I don't know why the hell she can't.

He'd started out as just another skinny, rather homely graduate student, working on a master's degree in English primarily to avoid the Vietnam draft. But to his surprise, he found the material fascinating, especially when he began to read in the Victorian era. At first, he was intrigued by Disraeli, who was Jewish like himself, until he discovered that the great Lord Beaconsfield had renounced his religion. This, Michael considered not so much heretical as undignified.

In the end, as Anneke had discerned, it was Oscar Wilde who captured his imagination. Oscar, the great iconoclast, who had lived his life on his own terms, who had done what he damn

well pleased and moreover had done it with style and wit. In the first flush of hero-worship, Michael had even experimented with one or two homosexual liaisons, but had concluded almost regretfully that he was irredeemably hetero. But, living through the turmoil of the late sixties and early seventies, he was like Oscar, he felt, in one thing at least: He was a man out of his time.

He was vastly unconventional, but in his own rather than the hippie fashion of the time, and was thus unacceptable among both rebels and establishment types. For his part, he viewed the antics of both his peers and his elders at the University with equal distaste, yearning instead for the expansive, leisured intellectualism of Victorian Oxford. To assuage this hunger, he began buying pieces of Victoriana.

"Man, you must be joking," his roommate declared the day he brought home the huge carved-mahogany breakfront to their student-slum apartment. "That is, like, truly gross." .

"It's a masterpiece," Michael said loftily. "Look at the detail in that carving, and the dovetailed drawers."

"Well, you can't put it in our living room," the roommate said positively. "Everyone would just freak out."

"If they don't 'freak out' over Day-Glo orange walls and purple curtains," Michael replied coldly, "I imagine they can endure a brief exposure to fine furniture."

"Well, I can't," the roommate snapped. "I don't mind the plummy act and the weird clothes." He glared pointedly at Michael's ruffled shirt and pegged black pants. "At least they're good for comic relief, y'know? But I'm not gonna let you bring that piece of elephant shit into my apartment."

Well, it had been time to get a place of his own, anyway: someplace where he could, in the barbarous phrase of the moment, "do his own thing." He found his own apartment, finished the master's degree—he had a habit of perseverance—and continued to buy and, increasingly, sell Victoriana.

As it turned out, he'd been lucky, although it hadn't seemed so at the time. In 1970, no one wanted the huge, ornate styles

of a century ago; he was able to buy cheaply, at yard sales and farm auctions, and resell for small but increasing profits to those few collectors who were interested. His taste was excellent and his business sense, it turned out, even more so. He began to make a name for himself in the small world of Victoriana collectors and dealers. Now finally, collectors were rediscovering the Victorian period, and he found himself near the top of a growing market. He no longer had to grub around in dirty barns at seven A.M., scrambling for bargains, and he neither missed nor mourned his youth. He greatly preferred the present, with its carefully paced auctions and elegant antique shows, where he sold only the finest merchandise to discerning customers. He was one of the few who had in fact done his own thing and made it pay.

At a price, of course; but then, everything in life had a price. How did that aphorism go? "Take what you want, and pay for it, says God." His early experiences had left him cautious of other people, and something of a loner. He had a wide circle of acquaintances, and never lacked a dinner or drinking partner, but he had been careful to keep his relationships discreetly superficial.

Yet now, as he moved toward his fifties, he (like a Baby Boom cliché, he realized sardonically) was beginning to ponder the metaphysical conflict between freedom and isolation, and wonder about the wisdom of being the cat who walked by his wild lone. It did not escape him that Oscar Wilde had died alone, disgraced, and virtually friendless.

"Let me check that list of Show hosts one more time," he said to Alice, shaking off black nostalgia.

At least she'd found a parking spot, Anneke thought, pushing open the glass-paned door squeezed between two Main Street storefronts. Inside, a flight of narrow stairs leading upward was softened by rich red carpeting and a heavily carved oak banister, under an elaborate Victorian chandelier on semipermanent

loan from Michael. Much of the furniture came from the same source, Anneke recalled as she pushed open the door to the large, one-room office; it was undeniably beautiful, but at the moment she was in no mood to appreciate the effect.

"This had better be quick," she warned him as she set down her briefcase on the big walnut conference table.

"For me as much as for you. The cavalry never looked so good before," he eyed her turquoise silk shirt, pleated gray pants, and silver-and-turquoise jewelry with approval.

"Never mind the butter," she said severely, "just get to the bread. What's the crisis?" She listened to his explanation with relief. "Good Lord, even Lydia ought to be able to do that. I'll run it for you this time and leave her instructions for the future. In words of one syllable this time." She moved to the computer, which was stationed in a far corner of the room but still contrived to look fantastically out of place in the antique-filled office. So did the nondescript woman in the unbecoming flowered blouse, shuffling papers at the other end of the conference table.

"It's Alice Cowan, isn't it?" Anneke asked, recalling the woman's face. "We met Saturday at a garage sale." So this colorless, obscure woman was one of the other suspects. She looked a wildly unlikely villain; well, Anneke thought, she ought to qualify under the least-likely-suspect rubric.

"Yes, you were with Joyce McCarthy, weren't you? It's nice to see you again." The words were spoken conventionally and Alice returned her attention to the papers in front of her. Anneke, feeling rebuffed, booted the computer and went to work.

"There, that should do it," she said after a few minutes. She pushed computer keys and the big dot-matrix printer clattered to life. "I'll send you the instructions tomorrow."

"Don't send them to me." Michael laughed charmingly. "I wouldn't know d-Base from first base, let alone how to move things around inside that infernal machine."

"It's just a query, isn't it?" The question came, surprisingly, from Alice.

"Yes it is," Anneke replied. "Do you have computer experience?"

"Not really." Alice colored and shook her head. "My son had an old computer before he went away to college, and I played with it a little."

"Well, you're right. You just run the query, then either set up a report or, even simpler, export it to a text file and print it from your word processor."

"If it's all numeric, can you export it to a spreadsheet?"

"Sure, as long as you structure it correctly." Anneke looked at Alice curiously; at this moment, with her face mirroring her concentration, she seemed a different woman, alert and intelligent rather than dim and withdrawn.

"Enough technobabble," Michael interrupted, ripping the printouts free of their stack. "It's party time."

"Party?" Anneke asked.

"Peter Casaday's open house. He does the wine-and-cheese routine for association members every year right before the Show."

"Oh? How come?" So one more of the suspects was involved with the association. "He's not a dealer, is he?"

"No, but since his studio is in the Show's line of march, so to speak, we include him in our program. The party is a kind of thank-you. Also good business exposure for him," Michael added shrewdly. "And I," he announced, waving the printouts, "can now enter in triumph. Mother Martha will be exceedingly put out. Ladies, shall we proceed?" He held out arms for Anneke and Alice.

"Me?" Alice faltered. "Oh, I can't go. I wasn't invited."

"Invited? Nobody was invited; nobody ever is in these barbarous times. You've more right to be there than most of those spongers. Besides, I want to march in with two beautiful women on my arm."

Why isn't there a man alive who understands how offensive that particular line is? Anneke thought with distaste. Still, she rather wanted a look at Peter's studio, her errands could easily wait, and she certainly didn't want to be mistaken for Michael's date. Alice's presence would prevent that, at least.

But before she could add her pleas to Michael's, Steve Olewski's voice interrupted.

"Still here?" he asked, stepping into the room gingerly, like a dubious cat. "Oh, Anneke. That must mean another computer screwup."

"Just a screwup by the ineffable Lydia," Michael countered. "Aren't you joining the hordes at Peter's?"

"Wouldn't miss it for the world." Steve agreed. "Closest thing Ann Arbor allows to a wet T-shirt contest." His own T-shirt was adorned with a picture of a wild-eyed cat in a food processor that made Anneke feel slightly queasy. "I just popped in to use the library for a minute."

"Well, we're on our way over to Peter's," Michael said. "Will you please be sure to lock up when you're done?"

"Yes, master." Steve bowed mockingly, but his eyes were already scanning the rows of reference books lining the back wall. Michael hesitated for a moment, then shrugged and shepherded the two women through the door and down the stairs to the street. Anneke, amused, let herself be shepherded; Alice, apparently feeling she faced a fait accompli, also went along without further objection.

TEN

Main Street had been lucky enough to be unfashionable in the early 1960s, and thus escaped the building boom that had ravaged much of Ann Arbor. The old business district remained structurally intact, a three-block strip of turn-of-the-century buildings only two or three stories high. Many of them were now being cleaned and restored as people finally came to appreciate the charm—and the commercial appeal—of old-town areas.

Peter Casaday had the upper two floors of a three-story building that had as yet been neither cleaned nor restored. The street-level door, crammed between a trendy Cajun restaurant and a discount shoe store, stood open to reveal a narrow, dark flight of wooden stairs covered with brown rubber no-slip treads, and walls the approximate color of eggplant. Anneke picked her way cautiously up the steps, wondering if she should have bothered to come, but when she crested the top step her eyes widened in amazement, then narrowed against the explosion of color and light that assaulted them.

The huge room, taking up the whole of the second floor, was so anarchically bright that at first she had trouble focusing. There was the picture-frame business along one side, its long, wide white countertop currently serving as a buffet. There was a kind of living-room area, or at least a sitting area, consisting of a mad mix of furniture that included a red velvet beanbag chair, an undulating, reclinerlike object in purple fabric, barely a foot off the floor, and a huge Day-Glo yellow chair in wet-look vinyl. There were floor cushions in coruscating psyche-delic colors, and patterned shag rugs, and a variety of brightly lit objects that included two Lava lamps, a tube full of sparkles, and a mirror with lights twinkling behind the glass. Everything in the room seemed to glow, or sparkle, or twitch.

"A bit much, would you say?" Michael watched her reaction with amusement.

"My God," she breathed. "It feels like an explosion in a Crayola factory."

"Perfect!" He roared with laughter. "Come and meet our host, and then we can proceed to the serious business of drink-ing. If you can stand Peter's plonk, that is." He plunged into the maelstrom, and Anneke and Alice followed behind. Alice was looking around with evident interest and a kind of calm aston-ishment; she seemed less nonplussed than Anneke herself.

They worked their way across the room, skirting a spiral metal staircase leading upward from the middle of the floor, to where Peter was standing surrounded by a knot of people. In the first rush of sensory overload Anneke had hardly noticed the occupants of the room, but now she realized there was a good-sized crowd.

Actually, she noted, her analytic mind automatically clicking over, there were two very disparate crowds. One was composed of antique dealers and a small number of local businesspeople, most of them standing and milling, plastic cups in hand. She spotted Joyce with two State Street shopowners, looking glumly

at a lumpy, mushroom-shaped object that might have been a chair or a footstool or, for all Anneke knew, a family pet.

The other set of guests was conspicuously, not to say flamboyantly, younger. They wore layers of multicolored clothing, or studded garments of black leather, or various combinations of the two, under hair in chopped, uneven, spiky styles in every color of the rainbow. Anneke was particularly taken with a tall, thin girl in black leather miniskirt, red lace bustier, and royal blue crocheted shawl, topped off by particolored hair of matching royal blue and black. Unfortunately for the effect, she had the pinched, rather earnest face of a serious student.

The younger crowd at least was able to sit, Anneke laughed to herself with a brief lament for the flexibility of youth. They sprawled on the floor cushions or the floor with easy impartiality, chattering to each other from positions a contortionist might well envy.

"Good afternoon, Peter." Michael had worked his way to the group by the window. "Still collecting outstanding examples of good taste in our time, I see."

"Ah, the great Michael Rappaport." Peter's face was slightly flushed; he had one arm around a beautiful blond girl with a pale, ethereal face, who wore a floor-length cape of shimmering white-gold over a light beige jumpsuit in some silky fabric. As he greeted Michael, Peter's arm tightened around the girl's shoulders. "Here he is, children, the Grand Old Man of the Ann Arbor antiques world." One of the young people tittered; Peter and Michael smiled at each other with ferocious amiability.

"May I introduce Anneke Haagen?" Michael said with pointed formality. "And I believe you know Alice Cowan?"

"Sure. Hi." Peter gave Alice a brief nod and dismissed her. "I know you too." He looked at Anneke with more interest. "You were with Joyce Saturday, weren't you? Find anything interesting?"

"Anything . . . ? Oh, yes, a few things," Anneke responded,

concluding that the double meaning of his words was accidental.

"Oh, hey, that's right, you found the body, didn't you? Hey, I'm sorry." He didn't look sorry exactly—more curious. "Anyway, glad you could come."

"Delighted to be here." She returned Peter's scrutiny. He was dressed in the height of fashion, 1968 style. Blue denim bell-bottom jeans, low on the hips, the legs slashed with bright paisley. Fringed suede vest, studded with embossed silver disks; pale blue shirt tightly fitted to his body, with wide lapels and full, billowing sleeves. He should have looked bizarre beyond imagining, but instead, Anneke admitted, the effect was decidedly impressive. In his tight, body-conscious clothing, Peter seemed to exude sexual power.

"What do you think of it all?" Peter asked the question as though it were a test of some kind.

"It's hard to say," Anneke answered slowly. "The initial effect is overwhelming."

"You've become accustomed to a colorless world. Take another look."

She let her eyes roam the big room once again. This time she could pick out individual pieces, and she had to admit that some of them, at least, had a kind of mad elegance. That purple recliner, for instance, was actually a gorgeous flow of color; standing on its own, against white walls, it would have been superb. So would the cheerfully patterned red-and-yellow shag rug. But the chaotic mix of color and pattern never let the eye stop to appreciate the individual pieces. And many of them were pure mass-market schlock, like the beanbag and the bead curtains, no more attractive for being twenty-five years old.

"It's very powerful," she said at last, picking her words carefully. "I like some of it a good deal—that purple piece, for instance. But the room itself almost feels alive, doesn't it? Hard to live in for most people, I should think," she mused almost to herself. "But . . ."

"Yes?" he asked impatiently.

"But if you're the kind of person who *does* fit a room like this, the rest of the world must seem very joyless."

"Joyless?" He seemed taken aback by the word. "Far out. Hey, you should take a look at the studio upstairs, too." He pointed to the spiral staircase. "And get yourself something to drink; the bar's over there." He waved toward the buffet.

It was a clear gesture of dismissal. Anneke murmured appropriate words and moved away, Michael following.

"This *ambiance* definitely requires strong spirits," he declared, giving the word its French pronunciation.

"Or an equivalent," Anneke said, catching the drifting scent of marijuana. She looked over the rows of bottles, saw that as usual there was no red wine, and accepted a plastic cup of mediocre champagne. Only as she took her first sip did she realize with a slightly guilty start that she'd forgotten completely about Alice. She finally spotted her in a corner, half hidden by an ungainly fig tree, in conversation with Martha Penrose. Martha, Anneke noted, had managed to commandeer one of the few normal chairs in the room.

". . . going to miss this place," Michael was saying.

"Sorry?"

"It's just been sold, or anyway it's about to be."

"What is? This building? They're not planning to tear it down, are they?" Anneke asked in alarm.

"No, nothing like that. John Maravich is heading the group buying it. They're going to do a complete renovation—turn the ground floor into retail space and the upstairs into luxury offices. I happen to know he wants this floor for his own office."

"So Peter's going to be bounced." Anneke didn't bother asking Michael how he knew all this; he was a magnet for local gossip. "How long has he been here?"

"Nearly five years, but he never did have anything beyond a month-to-month lease. And he'll never find another setup like this in Ann Arbor, at least not one he can afford on the income

from picture framing and a few art fairs." Michael spoke with distinct satisfaction. "Ah well, *plus ça change, plus c'est la même chose.* I'd better deliver these computer printouts."

Anneke sipped champagne as he drifted away, discovering in herself an ambivalence toward mingling. She'd come to the party in the first place with some vague notion of playing detective, but now that she was here the idea seemed . . . distasteful? No, actually, more than a little silly. She grinned to herself, looking around at the roomful of innocent revelers. She took another sip of the nasty champagne, grimaced, and set the cup down on the corner of an acid-green plastic table in the shape of a foot. Then she headed over to say hello to Joyce.

". . . ever since he stole those gold earrings from me." It was Alice's voice, surprisingly vituperative, that slowed Anneke's progress across the room.

"I can't say I'm surprised." Martha Penrose clucked sympathetically. Steve's never seemed overmuch concerned about *ethics.*" Anneke paused behind a potted rubber plant, pretending to examine a Jefferson Airplane poster.

"It was completely dishonest, that's what it was," Alice continued. "He said he'd bought them as part of a set, with the necklace. But he'd already paid for the necklace, and the earrings were still pinned to the table." Her voice rose, full of anger. "He just grabbed them and ran before I could even argue."

"Well, garage sales often do bring out the worst in people," Martha said comfortably. "Joyce once paid for an entire set of dishes while I was actually packing them into cartons, then had the nerve to tell me she'd already bought them." She sighed. "She's friendly enough, but I'm afraid she's rather *greedy.*"

"Talking about me?" The newcomer, to Anneke's amusement, was Steve, apparently finished with his researches across the street.

"We were talking about Joanna, poor thing." Martha's calm voice didn't miss a beat.

"Yeah, she was a greedy broad, wasn't she? Seems to've done her more harm than good, though," Steve replied flippantly.

"That's not very nice," Martha remonstrated.

"Neither was she," Steve said. "Not very lucky, either. Crazy, hitting a Big Score and getting yourself killed for it."

"Are they sure that's why she was killed?" Alice asked, her voice nervous.

"Why else?"

"I wonder what it was she found," Martha said, and there was just the slightest hint of avidity in her voice.

"I don't want to think about it," Alice declared.

"Oh, I don't know," Martha said mildly. "After all, we know the *sort* of thing it would have to be."

"What do you mean?" Alice's voice wavered.

"And that ought to help us figure out who might have done it." Martha ignored Alice's question. "Don't you agree?" she asked brightly.

"I don't know what you're talking about," Alice protested harshly. "I don't want to think about all that."

"Oh, come off it. You damn well do think about it, don't you?" Steve taunted. "We're all thinking about it, wondering what she found big enough to kill for. And wondering if it was something we saw and passed up. Except," he said, slowly drawing out the word, "one of us *isn't* wondering."

"What do you mean?" Alice's voice was shrill.

"Oh, get real." Steve snickered. "You know damn well that one of our happy little gang of garage-sale scavengers already knows what Joanna's Big Score was."

There was the sound of scraping chairs, punctuated by sarcastic laughter. When she turned and peered past the rubber plant, Anneke saw Alice and Martha stalking across the room, and Steve sitting on the floor, his sharp-featured face creased with a broad, mocking grin.

She made her escape past a print of red-and-purple squares and fetched up near a pile of floor cushions, where a tangle of

younger guests were passing around a badly-rolled joint in a feathered roach clip.

". . . guess I'll toss in that Detroit River watercolor." The speaker was a plump, dark girl in a black jumpsuit festooned with white plastic jewelry. "It should sell to that suburban crowd. Besides, I did get an A from Jackson for it."

"You're lucky," a pretty brown-haired girl in an embroidered dashiki commented. "My jewelry is much too avant-grade for a batch of tourists from the 'burbs." She touched her adornment, a red plastic construction that wound around her neck and up over one ear and looked spectacularly uncomfortable. So the younger crowd were mainly art students, Anneke concluded. "Now that's the kind of stuff I could do if I could afford the materials." She pointed to Anneke.

"This?" Anneke's hand went to her own necklace, a modernistic piece in chunky cast sterling and turquoise.

"Yeah. That's nice stuff. Who did it?"

"I don't remember," Anneke confessed. "I bought it from a woman at a perfectly terrible art fair a couple of years ago—one of those mall promo fairs. The woman who did this was so ridiculously out of place that her stuff stood out like a beacon. Everything else there was calico lampshades and heads carved out of dried apples."

"And deer-antler lamps. I know exactly the sort of fair you mean." She took another puff on the joint and handed it to Anneke, paying her the compliment of accepting her into their group. Anneke took a quick, shallow puff and passed it along; she had nothing against an occasional hit of pot, but she'd passed the age where she enjoyed sharing a soggy communal joint.

"Nice of Peter to let us hang stuff here during the antique show," a thin boy with a pigtail and three earrings said, taking a puff of the joint and passing it along.

"Oh, he gets his own kind of dividend." The dark girl did an exaggerated Groucho Marx leer.

"Who is it this month?" the blonde asked. "Still Lesley?"

"Yeah. Been going on all semester. I'm damned if I know what she sees in him," the boy said fretfully.

"You're kidding." Both girls looked scornful. "Take another look." The dark-haired girl rolled her eyes. "We're talking major stud here."

"Besides," the blonde added, "he really is an artist."

"He's okay"—the boy shrugged—"but he's never going to get anywhere much."

"Well, at least he hasn't sold out to the money men," the blonde snapped. "*You'll* probably wind up doing hemorrhoid commercials."

"Maybe so," the boy was uninsulted, "but at least by the time I'm Peter's age I'll be making some bucks." He waved an arm around the room. "Is this really the way you want to be living when *you're* thirty?"

Anneke felt suddenly ancient. And hungry, she discovered. Maybe a contact high giving her a case of the munchies? She stood and moved away from the young artists, working her way toward the buffet. Joyce was there, spreading an unidentifiable white substance on a cracker.

"Ah, food." Anneke took a small paper plate and speared chunks of cheese and vegetables onto it.

"Try this." Joyce pointed to the bowl of white stuff. "Crab-and-roquefort spread. Delicious." Anneke spooned a mound of it onto her plate, added a large dollop of bean-and-salsa dip, and filled a large plastic cup with club soda. Then she eased her way back through the crowd around the buffet, with Joyce following behind.

"I feel like I'm starving," Anneke said, looking around futilely for a place to sit.

"Well, it's past dinnertime, after all." Joyce's voice came muffled past a mouthful of food. "Let's go over there." She led Anneke to one side of the room, where they set their drinks on a chrome-and-glass étagère laden with peculiar ornaments,

many of them decorated with peace symbols. Among the lot Anneke recognized the amethyst geode she'd seen Peter buy Saturday. The lavender crystals glowed in the light of a weird lamp that looked like a transparent vacuum-cleaner hose filled with Christmas lights.

"The food's surprisingly good," Anneke said around a mouthful of tangy Cheddar.

"Better than last year." Joyce spread something pinkish on a cracker. "I seem to remember a lot of soggy chips and not much else."

"By the way," Anneke asked curiously, "did you really buy a set of dishes at a sale that Martha was already packing up?"

"Is she spreading that story again?" Joyce demanded. "Dammit, that was a sixty-piece set, and I did exactly what you're supposed to do—took one place setting with me to show the seller, and paid for the whole set. *Before* Martha even got there, I might add. Christ, you aren't expected to carry the whole goddamn set around with you. Let me tell you, Martha knew damn well I'd already bought those dishes—she was the one trying to run a game on *me*."

"Sorry, sorry." Anneke threw up her hands placatingly. "I forgot how seriously you pros take it."

"Maybe too seriously." Joyce's face sobered, "I still can't really believe Joanna found something worth killing for." She sighed. "Nothing new from the police, I suppose?"

"Not that I know of. How's Ellen doing? I don't see her here."

"She's not." Joyce gnawed her lower lip. "I don't know. I think it's beginning to get to her. She seems more tense and anxious every day. I wish to hell the police would *do* something."

"About traffic for the Show?" Peter came up behind them, carrying a glass of champagne. And not his first, either, Anneke guessed; his handsome face had the high color alcohol often produced in fair-skinned blonds. On Peter, the effect was of a young Pan.

"No, although I wish they'd do something about that, too," Joyce answered. "We were talking about the murder."

"Oh, yeah. Weird, really, isn't it? Poor Joanna."

"Did you know her well?" Anneke asked. Peter was the first person she'd heard express sympathy for the dead woman.

"Not really. You know, just to run into at sales."

"Most of the other regulars didn't like her much," Anneke persisted.

"Oh, she was okay." Peter shrugged. "She could be a pain sometimes, but who can't? And she had pretty good taste."

"Of course, you're not a dealer," Joyce pointed out. "You weren't in competition with her."

"Sure, you're right. I'm not in competition with anyone on the sale circuit." He grinned suddenly, completing the resemblance to a beautiful Pan. "That's why I get along so well with everyone. No one wants the stuff I buy, so I don't get involved in the feuds."

"Oh, I wouldn't say *feuds*, dear." Martha joined them by the étagère, carrying a glass of clear, fizzy liquid. "But of course we are all rather *competitive.*" She smoothed her flowered silk dress primly.

"Well, luckily for me no one on the sale circuit is competing for sixties stuff yet." Peter said.

"Some of it *is* rather . . . bizarre, wouldn't you say?" Martha reached out absently and flicked the vacuum-hose lamp off and back on. "Still, there are always people around with the *oddest* tastes. And after all," she said sweetly to Peter, "there *are* other people who like peculiar modern things, or you wouldn't be able to sell any of your art, would you?" She indicated the wall behind her.

"Did you get these at garage sales?" Anneke asked, examining the ill-assorted collection of prints. They included a Wyeth poster, an explosive splash of green and black, and a stylized, dyspeptic-looking black-and-white cat.

"Yeah," Peter said dismissively. "Never pay more than five

bucks apiece, and that's more than most of them are worth. Still"—he smiled tightly—"they do sell sometimes."

"Don't you ever find any good art at sales?"

"Not really, no." He darted a glance at her. "The Rembrandt-in-the-attic bit? Not bloody likely," he said scornfully. "Hey, if you're interested in art, come upstairs to the studio. Come on," he insisted as she hesitated. "I'd like your opinion. You too," he said to Joyce and Martha.

"I've already been upstairs, thank you," Martha replied, giving the vacuum-hose lamp a last abstracted flick.

"And I have no eye at all for contemporary art," Joyce said firmly. "Besides, I want to talk to Bob Jordan." She indicated a man Anneke recognized vaguely as a chamber of commerce staffer.

"I'll be glad to take a look," Anneke agreed, curious about Peter's work.

"Take your Dramamine," Michael Rappaport warned, coming up behind her.

"Beats the No Doz she'd need to stay awake in one of your rooms," Peter retorted. "Here, this way." He took Anneke's arm and led her to the foot of the staircase, where he waved her upward with a florid gesture. He seemed possessed by a kind of hectic gaiety. Thankful for the hundredth time that she never wore skirts, Anneke wound her way toward the ceiling and stepped out above it into another huge room, open and partitionless like the one below it.

ELEVEN

Up here the effect was, if anything, even more anarchic than on the lower floor, mitigated only by the fact that there were fewer people. A king-sized mattress on the floor in one corner was covered with a hugely patterned throw in black and white, with multicolored plastic bead curtains serving as a headboard. Two more of the inevitable vinyl beanbags crouched between a cantilevered chair in a single, elegant sweep of orange plastic, and an enormous, undulating recliner in chartreuse fur. Again, Anneke could pick out one or two pieces of inarguably fine design, drowning in a sea of mass-market junk.

But the bulk of the room was an artist's studio, complete with easel, stacks of canvases, paint-splotched floors, and the ineradicable aroma of turpentine. Anneke turned her attention to the work area, where half a dozen young people were gathered. Two of them she recognized: Peter's ethereal blonde, and Steve Olewski.

"We'll use your sculpture," the blonde said firmly to a thin-

faced boy with lank brown hair and a strained expression, "but not the oil. No landscapes."

"But the sculpture won't sell at a show like this," the boy argued, glaring at a waist-high chunk of twisted sheet metal. "And the oil is my best work—it was my senior project."

"We're not hanging any representational art this year," the blonde replied sternly. "Peter wants an entirely abstract show."

"Does Peter always get everything he wants?" Steve drawled, leaning casually against the paint-stained workbench and flicking an eye toward a point behind Anneke.

"Generally, yes." It was Peter who answered, moving around Anneke to confront Steve. He smiled charmingly, and his voice was as casual as Steve's, but his eyes glittered in his flushed face.

"Evverrrything?" Steve dragged out the word, leering at the blonde. "Pooooor Lesley." He stepped forward and draped one arm over the girl's shoulder.

Several things seemed to happen at once. Peter grabbed Lesley's arm to pull her away from Steve. Lesley yanked her arm out of Peter's grasp, jabbed her elbow into Steve's midsection and aimed a well-timed kick at his shin. Steve jumped back to avoid Lesley's assault and his arm struck the top of the workbench, where it sent a sculpture of multicolored glass rods hurtling into the air. A small, black-haired girl screamed and lunged forward, missing the sculpture in its plummet to the floor but catching Peter smartly in the groin with her head.

Rocky III, choreographed by the Three Stooges, Anneke thought, desperately choking back the hysterical laughter that threatened to engulf her. Steve was rubbing the leg Lesley had kicked, his face peculiarly expressionless. Peter was doubled over, sweat beading his forehead. The black-haired girl was sitting on the floor amid shards of glass, swearing in a low, steady monotone. Only Lesley herself remained coolly unruffled.

"Well, it serves you both right," she said curtly. "I'm not

some piece of property, you know? I'll decide who puts their hands on me."

She might have the face of a Botticelli madonna, but she has good modern attitudes, Anneke decided, feeling real admiration for the girl. Lesley picked up a small crocheted purse, slung it over her shoulder with a gesture of disgust, and disappeared down the spiral staircase, leaving Peter and Steve standing *en tableau* by the workbench.

"Get out of here." Peter forced the words through clenched teeth.

"No problem." Steve was casual, and his usual careless smile was back on his face. "I'll catch up with Lesley on the way out."

"You heard her say to leave her alone."

"I heard her say she makes her own choices, remember?" Steve raised a mocking eyebrow. "Maybe she's decided you're too old for her."

He dropped through the staircase and disappeared; Peter, his face contorted with anger, charged after him. And only then did Anneke realize, from the peals of laughter behind her, that Michael Rappaport had followed her and Peter up to the studio.

"I wouldn't have missed that for an Oscar Wilde first edition," he whooped.

"Hush, Michael." Anneke tried to put severity in her voice, but her own welling laughter defeated her. "Stop it," she choked. "It's not funny."

"Not funny? Not *funny?* My dear, I shall dine out on this story for the next month. Possibly the next year. Oh, my." He gasped for air, then burst into renewed laughter which set Anneke off as well. The remaining young artists were themselves convulsed in giggles; even the black-haired girl was grinning.

"That's enough," Anneke said finally. "If I laugh any more I'm going to be sick. I didn't come up here for a Marx Brothers exhibition." Why had she come? Oh, yes. "I want to see some of Peter's work."

"Whatever for?" Michael emitted one last hiccup of laughter and wiped his eyes with his hand.

Why *had* she wanted to see Peter's paintings? Anneke turned toward the wall behind her and studied the canvases hung and stacked against it. Bright color, abstract—she had expected that. A good deal of flair. She was no art critic, but she could recognize craftsmanship when she saw it. Peter had a certain amount of talent, she concluded; more than that, especially in the area of contemporary art, she couldn't say.

She stopped in front of one large painting and studied it more closely. It appeared to be a kind of fractured portrait, done on such a huge scale she had to step back to focus on it. Individual features were scattered randomly across the canvas—a nose here, an eye there—all painted in a large, screened-dot pattern. Picasso out of Roy Lichtenstein, Anneke thought.

She turned away and found her eye caught by a different canvas, unframed, a strong, almost brutal splash of black and red and blue, with bits of newsprint sticking out from under the paint. It looked like angry graffiti, Anneke decided. And not Peter's, she realized, spying the signature "L. Shea" in the corner. One of the students, presumably.

"Had enough?" Michael asked.

"I think so. At least, my stomach thinks it's ready for dinner." They descended the staircase to find that the party was winding down. Joyce was gone, Anneke saw after a quick check of the room; so were most of the older crowd, in fact. But many of the younger people were settled comfortably on the floor, drinking beer or passing around joints. She saw Peter in one of the beanbag chairs, with Lesley leaning against his knee. Apparently they'd made it up, then; Steve seemed to be gone, anyway.

"If you don't have any plans for dinner," she said to Michael impulsively, "the Full Moon has great hamburgers."

"And sidewalk tables," Michael sniffed, wrinkling his nose at the sweetish smoke drifting through the room. "Let's go."

* * *

Someone had messed with the stereo; the sixties sound had been replaced by something god-awful—heavy metal, repetitive, above all loud. Most of the older guests had gone; in the center of the room half a dozen kids were dancing, jerking and heaving to the music in serene isolation. When had dancing become a solitary activity? Peter wondered.

He slumped back in the beanbag chair, feeling the beginnings of a muscle spasm where Lesley leaned against his leg. The party had been a roaring success, a fitting farewell blast. So why did he feel so lousy?

Maybe he was hungry; he hadn't eaten much of the party food and it was already—what? Seven-thirty? He checked the time on the Peter Max clock he'd bought Saturday, part of a small Max collection high on one wall. It was a twelve-inch circle of shiny, wet-look vinyl in strong, bright colors that undulated around the black hands. Great design, of course, but jeez, what cheap stuff it was. Vinyl over cardboard, for God's sake.

How old was Max when he hit his peak? Jesus, he must have made a fortune with this stuff—real mass-market art. And after all, what was it? Really just warmed-over Art Nouveau done in clashing primaries. But back then, people just lapped it up. Nowadays, Peter lamented to himself, everything is either "tasteful earthtones" or that Laura Ashley crap that makes a room look like a gangster's funeral. I'm as good as Max, he thought bitterly, just not as lucky. My problem isn't lack of talent, it's that I was born at the wrong time.

It was an article of faith for Peter, this conviction of asynchronicity. Not like these kids, perfectly suited to their era. He looked at the group clustered around his chair, listened to them chattering about painting, and galleries, and the upcoming Show. Except they also chattered about grades, and job interviews, and "opportunities in the art market," for chrissake. Money and status were all they cared about.

"Does the *Gargoyle* pay for cartoons?" a pudgy kid named Jeff asked, proving Peter's point.

"Only a few bucks," the girl in the red plastic necklace answered—Catalina, she called herself, Peter remembered. "But it looks good on a résumé." Their voices were unnaturally loud and harsh, straining for volume over the noise from the stereo.

"And y'know, cartooning isn't a bad job market these days," a girl with spiky black hair offered. "Not just Hollywood, but Madison Avenue, too—they're using a lot more animation in commercials lately."

"Sure, because artists command lower residuals than live actors do," Jeff said disgustedly.

"Christ, is this the sort of thing they're teaching in art school these days?" Peter snorted. "Moneygrubbing 101?"

"Well, artists have to eat too." The black-haired girl was unoffended. "I suppose you think cartoon work is selling out."

"Selling out is internal, not external," Peter said, sounding sententious even to his own ears. "Take a look at Crumb's work sometime—hell, he was a cartoonist who really set the world on its ass. You shoulda seen my mother the first time she saw one."

"You showed Crumb to your mother?" Jess asked in astonished tones.

"Not on purpose; I left one in the john by accident." Peter laughed, remembering. "Christ, you should have seen the shit hit the fan." That's what they didn't understand, these kids; that the real joy of art was in the outrage it could provoke among the sodden masses.

His mother's shock and outrage, in fact, had provided him with his first taste of the joys of rebellion, and the sudden awareness of the power it conferred to the powerless. After all his comics were found and burned, he retaliated by creating his own, and to his own surprise discovered he actually had a talent for drawing. Moreover, he discovered that the persona of the

rebellious artist conferred real status, not only among his high school classmates but even among adults.

Both in high school and later, in college, it was the great Pop Art masters who captured his imagination, not so much for their work as for their rebellion. In truth, he found the scribbles of Jim Dine incomprehensible and the cartoonish multiples of Andy Warhol boring. But, by God, they'd knocked the art world on its ass! And become celebrities and millionaires in the process. He was as good as they were—all he needed was to find his own personal View, his artistic voice, one that the art world would perceive as brilliantly innovative, shocking, and outrageous.

They were looking at him oddly, not only unimpressed by his anti-establishment fervor but seemingly uncomfortable with it. Lesley passed a joint back to him over her head, and he took a deep, defiant drag. The hell with them; they were the people he was rebelling against. They would always be nobodies.

Yet he was uncomfortably aware, looking at their youthful faces, that his artistic clock was ticking ruthlessly onward. It was definitely time for a change in his life, he mused, watching the party wind down around him. Time to move on. For the first time, the thought gave him more satisfaction than dismay.

TWELVE

She had to pull herself together, Ellen Nakamura told herself sharply Wednesday morning. Concentrate on business and keep her mind off everything else. The brass foo-dog incense burner grimaced in her hand; put it in the carved corner unit, as part of the Chinese brass collection? Or should she display all the various foo dogs—at last count there were thirteen of them—together in one snarling mass? But that would mean she'd have to include the ugly blue ceramic dog, twice as big as the others and privately nicknamed Foo Yung. Maybe she should just admit the ceramic was a mistake, take it to the Treasure Mart and be done with it. It was junk anyway, not even worth its ten-dollar price tag. Not at all the sort of thing she wanted to deal in; not like the celadon vase . . .

She pushed the vase out of her mind with an effort, set the brass creature on a small lacquered table—nice piece, that—and looked around the room, her own personal piece of Remains to Be Seen. She waited for the feeling of pleasure it

usually gave her. She and Ted had done it all themselves—painted the walls a pale blue, stained and polished the oak woodwork to a rich, dark glow, even laid the deep maroon carpeting. And the stock was pretty good quality—not what she hoped for in the future, of course, but no Hong Kong schlock, either. Still, not like the celadon vase.

With a sigh she bent down and opened the door of a small lacquered cabinet. Even in the darkened interior the vase seemed to glow; she reached in and clasped her hands around the cool porcelain, feeling the wonder of it through her fingertips.

"Oh, good, glad to see you've got it stashed in a safe place."

The vase jumped in Ellen's hands, rocking slightly on its shelf. Thank God she hadn't been holding it aloft. She steadied it quickly and shut the cabinet door, turning to put her back against it.

"Sorry, didn't mean to make you jump," Steve Olewski apologized. "Especially with a Song dynasty vase in your hands."

"No problem." Ellen smiled casually while her mind raced. He knew what the vase was, had made an exact identification. So he also knew what it was worth; the first instinct of any professional dealer was to look up catalogue values. How he'd found out didn't matter; the important question was what significance he placed on the information. "All ready for the Show?" she asked, maintaining the mild tone of a normal conversation.

"Damn, you're good." Steve looked at her with open admiration. "I'll bet you didn't blink an eye when you first saw it, did you?"

"What on earth are you talking about?" Ellen asked, putting mild curiosity into her voice. It wouldn't fool him, of course, but it would force him to make the next move.

"Look, relax, okay? You know I'm not going to blow the whistle on you, don't you?" He moved closer to her. "You look

wiped out. You've been worrying, and you shouldn't. No one's going to find out." He put a hand on her shoulder. "Come on back to the kitchen and have a cup of coffee."

"Thanks, but I need to do some cleaning up in here." How insistent would he be?

"Sorry." He grinned, shaking his head. "I'm not taking no for an answer." His grip tightened on her shoulder. "Come on. There's nothing that a good hit of caffeine won't help."

She allowed herself to be led unprotesting to the kitchen, where he ceremoniously pulled out a chair and seated her at the big table. He poured them each a mug of coffee and sat down next to her, turning the chair backward and straddling it.

"Now," he said, propping his elbows on the back of his chair, "I don't want you to worry, okay? Only you've got to be careful, you know? If I could find out, so could other people. That husband of yours, for instance. Or even the police."

So he'd figured out that Ted didn't know about the vase either. Damn, worse and worse. For the first time she noticed the T-shirt he was wearing today, black like his mop of curly hair, with white lettering that said: "I am desperately interested in your inconsequential problems." She suddenly sickened of game-playing.

"What do you want?" she asked abruptly.

"Want? Hey, is that what you think?" He sounded hurt. "Look, this isn't blackmail or anything. You're a friend; I wouldn't do that to you." He hitched his chair closer to hers and laid his hand on her arm, lying bare on the table. "The way I figure it, the woman was a wart on the face of Ann Arbor. What the hell, she had it coming."

So that was what he thought. She looked at his hand on her arm, a big hand sprinkled with coarse black hairs, ragged nails on thick, spatulate fingers. She kept her arm still by an effort of will that nauseated her.

"After all," he continued when she didn't speak, "we are friends, right?"

"Of course we are." She freed her arm very casually, patted the back of his hand, and reached for her coffee mug. "And with the Show in four days, we've both got enough on our minds. You know, you drew a pretty lousy location." She advanced the new topic like a bishop's gambit in a chess game.

"Yeah, I know." He took the bait, his face darkening with anger. "I've got a feeling that Martha Penrose screwed around with the draw."

Ellen nodded. "It *is* a strange coincidence that she drew the corner spot again."

"Ah, that woman." Carmela Aguilar entered the kitchen and headed for the coffeepot. "One of these days she will bite off more than she can chew, and the result will not be pretty." She poured coffee and drank deeply from the mug. "I tell you, if I have to explain to one more tightfisted housewife why we do not haggle over prices, I will take a hatchet to them all. Steve, it is your turn at the cash register, thank God. I am just going to sit here for a while and put my feet up." She suited her action to her words.

"Sure." Steve jumped to his feet. "And look," he said to Ellen, "don't worry, huh? That's what friends are for—to help each other out." He grinned and ruffled her hair, and she managed a smile in return.

"What was that all about?" Carmela looked at her shrewdly. "God, you look terrible."

"Thanks a lot," Ellen said sarcastically. Now that Steve was gone she let her face relax fractionally.

"Well, it is the truth." Carmela was unapologetic.

"I haven't been sleeping too well, that's all," Ellen said.

"You must not let them get to you," Carmela declared. "Soon they will find the murderer and we can all forget about it."

But I can't forget about it, Ellen thought. I can't think about anything but that damn vase. Worse than that, I'm not even getting any pleasure from it. Even from the beginning it had too

many bad vibes associated with it, but this crap from Steve was the last straw.

I could just take the bloody thing outside, drop it on the sidewalk and sweep the pieces into the gutter; at least that would get rid of the evidence. But even as she formed the thought in her mind, her stomach wrenched at the idea of destroying such luminous beauty. The feeling was worse even than her nausea at Steve's touch. No, she couldn't, physically could not, do it.

She'd have to do something else.

THIRTEEN

• • • • • •

Wednesday, when what Anneke wanted most in the world was a calm, quiet session with unemotional algorithms, turned out to be a crisis day.

"It's the Wellspring," Ken Scheede said when she walked in, referring to a "healthy-food" restaurant near campus. He held his hand over the mouthpiece of the telephone.

"What's the problem?" Anneke asked with foreboding.

"Apparently someone pushed the wrong button and erased their entire personnel file."

"Nonsense. I set up that system so it takes four different procedures to erase a main file. I knew they'd be using a steady stream of amateurs. And anyway, why don't they just recopy it from their backup disk?" One look at Ken's face gave her her answer. "They haven't been backing up their data regularly, have they?" With a sigh that was closer to a growl—how could people have such sloppy minds? she thought savagely—she sat down at her desk and picked up the phone.

After dealing with the hysterical restaurant manager—someone would be over this afternoon to attempt a retrieval, no promises—she spent half an hour with a self-important economics professor who wanted her to develop a six-level factor analysis of international commodities trading. Apparently he had come to A/H because he figured a woman would work cheaper than a man and wouldn't care if he took credit for the work. Then there was a pitched battle between Carol Rosenthal and a sophomore named Aston Phillips, about rights to a wind-surfing-simulation game they were coauthoring—supposedly on their own time, although this morning Anneke had her doubts.

"All right, that's it," she barked out finally. "Ken . . . where the hell is Ken?" she snapped at the two combatants.

"In class," Carol muttered mutinously. "I'm on this morning, along with him"—she gave Aston a look full of loathing—"and Jackie comes in this afternoon."

"Good. Then until Ken gets back you're in charge," Anneke told Carol. "And you," she said to Aston, quelling his incipient protest with a glare, "can get your . . . aspirations over to Wellspring, so you can see what it's like to work with real idiots. As for me, I'll be working in the Sun room. No interruptions. That means no phone calls, no clients, no visitors, no problems. Understand? Good." She picked up her briefcase and coffee mug and retreated before she said anything more.

Inside the windowless room she took a deep breath, letting her irritation subside. She sat down at the Sun's terminal and patted the keyboard. Thank God for computers. Computers were never guilty of laziness, or boorishness, or sheer sloppy thinking. Computers didn't bog down in messy emotionalism. The Sun didn't feud with the IBM over which one would run the women's athletics survey, or sulk when she transferred data from one to the other. Sometimes, in fact, computers were the ideal companions.

She spread out the women's sports questionnaire, for which

the client, an organization of women students, wanted a batch of fancy—and unnecessary—statistical analyses. On the other hand, maybe the stats were necessary on political grounds: Complexity increases credibility. In which case she'd be better off running the whole thing through the more powerful statistical programs on MTS.

The thought of MTS reminded her that she hadn't checked for electronic mail in a couple of days, but on second thought she decided it could wait. She absolutely could not face the possibility of a second message from Dennis. Not today; the thought of yet another emotional onslaught was unbearable.

For the next several hours she lost herself in the cool, precise world of electronics and mathematics. The survey results took shape nicely; she'd have to do them a batch of pie charts, which always impressed the hell out of people; and maybe a couple of histograms. . . . The telephone buzzer shattered her concentration like an explosion.

"Yes?" She looked at her watch as she spoke into the receiver, amazed that it was nearly two o'clock.

"Ms. Haagen, I'm sorry," Carol's voice was almost tremulous. "I know you said you didn't want to be disturbed, but . . ."

"It's all right." Good Lord, she must have scared the girl to death earlier. "What's up?"

"Well, I wouldn't have bothered you except, well, it's the police, and they sound pretty insistent."

"Oh, damn. If they've screwed up that printer program again I'll . . . hell. All right, thanks, Carol, I'll take it."

But when she pushed the line button and spoke into the receiver, it was Genesko's voice that answered.

"Hello, Ms. Haagen. I hope I'm not disturbing you."

"No, not really. I was just about ready to come up for air anyway."

"Good. I've got a question about a computer procedure I think might be helpful. I wonder if I could talk to you about it. Perhaps later this afternoon?"

"Yes, I suppose so," Anneke said reluctantly, suppressing her first instinct to refuse. "I assume this has to do with the Westlake murder?"

"Yes, it does, but I'd rather explain it to you in person, if you don't mind. Would four o'clock here in my office be convenient?"

"That will be fine." Anneke hung up and leaned back in her chair, staring at the monitor in front of her but not seeing it. So much for peaceful, emotion-free work. The very word "murder" was emotion-laden. Joanna Westlake had been killed out of greed, or envy, possibly mixed with hatred or fear or any of a dozen other unpleasant human passions.

In the pressure of the day's work, she had spared only a brief thought for the murder, and that thought had been chiefly relief that it was not her problem. She had done all she could, and more if you counted last night's party, and she had obviously found out nothing that was any use—likes and dislikes, suppositions, gossip and scandal weren't evidence. After all, what had she picked up in her idiotic detective role-playing game? Ronald Westlake's affair? Feuds and animosities among dealers? The dreary clash of male egos? It was all just sloppy, emotional nonsense.

Shaking her head, she logged off the Sun, stopped for a word with Carol, and headed outside for a late lunch.

"What I'd like to do," Genesko explained, "is use the computer to sort and map this data." He pointed to a stack of typewritten paper, presumably the same stack Anneke had seen on her last visit to his office.

"Exactly what sort of thing did you have in mind?" she asked warily. There were people who hated and feared computers; by the same token, there were people who endowed them with supernatural powers.

But Genesko's idea, to her relief, made sense. In fact, it was

rather clever, she thought, reluctantly impressed. She didn't really want to be impressed any further by this man.

"We have a mass of statements outlining people's movements," he explained. "If we could map them—produce a visual chart of each track, with locations and times—we'd have a better understanding of how these people interacted on Saturday, who was where when. If nothing else, it might help us eliminate one or two suspects."

"Hmm. Tricky but not impossible." Anneke's mind was already formulating procedures.

"The trouble is," Genesko warned, "we'd need it fast."

"Well," she said, thinking aloud, "there's a program you've already got that I might be able to hack it into. It wouldn't be pretty, but it should do the job." She could give the women's athletics survey to Aston to finish—it was nearly done anyway, and reading the results would be good for him, the little pig.

"Would it be possible to add in data about the items purchased at each sale?" he asked. "That's less crucial, but it would help organize two lines of investigation into one."

"Organizing data is always the first problem, isn't it?" How would one go about organizing a criminal investigation? she wondered. Were there recognizable parameters to what was essentially a series of random human acts?

"The classic approach is to identify means, motive, and opportunity," he said, seeming to follow her train of thought. "But of course that's an oversimplification."

"In this case, don't too many of the suspects fit all three categories? The means was an ordinary rock, half a dozen people had the opportunity, and the motive was presumably theft."

"Well, yes and no." He leaned back in his chair. "That's construing 'motive' too narrowly, especially in this case, where we're not dealing with ordinary street theft. It's more accurate to say that Joanna Westlake was killed because she had something someone wanted or needed."

"Needed?"

"Well, thought they needed. You'd be surprised at what people sometimes think they need."

"I don't think I would." Anneke made a face. "It's awfully easy to confuse needs and wants, isn't it?" That had been the trouble with Dennis, she thought, struck by the notion; he'd never learned to differentiate. She had become, disgustingly, something he "needed." "It isn't always a question of money, either," she said slowly.

"Not by any means." Genesko looked at her thoughtfully, and she felt a momentary disquiet, as though he were reading her mind. "Still," he continued matter-of-factly, "monetary gain is usually a good place to start. Take Steve Olewski, for instance. Four or five years in Ypsilanti as an NVMS—that's 'no visible means of support,' but take your best guess. His antique business makes him a bare living, but he has no apparent assets beyond his shop. He still lives in a one-room apartment in Ypsi, and as far as we can tell he's clean—at least, he hasn't been suspected of fencing, which I admit surprised me, considering his background."

He riffled through a different stack of papers. "Or consider Ellen Nakamura. She's a graduate student struggling to pay tuition. Her husband is a first-year professor on a low salary, who owes thousands of dollars in student loans that they're going to be years repaying."

"Well, what about Peter Casaday?" Anneke challenged. "He's about to lose his business, his studio, and his apartment, and I doubt that he's got a fortune stashed away."

"Very true." Genesko regarded her quizzically, then shuffled papers and read aloud. "Peter Casaday, twenty-nine years old, last year's income from all sources twenty-two thousand dollars, most of it from his framing business. Above starvation level, but not what you'd call wealth, either. Especially if you want to live in Ann Arbor. And his lease, as you obviously know, is about to be canceled."

"Still, I suppose the others could use extra money too," Anneke commented. Why on earth is he telling me all this confidential stuff? she wondered, feeling uncomfortably voyeuristic. Still, she was curious enough to hope he'd continue.

"Well, Martha and Howard Penrose own their own home, live on their pensions and antique income, plus a good-sized annuity. They don't seem to have any serious financial constraints." He put a mild stress on the word "seem." "Alice Cowan's husband"—this time he emphasized the last word slightly—"has a good deal of money, all of it in his name, plus a mid-six-figure yearly income. Michael Rappaport's reported income last year was in the eighty-thousand-dollar range, but he lives up to nearly every dollar of it. And he passed his fiftieth birthday last year."

"Murder strikes me as a rather extreme response to a midlife crisis," Anneke remarked drily.

"But not unheard-of." She wasn't sure whether the note in his voice was amusement or something else.

"What about Ronald Westlake? —I know, I know," she said stubbornly, "he has an unshakable alibi. But are you aware that he's involved in a long-standing affair?"

"With Professor Carla Bridges, also of the Residential College." Genesko nodded. "You picked that up too, did you?"

"What about her? She could have as strong a motive as Joanna's husband."

"She was at the same seminar, I'm afraid."

"Oh." Anneke felt like a punctured balloon. "And she never left either?" He shook his head, and she gave him points for not smiling.

"Did you learn anything else that might be relevant?" he asked. She looked at him sharply but could detect nothing patronizing or amused in his demeanor. The question seemed entirely serious.

"Nothing you don't already know," she said briefly. "Still,"

she continued after a moment, "money isn't the only motive for theft."

"Absolutely not," Genesko agreed. "There are all kinds of greed in the world."

"Greed. Yes." Anneke recalled the avid looks she'd seen on dealers' faces. "You know," she pursued the thought, "some of these people are dealers, but all of them are collectors. In fact, I'd guess that's how most dealers begin, as collectors who turn professional."

"And?" Genesko prompted.

"Well, if one of them came across something really special—say, for instance, Michael found an autographed photo of Oscar Wilde—would he sell it?"

"It would depend, I suppose." Genesko considered the question. "If he needed the money badly enough, I suppose he'd have to, wouldn't he?"

"If he needed the money for a . . . I don't know, a triple bypass, maybe, but not for anything much less critical." She laughed at Genesko's politely skeptical expression. "You don't have the collector's passion, do you? Believe me, there are people who would kill simply to possess some object they're obsessed with."

"Oh, I know there are. There are cases on record. But pure financial gain seems to me more likely." He looked at her for a moment. "Is there anything you'd actually kill for?"

"A Donald Deskey dining set," she answered immediately. "All right." She smiled ruefully. "I don't suppose I'd really kill for it, but I can understand the feeling. Isn't there anything you'd kill for?"

He gave the question serious consideration. "Not something tangible," he said after a moment's thought. "Things—objects—just don't seem to mean that much to me."

"You're a tosser, not a keeper," Anneke said. "Even so, wouldn't you consider killing for that?" She pointed to the Super Bowl ring.

"To keep it, perhaps, but for its symbolic value. Certainly not for its beauty." He raised his hand, and Anneke noted that his middle finger was bent slightly out of line. The chunky ring was big even on his huge hand. "And if you think this one is ugly," he said with a sudden, broad grin, "you should see the others."

It was the first time she could remember seeing him smile openly; it changed him utterly, from a somber, almost menacing authority figure to a man of enormous personal charm. For a moment a flow of warmth washed over her, followed almost immediately by a feeling that was nearly terror. Charm was how it always began, she told herself, alarm bells going off inside her. She tried to visualize him in Steeler black and gold, snarling hatred at opposing quarterbacks. She fixed the picture in her mind, reminding herself that this man could be as dangerous to her as he'd been to Kenny Stabler.

"That's right, you have a collection of them, don't you?" she said finally.

"Well, only three."

"Only three." She allowed herself to laugh outright. "I'd say for Super Bowl rings that represents a sizable collection. Anyway," she continued more soberly, returning her mind to the original subject, "you do see what I mean. If this thing, whatever it was, triggered some insane collector's passion, then you can't analyze it as murder for profit in the ordinary sense."

"That's true. And it means," Genesko continued, "that whatever was stolen may never turn up on the market, because the murderer has no intention of selling it. On the other hand, since we don't know what it is, we can't circularize the usual pawnshops anyway."

"If it's the kind of thing we're talking about," Anneke pointed out, "you'd do better to check out Sotheby's and Christie's."

"Oh, we've done that." He smiled slightly at her look of surprise. "Just in case any major consignment is offered from Ann Arbor."

"I read somewhere that police work is primarily a matter of slogging routine," Anneke returned his smile cautiously.

"Well, most jobs are, aren't they?" He spread his hands on the desk, palms down. "Routine is just another word for an orderly approach to a problem. Once you organize your data, your mind can begin to see the pattern emerge. Learning to recognize patterns is the key to doing most jobs well, isn't it?"

"I suppose it is," Anneke agreed, struck by the thought. "Certainly it is in programming. On the other hand," she added with a certain irony, "in writing a computer program there may be more than one acceptable pattern."

"But only one 'best' pattern, surely?"

"I suppose so." She pondered his theory. "There's one other problem, though: The human mind demands pattern, so much so that it imposes order even where it doesn't exist."

"Of course." He understood her objection immediately. "That's the basis of the Rorschach inkblot test. There's no question that that's a risk, but what's the alternative?" He spread his hands in a gesture of inquiry. "Besides, I think there's an even worse risk."

"Oh?"

"Too much routine, too much order can suppress intuition and innovation. You can get so accustomed to the existing patterns that you don't see new ones even when they're right in front of you." The words were spoken in his usual mild, impersonal tone; perhaps she only imagined the undercurrent of some secondary meaning, because her own train of thought was expanding his own.

"Well, if you want that program I'd better get onto it," she said. "I'll let you know when I've got it finished."

"Before you leave," he said as she rose, "I've been asked to attend a hospital fund-raising dinner next week. I wondered if you'd be interested in joining me."

"Thank you, but I'm afraid I'm busy." The words came automatically, with the ease of repetition, the same polite

phrase with which she'd turned down all such invitations in the last half-year. Only after his murmured "That's too bad" did reality kick in.

The reality, she realized as she walked down the institutional-gray corridor toward the parking lot, was that she wished she'd said yes. Or rather, she told herself firmly, she wished life were uncomplicated enough to make yes a possible answer. Well, it wasn't. The complexities of algorithms were all she could handle for the foreseeable future.

FOURTEEN

Aston surprised her by being genuinely interested in the women's sports survey, and Ken Scheede, with no Thursday classes, ran interference with the other problems. Genesko's program was interesting as well as troublesome, a programmer's delight that engaged all of Anneke's attention throughout the day. It was after six o'clock when Ken's voice brought her up for air.

"Anything you want me to do before I leave, Ms. Haagen?"

"What? Oh, no, not that I know of." She stretched aching shoulder muscles. "Everyone else gone?"

"For the moment. Carol's coming back in later tonight, to work on that graphics program."

"Fine." Anneke had long ago concluded that the combination of programming skills and a preference for keeping weird hours must have some sort of genetic linkage. One reason she had such good luck with programmers was her willingness to let them work whatever preposterous schedule they preferred.

"How're you coming?" Ken asked curiously. She had told him, without going into specifics, that she was doing a rush job for the police.

"Slowly. Too damn slowly. In fact," she decided, "I think I'll grab a bite and finish up at home. I hope."

"Well, if you need any help . . ." His voice held the normal eagerness of a good programmer scenting an interesting problem.

"Thanks, but I think I've finally got a handle on it." Ken had worked on other police projects, but this was the first case-related request she'd had, and it seemed to call for greater confidentiality. "See you tomorrow."

She bought a turkey-and-cheese croissant from a shop across the street and took it home, where she relaxed for half an hour watching "Wheel of Fortune" on television. The computer version was more fun, she decided. She logged her Compaq into the police computer, reviewed what she had done so far, and shook her head in annoyance. If only they had better graphics capability . . . six different lines—no, seven, counting Joanna . . . if she set this operation up as a subroutine . . .

She'd left the television on, but it functioned purely as background noise so she almost missed hearing it. Only the words "Ann Arbor" penetrated her consciousness, and even then it took her a minute to adjust her mental focus from monitor screen to television screen.

". . . found here in these woods by a pair of joggers at approximately five-thirty this afternoon." Anneke swiveled her chair so she could see the television through the arched door of her den; the speaker was a thirtyish man with high cheekbones and an improbable hairdo. "According to police, she had been dead for several hours."

Oh Lord, another murder. Anneke swiveled back to her monitor. Well, it would have to be either a murder or a protest demonstration; Detroit TV stations never covered any other

Ann Arbor news. She listened to the rest of the report with only half her attention.

"The victim has been identified as Lesley Shea, a nineteen-year-old student at the University of Michigan Art School. At this time police have not determined whether the victim was sexually molested, but we at Channel Three NewsVigil have learned exclusively that police believe she was killed elsewhere and her body placed here, along this beautiful and usually peaceful stretch of the Huron River, after her death."

And still, all Anneke felt was distaste for the smarmy newsman. She turned once more toward the TV screen.

And it was Lesley. The picture filling the screen had the posed, air-brushed quality that shouted high-school yearbook, but there was no mistaking that beautiful, ethereal, intelligent face surrounded by its pale cloud of ash-blond hair.

"No!" Anneke said aloud, explosively. "Oh, goddammit to hell." She jumped from her chair and ran into the living room, where the anchorman now shared a split screen with the reporter.

". . . have any suspects?" the silver-haired anchorman was asking.

"Not yet, Carlton," the reporter answered. "They're asking anyone who saw the girl today to get in touch with police at this number." A phone number appeared across his chest, and he recited it carefully twice.

"And of course Channel Three NewsVigil will bring you any new developments first, as soon as they occur. Thank you, Griff." The anchorman turned back toward the camera and the split-screen effect dissolved. "Next on NewsVigil—a suburb goes to war over a proposed leash law for cats, after this message."

Anneke watched, unseeing, as a family crisis was resolved by a trip to a fast-food outlet. A wave of cold anger threatened to overwhelm her—that beautiful, classy girl—it was unspeakable, obscene to think of her murdered, to think of her dead body a

subject for the titillation of a slimy toad hyping television ratings points. . . . She discovered that she was shaking, and that her vision was dimmed by unshed tears.

Taking a deep breath, she stalked to the lacquered Art Deco cabinet, poured herself a sizable dose of Bailey's Irish Cream and downed the thick, sweet liquid at a gulp. Then she stalked back to the den, picked up the telephone, and started to push buttons. But after three digits she stopped and replaced the receiver.

Calling Genesko would be foolish. For one thing, there was no reason to assume he was even assigned to this case. For another, what could she tell him? That she'd met the girl, seen her behave coolly and intelligently in a difficult situation, been vastly impressed with the mind and personality behind the beautiful face? Well, she could report that Lesley Shea was the sort of girl who brought out strong passions, or at least strong testosterone reactions, in men, Anneke considered, recalling the squabble in Peter's studio.

Her eyes fell on the computer screen, its cursor blinking patiently where she'd left it. She'd coded each suspect by initials—EN for Ellen Nakamura, PC for Peter Casaday, SO for Steve Olewski, and so on. For the first time it occurred to her to wonder if Lesley's murder was connected to Joanna's. Her hand reached for the phone once more, but again she stopped.

If I finish this damn program tonight, she temporized, I can call him first thing in the morning. And then, if there is a connection, maybe I'll have something that can help. Grimly, she sat down at the Compaq and attacked the program again, seeing it now from a different perspective. Before, it had been merely an intellectual exercise, devoid of emotional content; now she was intensely aware of its ultimate purpose—not merely to create the correct tracks on a screen, but to provide a pattern to catch a murderer.

The new awareness, she discovered, made it harder rather than easier to finish the job.

The morning papers carried more detail about Lesley, but little further about the investigation. Anneke read it bleary-eyed, after four hours of restless sleep. Lesley had been the youngest of three daughters of a Birmingham family. Her father was an accountant, her mother a real estate broker, and one sister was a senior at Berkeley, majoring in business administration. An unlikely group to produce an artist, Anneke thought; or perhaps a likely one, although Lesley had seemed more self-assured than rebellious.

She put down the paper, drained her third cup of coffee, and went into the den. At least she'd finished Genesko's program; she could call him now with a clear conscience. But for the third time she paused with her hand on the receiver.

There was something else she wanted to do first. She'd been trying all morning to talk herself out of it, using pejoratives that included "meddling," "interfering," and worse, but to no avail. It was something she simply had to do.

She took a small Sonia Delaunay print off its hook on the wall, positioned her heavy cat's-head letter opener above it, and brought the handle down sharply. There was a satisfying cracking sound, and the glass over the print split neatly from side to side. Anneke slipped the result into a paper bag, put the bag into her briefcase, and set off on her errand.

"I banged a stepladder against it," she said with an embarrassed laugh. The embarrassment, at least, was entirely sincere.

"Easy enough to repair," Peter Casaday said. "You want the back museum-sealed the way it is now?"

"Yes, please." Now that she was here, Anneke really didn't know quite what to do next. Against all expectations, Peter didn't even seem to recognize her.

The shop, empty now except for the two of them, seemed to Anneke less bizarre than it had Tuesday evening, but rather more tacky. The furniture, seen in clear daylight, was thread-

bare; the various artifacts, stilled and unlit, were merely ugly. The mirror was just a mirror, the vacuum-cleaner-hose lamp looked more than ever like an out-of-place household appliance, and was there anything in the world more repulsive than a quiescent Lava lamp?

And Peter himself looked dreadful. His eyes were bloodshot and red-rimmed, his face was pasty under a half-completed shave, and his hair lay lank on his head; without the careful blow-drying, Anneke could make out the beginnings of a receding hairline.

"Name, please?" The hand gripping the pen as he prepared to write out her receipt wavered slightly.

"Anneke Haagen." She spelled both names automatically, and his pen followed her. Only when he reached the second "a" in her last name was there a flicker of recognition.

"Oh, yeah. You're that friend of Joyce's." He tore off the receipt and handed it to her without further comment. She cast about rather desperately for a conversational opening, mentally swearing at herself for poor preparation. She might have expected this, after all. Should she simply offer her condolences, or would he put her down at once as a snooping busybody overcome with prurient interest? And if it came to the point, didn't that particular shoe fit uncomfortably well?

She was saved from ignominious retreat by footsteps on the stairs behind her, and a voice that caused Peter to wince visibly.

"Christ, couldn't you at least close up for the day, you bastard?" The voice was high-pitched and breathless, robbing the words of much of their intended brutality. "Afraid you might lose a couple of bucks?"

The girl was tall and dark, lanky and somehow unfledged-looking. Her eyes were red and swollen behind fashionable small eyeglasses, and her long hair hung flat and lifeless down her back. She wore a short blue denim skirt, yellow blouse, and scuffed brown sandals, as if she'd dressed by grabbing the first clothes at hand.

"I never thought of it." Peter blinked with surprise. "I guess I should have." He straightened his body, visibly pulling himself together. "Karen, I'm sorry. I guess I should've called or something. I just . . ."

"Forget it," the girl said dully. "I only came to get her stuff. Her parents are coming down this afternoon to clear her things out of our room." So this was Lesley's roommate, Anneke realized.

"You're too late." Peter shook his head. "The police already took everything of hers that was here."

"Oh." The girl seemed nonplussed. "Then I guess . . . Did they take all her paintings too?"

"No." Peter seemed surprised. "They're here for the Show."

"Oh no they're not. They belong to her parents now, not to you." The girl glared at him angrily. "You're not going to sell off her best work. I know you—you'll keep them for a couple of years and then try to pass them off as your own work. You know damn well Lesley had five times the talent you'll ever have." Her voice was shrill, rising toward hysteria.

"And ten times yours," Peter responded savagely. "You want them, you can have them." He stormed out from behind the counter and across the room. "Here," he shouted, knocking over a stack of canvases that leaned against the wall. "This one was hers . . . and this . . . and this one." He picked up each unframed canvas as he spoke and tossed it across the room into a heap on the floor. "There they are. Now get the hell out of here and leave me alone."

"Don't worry, I will." The girl fell to her hands and knees and scrabbled at the paintings, trying to gather them into a manageable stack, all the while sobbing openly. Peter stood and glared at her tight-lipped, his arms folded. Both of them seemed to have forgotten Anneke's existence.

"Here, let me give you a hand." Anneke knelt next to the girl and efficiently gathered up the paintings. Then she put out a hand and helped Karen to her feet, fished in her purse for a

Kleenex, and waited while the girl mopped her eyes and blew her nose. She felt a kind of irritated sympathy for the child, like a housemother dealing with a bright but antisocial student.

"I'm sorry about Lesley," she said when Karen had gotten herself back under control.

"Did you know her?" the girl asked eagerly.

"I only met her once, but I was very impressed with her." Anneke noted Peter's look of surprise and dawning memory.

"Yes, that was it, she was impressive, wasn't she? She was so ... so ..." Karen gulped and tears started to flow again.

"Look, let me help you carry these things out, and I'll buy you a cup of coffee," Anneke said decisively. "No, really, I could use one myself," she insisted with emphatic honesty. "Come on."

There was an outdoor café a few doors down from Peter's studio. Anneke introduced herself, led Karen to a table, and ordered coffee and, over the girl's weak protest, a plateful of muffins.

"My dear child," she said acerbically, feeling more than ever like a housemother, "eating is not disrespectful to the dead, nor is it a sign of insufficient grief. Now, for heaven's sake, get some food into you."

Karen seemed to take her at her word. While she gobbled muffins, Anneke took the opportunity to examine Lesley's paintings, propped on an empty chair. They were good, she concluded, although she couldn't at all justify the conclusion. They were mainly slashing abstractions—strong, almost savage in their use of color—but there was something sure and disciplined in their structure. They were also, Anneke decided, as unlikely a style for the ethereal Lesley as she could imagine.

"They're wonderful, aren't they?" Karen said around a last mouthful of muffin.

"They're very different from what I would have expected," Anneke said, voicing her thought.

"I know." Karen was feeling so much better that she actually

giggled. "She really worked that Botticelli Venus act, y'know? She could've gone punk to match her work better, but she got a lot more attention this way. People'd see this airy-fairy, Lady-of-the-Lake baby-doll, and then she'd hit them with this kind of stuff and they'd just fall apart. Especially the old guys—you should've seen some of them, it was a total riot."

"She'd had some success, then?"

"Oh, sure." Karen really did look better now, less devastated, and she seemed to want to talk. "Look, she used that Venus-on-the-halfshell routine to get attention, sure. You know how it is." She looked at Anneke shrewdly, woman to woman. "Art is a man's world, after all. But she had real talent; the act wouldn't have gotten her anywhere without it. Hell, she already had a Chicago gallery that was going to take a couple of her things." Karen spoke the last words in tones of awe. "That's more than *he* ever managed," she added venomously.

"Peter, you mean?"

"Peter bloody Casaday, God's gift to women, God's joke on the art world." The words came out with the ease of repetition, as if that was the standard punch line to Peter's name.

"Lesley-must have seen something in him," Anneke pointed out mildly. "They seemed pretty serious about each other."

"Serious!" Karen's voice mixed scorn and indignation. "Never. She was just . . . I don't know. See, Peter was sort of the Catch, y'know? I mean, he's gorgeous-looking, I'll give him that, even if he is nearly thirty. But Lesley was never serious about him."

In fact, Anneke translated to herself, the truth was that Lesley, with the unconscious cruelty of the young, had been using Peter to score status points.

"I'll tell you something else," Karen continued. "He was really jealous, too."

"You mean about other men?" Anneke asked, recalling the scene with Steve.

"Yeah, that too, I guess, but that's really just male ego

hangup. What he was really jealous about was Lesley's talent. He couldn't stand it that she was going to make it big while he was never going to get past two-bit local street fairs." She drained her second cup of coffee. "I do feel better. Thanks, Ms. Haagen." She reached for the canvases and stopped. "Hey, I just remembered—what about the 'Fractured Unicorn'?"

"The what?"

" 'Fractured Unicorn,' " Karen said impatiently. "It was Lesley's best work—a big canvas, part collage, lots of black and red and blue with newspaper headlines worked into it. I'll bet the son of a bitch has it hidden away somewhere."

Anneke had a sudden flash of memory: the big painting in Peter's studio, signed "L. Shea." So that had been Lesley's work. She started to tell Karen about it, then paused; the girl's face was twisted with grief once more.

"Does it really matter so much?" Anneke asked finally. "Why not let it go for a while?"

"I suppose." The girl looked exhausted.

"Look, my car is just around the corner." Anneke stood and picked up the canvases. "Come on, I'll drop you off at your dorm."

They drove in near silence to Bursley Hall, across from the art school on North Campus. The Alfa's top was down and the June sun was warm on their backs, but Karen huddled in the passenger seat as though cold, and jumped from the car almost before it rolled to a halt. She grabbed the canvases and gave Anneke only the most perfunctory thank-you—as if she regretted talking to me, Anneke thought, swinging the car around.

When she reached Bonisteel Drive she turned east instead of west, then swung up Huron Parkway and out Huron River Drive, wanting time to think about the morning. Somewhat to her surprise, she decided that Peter was genuinely grieved by Lesley's death. And to her further surprise, she concluded that Karen's grief, while also undeniably genuine, seemed mixed

with some other strong emotion. After a moment she identified the emotion, tentatively, as envy.

She put the thought aside to negotiate a curve and pass two side-by-side bicyclists, then took up the thought again. Karen had been fond of Lesley, and proud of her. Yet what must it have been like, being roommate to beauty, brains, talent, and accomplishment? And why, if Lesley were in fact using Peter, did Karen harbor so much resentment toward the man? Was it possible that Karen was jealous of Peter's interest in Lesley?

It was certainly possible, Anneke thought gloomily, once more damning all messy human emotions. She swung the Alfa around in the Delhi Park entry without bothering to glance at the tumbling rapids and lush spring greenery, and pointed its nose back toward Ann Arbor.

FIFTEEN

• • • • • • •

Her first act, when she returned to her office, was finally to complete her call to Genesko. Disappointingly, he was out, and all she could do was leave word that his program was ready and ask that he call her back. Then, having wasted the morning, she determined to concentrate on work for the afternoon.

Genesko called, finally, after four o'clock, apologizing for his absence.

"I've been tied up with another murder, I'm afraid," he explained.

"Lesley Shea?" Anneke asked quickly.

"Yes. You sound as if you knew her?" His voice made the statement into a question.

"Not exactly," she hedged. "I'll explain when I bring you the program."

"I'll be in my office for the rest of the afternoon if you're free."

"Give me about half an hour," Anneke agreed, powering down her terminal instantly.

Genesko's greeting, when she reached his cramped city hall office, was friendly but businesslike. Anneke went first to the terminal, ran the mapping program, and explained its operation to him.

"It's quick and dirty," she warned, half apologetic. "It's built onto a graphing program, with no checking routines, no safeguards, just the bare operations."

"In other words," he said with a slight smile, "don't give it to Brad Weinmann to run." They both laughed. "Jon Zelisco's pretty good with computers. I think I'll pull him off the Shea house-to-house and ask him to do it."

"Is there anything new on Lesley's death?" Anneke asked.

"No immediate suspect, if that's what you mean. You said you knew her?" He poured two mugs of coffee, giving one to Anneke and taking the other back to his desk.

"I only met her once, Tuesday night at a party at Peter Casaday's studio. I was very impressed with her." Anneke picked up the mug and moved from the terminal to the chair next to the big desk, trying to arrange her thoughts in neat rows, like the stacks of paper on the desktop. Today there seemed to be even more stacks than before.

"The first time I saw her, she was with Peter and a few other people, mostly students. Or at least student types," she corrected herself, intent on absolute accuracy. Briefly she described the events at the party, including the fight with Steve—"well, scuffle really"—and its aftermath. When she finished, Genesko sat silently for a moment, digesting her account.

"Did you get the impression that Steve's advances were serious?" he asked finally.

"Well, yes and no." She pondered the question. "Let's say he didn't actually expect to get anywhere with her, but he would have been delighted to be wrong. Still, I think he was needling Peter more than he was making a move on Lesley."

"Was there anything in their behavior to suggest there had been a previous relationship between Steve and Lesley?"

"I would say definitely not," Anneke answered slowly, her voice far less positive than her words. It was not a thought that had occurred to her before.

"When you left, everything seemed fine between Peter and Lesley?"

"As near as I could tell. They were sitting together, and they both looked reasonably content." She laughed slightly. "Of course, I think they were both a little stoned."

"Would you say," Genesko pressed, "that they were in love with each other?"

"In love?" Anneke mouthed the words and made a face. "Hell, I don't know. I don't even know what it means—it's like trying to quantify emotions." The phrase triggered a thought. "Well, all right, let's quantify them, then. Put it this way: I think Peter cared a good deal more about her than she cared about him. Especially after what I heard this morning."

"This morning?" Genesko said quickly.

"Yes. I saw Peter this morning, and I had a talk with Lesley's roommate." To her relief, he did not ask about hows and whys, merely listened quietly as she reported the morning's events.

"I'm pretty sure," she concluded, "that this wasn't the cliché of the sophisticated artist seducing the dewy-eyed innocent. Lesley was no cloistered ingenue."

"Few women are these days," Genesko noted drily.

"Thank God," Anneke snapped with somewhat more asperity than she'd intended. "Anyway," she continued more temperately, "Peter certainly seemed devastated."

"Yes, he did." Genesko sounded thoughtful. "He was certainly an emotional wreck, I'll grant that. I just wish I were more sure exactly what the emotion was."

A point that hadn't occurred to her, Anneke admitted to herself. The trouble was, there were so damn many violent emotions messing up people's heads.

"She wasn't pregnant by any chance, was she?" As soon as the question was out, Anneke knew the answer, confirmed by the

negative shake of Genesko's head. No; not the sort of mistake a girl like Lesley would make. "The report I saw didn't say how she was killed."

"Well, she died of a cerebral hemorrhage." Genesko reached into one of the piles of papers and extracted a sheet. "Apparently brought about by a single, massive blow to the back of the head. About here." He pointed to a spot just behind his own ear, where dark hair curled crisply above his collar. Anneke moved her hand to her own neck, mimicking his motion.

"She was struck from behind? Does that mean someone sneaked up on her?"

"Not necessarily." Genesko shook his head. "It could just mean that she turned away from the killer."

"Couldn't she have fallen against something?"

"An accident, you mean? Almost out of the question," he said. "For one thing, the blow was far too forceful for that. It is possible that she could have been pushed against something, but it would have to have been a fairly violent push."

"A fight, you mean." Anneke visualized again the scene in the studio.

"It's one scenario," he agreed. "But however she died, it's positive that her body was moved after death. She definitely wasn't killed on that jogging path."

"Where exactly was it?" Anneke asked.

"Right here." He rose from his chair and pointed to the big Ann Arbor map behind the desk. Anneke stood and edged around the desk for a closer look. His index finger was fixed on a spot just north of downtown, the smoothly shaped fingernail indicating a wooded riverfront area that Anneke could not remember ever having driven past. She leaned forward and her cheek brushed the sleeve of his dark gray suit, the summery fabric light and very fine. She was suddenly intensely aware of his size, of his sheer physical presence.

"I don't think I've ever been along there," she said, drawing

back abruptly, hoping he hadn't noticed the small catch of her breath.

"It's a beautiful spot, almost a ravine," he said, returning to his chair. "The road runs along the top of an embankment, about fifteen feet or so above the riverbed. The jogging path is right along the edge of the river, hidden by trees; you can't see it at all from the road."

"A beautiful place to die." She grimaced.

"Except, of course, she didn't die there."

"I take it no one saw anything?" Anneke asked.

"No one saw anything, no one heard anything." He shook his head.

"Do you have any idea where she was actually killed?"

"Idea, yes." He leaned back in his chair. "There were traces of paint under her fingernails, and paint smears on her shoes."

"Paint smears." Anneke considered for a moment. "Not unusual, surely. After all, she was a painter." He said nothing, merely waited as though expecting something more from her. What more was there about paint smears? "What color was the paint?" she asked finally.

"The paint under her nails was primarily black and different shades of blue." He seemed satisfied with her question. "All of it was old, long dried, and there was only a small amount of it—microscopic particles, really. She'd apparently done her best to clean them off, but of course it's almost impossible to remove all traces of something like thick oil paint. The stains on her shoes, now, were different. They were large smears of gold, and she hadn't cleaned them off at all."

"So she'd dripped gold paint, or stepped in it. Gold paint." Anneke recalled Lesley's paintings. "There's something wrong with that. The black and the blue make sense, but gold just doesn't sound like Lesley's kind of palette." She frowned in thought. "Have you seen any of her work?"

"Yes." He nodded. "Not my kind of thing."

"Mine either," Anneke agreed, "but I think she was actually

pretty good. Still, that's not the point. She worked in big, bright colors, lots of primaries. Can you visualize gold as part of her color work?"

"No, and we didn't find any paint to match it—not in her own studio area at the art school and not in Peter's studio either."

"Gold paint . . . wait a minute," Anneke said sharply, an idea forming in her mind. "What kind of gold are you talking about? Can you describe it?"

"I can do better than that." He pushed a button and spoke into the intercom on his desk, then stood up and poured them each more coffee. Shortly a stocky, gray-haired woman in casual civilian clothes entered the office carrying something in a plastic bag.

"You wanted this, Lieutenant?" She asked the question as if she had a grievance.

"Thank you, Helen." He took the bag from her, and when she had gone he set it on the edge of the desk nearest Anneke, turning it so that the sole was facing her. "The mate to it is at the lab, but I wanted to keep this one for intensity reference. Take a close look at it."

She did so, and knew immediately that her surmise had been right.

The bag contained a woman's athletic shoe, size 7 or 8 Anneke guessed, in the blue-and-white pattern of a currently trendy national brand. A long smear of iridescent gold ran along the outer rubberized edge and down across the bottom near the instep, smearing the surface of the sole and clogging several of the deep treads.

"That's not paint," she said at once, positively. "It's gilt. You know, the kind that's used on picture frames. It comes in little pots, or in tubes, and you usually smear it on with your fingers."

"Picture frames. Yes, of course." He leaned back and looked at her, an expression of satisfaction on his face. "I knew it wasn't ordinary artist's oils, but I was waiting for the lab report. But

assuming you're right, this is the sort of thing a framing studio would be likely to have around."

"Well, so would most antique shops," Anneke pointed out. "They're always repairing old or chipped frames. I saw Steve covered with the stuff just last weekend at the shop." She stopped abruptly. "I didn't mean . . ."

"Yes, well," he said, "any dealer might have it around. You say it comes in tubes?"

"That's one form I've seen it in, yes."

"So she might have stepped on a tube and squirted it out over her shoes," he said, more to himself than to her.

"Yes, but look," Anneke protested, "even if she did step on a tube of the stuff in Peter's studio, that wouldn't mean anything, because she was in and out of there all the time."

"Take another look at the shoe," Genesko suggested.

Anneke did so, frowning at the smears of gilt. "Oh. Yes, of course."

"You see. She didn't walk more than a few steps after she got that paint on her shoe. The gilt on the surface of the sole would have been rubbed off if she had."

"I assume you examined the floor of Peter's studio?"

"Yes. And yes, there were traces of the same sort of gold on the floor, along with traces of twenty-seven other kinds and colors of paint. Exactly what you'd expect in an artist's studio."

"So Peter has to be a primary suspect, doesn't he?"

Instead of answering, Genesko looked at his wristwatch, a complicated stainless-steel chronometer.

"Look, it's nearly six o'clock and I can't even remember whether I ate lunch today." He gave her one of his rare, brilliant smiles, and again she felt a wave of warmth. "Why don't we continue this over dinner? Unless," he added when she didn't reply immediately, "you have another commitment?"

"No, no other commitment," she said at last. It was, she thought, like reaching for the last step of a staircase and finding yourself already at the bottom—that instant of panicky imbal-

ance, of dislocation as the floor seems to rise up to crash against your foot. "I didn't get much lunch either."

"Good," he said, rising, and Anneke knew, without knowing how she knew, that if she'd refused there would have been no third invitation. The fact was somehow important.

Outside, the June sun was still high in the sky, and Anneke took a deep breath, savoring the spring air. She was very aware of the man next to her as they crossed the parking lot, and uneasily conscious of her own awareness. The big Thunderbird was in its assigned slot, but instead of heading toward it, he led her toward the sidewalk.

"If you don't mind, I'd like to stay nearby," he asked her. "Is the Mackinac Hotel all right?"

"The Greenery? That sounds wonderful," she agreed, mildly nonplussed. She'd expected one of the small restaurants that lined Main Street; the Greenery was one of the most elegant and certainly one of the most expensive eating spots in Ann Arbor, catering heavily to visiting businessmen and the hotel-and-expense-account trade.

"If you like fresh tuna steaks," he commented, "theirs are excellent."

"I love fresh tuna," she replied. They chatted companionably about food as they crossed the street and ascended to the roof-top restaurant, where Genesko seemed known to the maître d'. They were seated at a table by the south-facing window, which provided an excellent view of wooded campus in the distance and grubby downtown rooftops nearer by.

"It doesn't look much like it did when I was a student here, I'll say that," Genesko noted after they had ordered—Anneke the grilled tuna, he the *boeuf en daube.*

"Well, the stadium hasn't changed." She pointed to the huge oval visible about two miles away.

"No, but the people inside it have. College football is a lot different for today's kids than it was for me." He wasn't talking

about plays or equipment, Anneke understood. "I'd hate to have to advise a kid playing football these days."

"Do you have any children?" Anneke asked, curious for the first time about his personal life.

"No, no children," he answered casually. "My marriage didn't last that long. How about you?"

"Two grown daughters, one granddaughter. My marriage lasted too long." She smiled to take the sting out of her words. "No football players, fortunately."

"You don't like football, I take it?"

"On the contrary," Anneke protested. "I love football. Watching the Steelers play football in the Bradshaw years was like . . . well, like walking into a Frank Lloyd Wright house. For a few moments, at least, you know what perfection looks like."

"Isn't 'perfection' stretching it a bit?" He raised an eyebrow. "Brad did throw an occasional interception, you know."

"More than a few. Believe me, I remember some of them." She laughed with him. "I didn't mean that the perfection was constant, of course it wasn't. But you watched for instances of perfection, for that awesome moment when Lynn Swann floated out over the end zone and you thought he'd never come down."

"He did, though," Genesko reminded her.

"Yes," she agreed soberly. "And that's why I'm glad I have no personal involvement. I know intellectually that football is a violent game, but as long as I remain an uninvolved spectator, I can think of it as Roadrunner violence."

"Of course." He nodded his understanding. "After the most explosive acts of violence, the participants pick themselves up, shake themselves, and trot off the field."

"I know the violence is real to the players," Anneke said, "but that's the way it can be to the spectators."

"All the fun with none of the emotional involvement?" He seemed to be challenging her somehow.

"Why not?" she answered, stung. "Why look for pain when you can avoid it?"

"There are too many answers to that," he said after a pause. "And I think you know most of them yourself."

SIXTEEN

Their food arrived then, and for a while they ate in appreciative silence. The tuna was wonderful, as advertised; so were the potatoes, in a light, unusual wine sauce. Anneke was just scraping up the last crusty bits when she heard her name called.

"Anneke! Finally! I knew if I came to Ann Arbor often enough I'd have to run into you again."

Her fork clattered against the plate.

"Hello, Dennis." She turned to greet him, arranging her face into polite but—she hoped—repressive lines. "How are you?"

"You know how I am. Why didn't you answer my message?" He stood, too close, over her chair. Genesko had risen politely, but Dennis pretended to ignore him, not an easy task considering Genesko's size.

"Because I had nothing to say." She turned toward Genesko. "Karl, may I introduce Dennis Grantham? This is Karl Genesko." It was the first time she'd used Genesko's given name; it felt odd, but she was damned if she'd introduce him by

rank, as a policeman. Let Dennis think what he bloody well pleased.

"How do you do." Genesko held out his hand. Dennis stepped back and stared contemptuously up at him, then pointedly shoved his hands in his pockets and turned his back. He'd been drinking, Anneke realized; his thin, elegant face was flushed and his eyes glittered. Oh, God, don't let him make a scene, she prayed.

"Anneke, did you know I've got the Alliance project? Half a million dollars in robotics software." Dennis sat down uninvited in the chair next to hers. "What a team we'd make." He reached for her hand, but she jerked it away.

"Dennis, don't be ridiculous."

"All right, I know robotics isn't your sort of thing." He spoke quickly, jerkily. "It doesn't matter. I've got other projects, and then there's your game, we've got to get that finished, you know, or maybe we could go after a couple of communication projects, I know you've always been—"

"Dennis, stop it," Anneke interrupted desperately. She was painfully aware of Genesko, still standing, a politely noncommittal expression on his face. "You know perfectly well I have no intention of working with you on anything, now or in the future. Will you please excuse us and let us finish our dinner?"

"Oh, I see. So it's like that." He turned in his chair, staring at Genesko as if seeing him for the first time. "Is this what you like?" he sneered, tilting the chair onto its back legs and looking up. "I didn't know you wanted your men by the pound." My God, he must be even more drunk than he looks, Anneke thought, choking back a wild desire to laugh. Either that or he's got a death wish.

"I think it would be better if you did leave, Mr. Grantham." Genesko's voice was quiet and without menace, but he grasped Dennis's arm as he spoke, and his hand nearly circled the other man's biceps.

"Oh, good, it talks. Hey, look everybody, it can make sen-

tences," Dennis called in a voice loud enough to draw stares. His hair had fallen over his forehead and his face was twisted into an ugly leer. Anneke couldn't imagine how she'd ever thought him handsome.

"Anneke, please excuse me for a moment." Abruptly Genesko released his grip on Dennis, whose chair fell forward with a thump.

"Good, he's gone." Dennis reached for her hand again. "This is the way it should be—just you and me. Anneke, dear Anneke . . ."

"Dear God, even for you this is unbelievable." Anneke could feel the stares of the other diners, and the heat from her own face, crimson with embarrassment. "I want you out of here, now, and if I have to make a scene I'll do it." She started to rise, ready to throw caution to the winds—how much worse could it get, after all? But suddenly two men appeared on either side of Dennis, two men in impeccably tailored dinner clothes who each grasped one of Dennis's arms and brought him to his feet in a single, smooth motion.

"If you'll just come with us, sir?" one of the men said quietly, while the other said to Anneke, "If you'll just excuse us, ma'am?" and in a moment all three of them had disappeared and Genesko was approaching the table as calmly as if he were returning from some ordinary errand.

"If you're finished with your fish," he said, slipping neatly into his chair, "would you like some dessert?"

"Dessert?" The wild desire to laugh, compounded of relief, pouring embarrassment, and sheer hysteria, was even stronger. "What on earth would be the appropriate climax to something like that?"

"Chocolate mousse, I should think."

Now she did laugh, out of sheer reaction, and pure admiration and gratitude, and because the whole thing suddenly seemed preposterously, blindingly hilarious. She tried to choke it back, holding her napkin to her face to muffle the sounds but

no longer really caring if the other diners were staring or not. When she finally looked up, Genesko was pouring champagne from a bottle that had materialized at the table.

"Thank you," she said with a final gasp, accepting the glass from him and taking a long drink of the cold, dry liquid.

"You're welcome." He did not pretend to misunderstand her. "It's usually better to work through channels in situations like this than to come on like Mark Gastineau."

"How often are there 'situations like this,' for heaven's sake?"

"For a football player, unfortunately, more than you'd think. The world is full of drunks out to prove you're 'not that tough.'"

"And of course it's a no-win situation." She nodded. "If you win you're a bully, if you lose you're a wimp. Still, it must take a good deal of self-discipline."

"Not really." He grinned suddenly, the wide, amused grin that lit up his face. "You see, I already know I am that tough. Now, how about dessert?"

"Why not?" she answered, surprised to discover she had an absolute craving for sugar. Metabolic reaction, she supposed. Or just self-indulgence. In any case, what the hell? "Yes, absolutely, chocolate mousse and another glass of champagne."

"Good." He signaled to the waiter. "I didn't think you were the slinking-away type."

He made no further comment about Dennis, nor did he ask any questions. The other diners, deprived of further excitement, returned to their own meals. The two of them ate the luxurious chocolate mousse and watched the setting sun reflecting off distant windows. When coffee had been poured, Genesko returned in businesslike tones to the question Anneke had raised in his office.

"You asked whether Peter Casaday is a suspect in Lesley Shea's murder."

"I did? Oh, right. Sorry, it seems about a year and a half ago," Anneke said, trying to switch mental gears. "I assume he is, if

only because of his obvious emotional attachment for her." She winced inwardly at her own words; she'd had enough misplaced emotionalism to last her the rest of her life.

"Well, love doesn't have to be obsessive, after all," Genesko commented, once again responding to her unspoken thoughts. "And in any case, Peter has one of the damnedest alibis I've ever heard."

"He does? What is it?" She bit back her acid response to his comment.

"According to him," Genesko recited slowly, "he received a call Wednesday afternoon from a woman who identified herself as Freda Sarkosian, of Bloomfield Hills. He stated that Mrs. Sarkosian asked him to visit her Thursday at one P.M., to discuss painting her portrait as a surprise gift for her husband."

"Nonsense," Anneke blurted. "Peter Casaday? Why Peter? Besides, I've seen his work; he doesn't do portraits at all, does he?"

"No," Genesko agreed drily. "He says he told her that, but she insisted. According to him, she said she had seen his work at one of the Ann Arbor art fairs, and she thought he could do a great portrait. 'Avant-garde' was the term she used."

"He said yes, of course."

"Right."

"So he was in Bloomfield Hills with this woman all afternoon?"

"Not so fast." Genesko's face wore the ghost of a grin. "Peter stated that he left Ann Arbor at noon Thursday, arrived at the indicated address at one o'clock, as requested, and discovered that the entire call had been a hoax."

"A hoax! So he doesn't have an alibi."

"Oh yes he does. You see, there really is a Mrs. Freda Sarkosian, a thoroughly blameless—and very wealthy—Bloomfield Hills matron who swears that, although she didn't call Peter on Wednesday, he certainly did show up on her doorstep on Thursday, at one o'clock on the dot. What's more"—Genesko

paused, waiting for the dawning look of amazement on Anneke's face—"after sorting it out and talking to him for the better part of an hour, Mrs. Sarkosian has in fact commissioned him to paint her portrait. And, I have the feeling, perhaps certain other personal services."

"But that's ridiculous," Anneke protested.

"The hoax? Or the commission? Or what goes with it?"

"Both. All of them. The whole thing." She waved her teaspoon at him. "I mean, why?"

"Ah, that is the question, isn't it?" Genesko agreed. "Assuming every word of Peter's story is accurate, exactly why did someone go to all that trouble?"

"To get him out of town?"

"To get him out of his studio, at least."

"Robbery?" Anneke asked dubiously.

"According to Peter, there were no signs of a break-in when he returned home, and he swears nothing is missing or altered in any way."

"A practical joke, perhaps? No." Anneke rejected her own suggestion. "Coincidence can't be that convenient."

"Well, it can, of course," Genesko contradicted her. "And Peter does have a number of undergraduate friends. But they all swear they had nothing to do with it, and I tend to believe them. They're pretty shaken up by Lesley's death."

"You say this woman gives Peter an ironclad alibi." Anneke decided to attack the problem from another direction. "Are you that positive about the time of death?"

"Positive enough. From an analysis of the stomach contents, we know she died approximately one hour after lunch, and three friends say she had lunch with them in the dorm at one o'clock."

"What about the voice on the phone?" Anneke took a sip of coffee and hastily moved on to another question.

"Well, Peter didn't recognize it, but he's sure it was a woman."

"A woman, or a girl?" Anneke asked.

"I don't think the distinction was ever suggested," he said, looking interested. "It's certainly worth asking."

"Well, the whole thing is beyond me." Anneke shook her head and took a last sip of coffee while Genesko signed the charge slip at his elbow.

They rode down in the elevator silently, constrained by the presence of other passengers, but when they reached the bottom Anneke paused.

"Is it customary," she asked, "for one police officer to be in charge of more than one murder case at a time?"

"As a matter of fact," he pointed out as he led the way toward the lobby door, "it isn't customary for Ann Arbor to *have* more than one open murder case at a time." They emerged into cool June twilight. "I do know what you mean, of course," he continued. "And the answer is, I don't know if the two murders are connected or not. At the moment, there isn't a single thing to link them together."

"Except Peter," Anneke murmured.

"Except Peter," he agreed. "But that doesn't really help."

"No. Just the reverse, in fact," she said thoughtfully. "If both of them were killed by the same person, Peter seems to be the only one who can't be the murderer." She thought for a moment. "What about alibis for the others?"

"The other suspects in the Westlake killing? No help there, I'm afraid. None of them can produce an ironclad alibi for the entire relevant period."

"No convenient seminar this time."

"No," he said, looking amused. He walked her to her car and waited while she fished her keys out of her purse.

"Thank you for getting me that program so quickly," he said. "I'm going to get Jon Zelisco on it first thing in the morning."

"You're welcome. And thank you for dinner. I enjoyed it." In fact, she had, she realized with some surprise, at least before and

after the scene with Dennis. There was something to be said for intelligent conversation with no emotional entanglements.

"Good. Perhaps you'll rethink the hospital dinner?"

"No, I'm sorry. I really can't." All her misgivings came back with a rush; when she looked at him, Dennis's face seemed superimposed over his. "I'm sorry," she repeated. Damn, I'm stammering like an adolescent, she thought furiously. I don't need this.

"No, I'm the one who should be apologizing," he said soberly. "If my timing had been this bad with the Steelers, I'd never have made a tackle. Thank you for all your help."

He sketched a wave, turned and was gone, leaving her as she wished to be, alone beside her tiny car. But instead of feeling relieved, she felt unaccountably forlorn.

SEVENTEEN

Did she owe him an apology? she wondered as she drove home. It felt that way somehow, but she was damned if she knew what she should be apologizing for. As a kind of penance, when she got home she dialed into the police department computer and checked out the status of the mapping program. To her surprise, Jon Zelisco's data were in an open file. My God, she realized with dismay, I rushed it through so fast I forgot to set up password protection.

The process was simple enough. But she'd have to stop by City Hall in the morning to show it to Zelisco. Which meant having to face Karl Genesko again, *and* for the sole purpose of admitting her own stupid incompetence.

She woke Saturday morning feeling fuzzy-headed and out of sorts, and thoroughly depressed by the prospect of the errand in front of her. It serves you right, she gibed at herself. Stick to cool algorithms and stay away from emotional *Sturm und Drang*. She would go straight to City Hall, correct her screwup, and

spend the rest of the day at the office. As for Karl—as for Genesko, she would be pleasant and businesslike and not refer to personal matters at all. In fact, she probably wouldn't even see him.

But as she pulled the Alfa into a short-term parking spot and descended to the pavement, she saw him striding across the parking lot.

"Anneke, good morning." His greeting seemed to have an expectant air. "More computer problems, or something else?"

"Computer problems, but my own stupid fault." She smiled as impersonally as she could manage, although she felt an internal constriction in her stomach. He was wearing a camel's-hair jacket—real camel's hair, Anneke guessed. "I made a howler on your mapping program."

"Serious?" He looked both sympathetic and curious. And something more, she thought warily. "Look, I'm on my way to the sheriff's office, out at the County Service Center. Why don't you ride along and tell me about it on the way?"

"I don't have much time," she lied, wavering. "I've got to get into the office. Will you be long?"

"No; I'm only going to pick up some papers." He neither urged nor dissuaded her.

"All right," she said at last, and then berated herself as she slid into the big black car. Stupid, stupid, stupid; I could have worked it out with Zelisco privately, left Karl a note or something.

"Jon says the program is working fine," he said when he had the Thunderbird heading east on Huron.

"I'm glad of that, at least," she said wryly. Briefly she explained about the lack of password protection.

"That doesn't mean it's publicly accessible, I assume?" he asked.

"Good God, no," Anneke replied, horrified. "All police data are at least two layers down. But it is accessible to anyone in the department with second-level clearance."

"That doesn't sound too serious, then."

"You wouldn't think that if someone came across Jon's file by accident, hit one wrong key, and erased a week's worth of data input," she retorted. "Besides, it's the sort of mistake no competent programmer should ever make."

"Well, if you're intent on self-punishment . . ." he began, and let the half sentence trail off even as Anneke was formulating an angry response. She waited, but he said nothing more, and when she glanced at him he seemed wholly concentrated on driving.

She watched the passing traffic for a while, increasingly aware of Genesko's physical presence beside her, wondering if she should refer to last night. She considered once more whether to apologize, and once more asked herself, defensively, what for. Dammit, this sort of emotional morass was exactly what she wanted to avoid, she thought with a resentful glance to her left.

His impassive profile brought her up short. But the emotional mess is entirely in my own head, she realized with a start. All he's done is invite me to a couple of dinners and discuss a murder case with me. I'm the one reading more into it. "Anything new on Lesley's murder?" she asked, forcing her thoughts into less problematic channels.

"Not really. The gilt on her shoe is a dead end at the moment. Half a dozen people, including Peter, admit to using the stuff."

"Still, Lesley didn't even know the other suspects in Joanna's murder, did she?" Anneke asked. "Isn't it most likely that it happened at Peter's studio?"

"But if someone other than Peter killed her—and Peter does seem to be out of it—why move the body? Why not leave her there to throw suspicion on Peter?"

"Unless the murderer knew Peter would have an alibi. Suppose the murderer was the one who made the call?" Anneke theorized.

"It still doesn't track," Genesko pointed out. "Say the killer

gets Peter out of the way, meets Lesley at the studio, and kills her. Even if that makes sense, which it only barely does, why go to all that trouble and then move the body?"

She was about to respond, but stopped when she realized she'd lost his attention. Instead, all his concentration was focused on the voice coming from the radio under the dashboard. Anneke could make no sense of the static-filled transmission, but Genesko's face darkened as he listened.

"Damn and blast," he muttered, looking angry for the first time since she'd met him. That must be the face quarterbacks used to see, she thought, almost alarmed by the intensity of his expression. "Sorry," he said to her, wrenching the steering wheel around and simultaneously flicking a switch on the dashboard. A blue flasher on the rear deck sprang to life with a blare of sirens as the big car slewed around and roared back west on Washtenaw.

Anneke gripped the arm rest and kept her mouth shut as they rocketed back toward downtown. Genesko drove fast and efficiently, weaving through traffic with a minimum of sideways motion.

Only when they had swung past the Stadium Boulevard intersection did she risk a question.

"What is it?"

"Another murder." He slowed for the South University crossing, swung past a left-turning Honda trying to beat him through the green light, and continued up Washtenaw. "A woman's body found in a car."

"You think . . . What kind of car?"

"Didn't say," he replied briefly, wheeling the Thunderbird in a two-point turn around the curve onto Huron. She wanted to ask where they were going but subsided; she'd find out soon enough. She sat back, against all odds finding the high-speed ride exhilarating. The big car turned off Huron onto Main, swung left onto Miller and then right on Brooks. After that she lost track in the tangle of suburban streets; not until Genesko

reached forward and cut the siren did she realize they had arrived at their destination.

They were on a wide, heavily wooded, curbless street whose houses were set far back on their lots. The house directly opposite was a large contemporary structure nearly hidden by the pine trees that almost filled the front yard. Parked on the street was a huge elderly blue Plymouth, flanked by a yellow-and-white fire department rescue vehicle and two police cars.

The Plymouth's door was open. Anneke could make out a small, plump body and an aureole of fluffy white hair.

"Oh, God, it's Martha." Genesko didn't answer; he was already out of the Thunderbird and striding toward the Plymouth, where Brad Weinmann stood waiting for him. Anneke, feeling rather breathless in the ringing silence now that the siren was off, unhooked her seat belt but remained where she was, listening to their voices through the car's open window.

"What have we got?" Genesko asked.

"Martha Penrose," Brad responded crisply. "Dead maybe half an hour, from the look of her." Anneke looked at her watch; it was a little after ten o'clock. "Apparently strangled," Brad concluded.

"Who called it in?" Genesko asked.

"Woman who lives in there." Brad jerked his head toward the house behind the pine trees. "She and her husband were on their way out to the hardware store when they spotted her car. They say they saw her leaning against the car window and thought she was sick, so they stopped to help."

"Did they touch anything?"

"They say not. Said they could tell right away she was dead. Well, you know what a strangulation victim looks like." Anneke felt a sudden, quick twist in her stomach.

"Hmmph." Genesko was noncommittal. "Print them anyway, just in case. Then I want a pickup order on the entire list of suspects in the Westlake killing. They're probably all out on the roads going to their goddamn garage sales, so put out descrip-

tions of their cars also. I want them brought in for questioning right away and as is, cars and all. And do *not* search the cars without their permission, for God's sake. Do that now, while I talk to the medics."

Brad trotted toward one of the squad cars. Genesko motioned to a young man in medical whites standing next to the Plymouth.

"I assume she was dead when you got here?"

"Afraid so, Lieutenant." The paramedic had a young, cheerful face under a shock of blond hair. "She was already starting to cool." Anneke, listening, felt her stomach take another quarter-turn.

"What did you touch?" Genesko continued.

"The car door, of course. We opened the car and turned her over slightly—she was lying on her side, sort of across the front seat. We saw the rope around her neck right away—it's still embedded in the flesh—and as soon as we realized what we had we backed off. We didn't touch anything else, including the rope," the paramedic concluded earnestly.

"Thank you, that makes it much easier for us," Genesko said warmly, eliciting a pleased smile from the boy. "I'm afraid you guys are going to have to hang around for a little while longer, but we'll be as quick as possible."

"That's okay," the paramedic said amiably.

"The pickup order's out," Brad reported, trotting back from the police car.

"Good," Genesko replied. "I'd like you to head back to City Hall and catch them as they come in. Don't question them until I get there, but ask for permission to examine the cars. If you get it, run full vacuum searches of every one of their cars. Maybe we can connect her"—he motioned toward the Plymouth—"with one of the others. I'm going to stay here until the crew is finished, then I'll come in." Anneke noted that a swarm of people were already busy around the big blue car. "Oh, one

more thing," Genesko added to Brad. "Will you please take Anneke back to City Hall with you when you go?"

Brad looked toward the Thunderbird in surprise. Anneke hastily gathered up her briefcase and descended from the car.

"I'm sorry about all this," Genesko apologized briefly. "Brad will take you back downtown." He returned to the Plymouth. Anneke smiled slightly at Brad and followed him to the patrol car, but as she passed the Plymouth she was unable to resist a look inside.

One look at Martha's engorged face convinced her she should have resisted harder. But as her eyes slid hastily away and down the body, they focused on the small pink-and-white tennis shoes on Martha's feet. And on the instantly recognizable smear of gilt along the rubberized edge.

She was so stunned by the gilt that she only had a moment to peer into the back of the big car. And in any case, there was hardly anything to see. Except for a large ceramic platter and what looked like a set of fireplace tools, the backseat seemed to be empty.

Brad blessedly refrained from asking her why she had been in Genesko's car. Indeed, he said very little on the ride back to City Hall; he seemed to be concentrating on the occasional static-filled bursts of sound from the police radio.

"Good, that's two of them," he said after a particularly long and, to Anneke, incomprehensible transmission.

"Two of what?"

"Two of the people Karl wanted picked up. Plus one who was at home."

"Oh? Which one?"

"Michael Rappaport."

"Of course. He doesn't usually do the garage-sale circuit," Anneke recalled. "You know, some of the others might not be doing sales today either. They've got the big antique show tomorrow. And besides—" She was interrupted by another burst of static.

"That's three," Brad said, barely listening to her. She lapsed into silence for the remainder of the trip, her mind going over and over that splash of gilt on Martha's shoe. But when Brad finally deposited her next to the Alfa and disappeared inside City Hall, she still had no notion of what it implied.

She did, however, have a parking ticket.

Swearing, she plucked the offending white rectangle from under the windshield wiper, then remembered the password problem. Well, as long as she already had the ticket. . . . She tucked the ticket back under the wiper and headed back into City Hall. She'd hook in the password protection, then go back to her own office and try to put in a day's work.

EIGHTEEN

But at the office, Anneke found herself paying the price of several days away from her desk. Instead of a long, soothing programming session, she spent several aggravating hours bogged down in mail, phone messages, and assorted paperwork, the curse of the small entrepreneur.

When she finally did get to sit down at the computer, she couldn't seem to concentrate on the staff scheduling program she was supposed to be developing for a local volunteer agency. Instead, she found herself computer-doodling, drawing shapes on the screen with text characters. After a while, she looked at her handiwork and saw

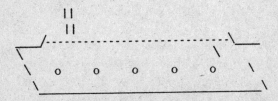

Irritably she cleared the screen and typed

across the top of the screen. Down the side she typed

JOANNA

LESLEY

MARTHA

She began to fill in the resulting grid—"rock" in the upper left, "rope" in the bottom left. At the top of the middle column she typed "theft," and then saw that she had no further entries for that column, and nothing at all for the third column except Peter's alibi for Lesley's murder.

She cleared the screen again and stared at gray blankness for a while, then tentatively typed ROCK. Indenting beneath it she typed: "Why was the rock taken away?" After another pause she typed JAP, followed by: "What did Joanna's last words mean?" And finally she typed GILT, and stared at the word for a long time without adding anything more.

She typed JOANNA   LESLEY   MARTHA at the bottom of the screen, and then went back and put brackets around the name in the middle. Lesley was the ringer, the odd woman out, as in one of those aptitude-test questions: "Which of the following words does not belong with the others?" Lesley had no connection with garage sales, or antiques, or either of the other victims, for that matter, except through Peter. And except for that wholly inexplicable smear of gilt on Martha Penrose's shoe.

Had Martha known Lesley? And did Martha ever repair and sell antique picture frames? Probably not, and probably so, in that order, and questions for the police in any case.

For the third time she cleared the screen, and typed JAP. Then she ran the letters vertically, so that they read:

J

A

P

Finally, she went back to horizontal, placed a period after each letter, and looked at the result.

J.A.P. Initials? If so, what could they stand for? A person? An object? A company? She powered down the computer and stood up.

"Aston, I'm leaving," she said to the only other person remaining in the office. "Have you finished the survey data yet?"

"Just about," he said, looking up from his terminal. "Should have it cleaned up and printed out before I leave tonight."

"Don't stay too late just to finish up," she told him. "Tomorrow is time enough." He nodded absently, already immersed again in his work. "Lock up when you leave, please." She took his abstracted nod for consent and headed out of the office.

Taking the Alfa out of the parking structure was a mistake, she realized as she approached Main Street. The three blocks between William and Huron were already filled with raw wooden structures and barricaded against traffic. Huge cloth banners overhanging the street screamed "Ann Arbor Antique Show" in purple lettering, and workmen swarmed the street, hammering, shouting, and otherwise preparing the booths.

She found a parking spot finally two blocks north of Huron and walked back to the Antiques Association offices, sidestepping crowds of gawking tourists who were making a weekend of it. She expected the association to be a madhouse the day before the Show, and her gloomy pessimism proved itself justified even before she crested the top of the carpeted staircase.

"I am not changing anyone's booth location, and that's final," Michael Rappaport was declaring in a voice somewhere between a shout and a squawk.

"But now that there's an empty booth, I don't see why I

should be stuck all the way up at Huron," Carolyn Herbert protested angrily.

"Yes, and Frank doesn't see why he should be in the middle of a block instead of at a corner, and Janice Cavanagh doesn't see why she shouldn't be able to spread out now that the space next to hers is vacant, and Marty Wellman doesn't see why his friend from Chelsea shouldn't be allowed into the show now that there's an empty space. And I," Michael roared, "do not see why you people cannot refrain from squabbling for just one, single, rotten day."

"Be careful, Michael. Your veneer of civilization is cracking," Carolyn said poisonously. She gave Anneke a look of pure acid as she sailed past her down the steps, leaving the office to the relative peace of phones ringing, typewriter clacking, and printer chattering.

"My God, can you believe the ghoulishness of human beings?" Michael raged. "I mean, I may not have liked the damn woman, but at least I'd have the decency to wait until the body was cold before robbing the carcass. May I assume at least that you're not here to demand the use of the former Penrose Antiques booth?" He glared at Anneke.

"So that's what this is all about," she said. "How on earth did the news get out so fast?"

"In Ann Arbor? You forget, my dear, this is a high-tech town. The grapevine is set at warp speed. Helped, of course, by the fact that the police questioned half the dealers in town today."

"They pulled me in off the street on my way to a sale." Alice Cowan, seated at the paper-clogged conference table, spoke for the first time. "I lost the whole morning of sales sitting around at the police station." She sounded more aggrieved than grieved over Martha's inconvenient demise.

"What did they ask you?" Anneke probed.

"The same things they asked me last Saturday," Alice complained. "Where I went, what I bought, who I saw, whether I talked to Martha this morning."

"And had you?"

"Talked to Martha? No, I never saw her at all this morning. In fact"— Alice looked thoughtful—"I hardly saw anyone. I ran into Joyce over on Avondale, but I can't remember seeing anyone else."

"Maybe people quit early to get ready for the show," Anneke suggested.

"Maybe." Alice sounded unconvinced. "But they were all out doing sales when the police caught up with them."

"I, thank God, was at home," Michael announced. "Although that didn't stop them from wasting an hour of my time asking me questions for which I had no answers. If I'd only had a woman there with me, I could have given them an alibi and sent them away. Although she would probably have cost me even more of my time."

"Well, at least you weren't cooped up in a dirty little room at City Hall for two hours," Alice complained. "And then by the time the police were through with me I had to come straight here to finish up this stuff. And on top of that, I've spent most of the afternoon answering phone calls from people who want Martha's booth at the Show."

"She had a choice location, I take it?"

"The best, right on the corner of Main and Liberty," Michael agreed. "She was one of the founders, you know."

"The trouble is, of course, that now it's going to be empty," Alice pointed out. "It's a high-visibility location, and it won't look good for the association to leave it vacant."

"Well, if I reassign it to anyone else," Michael complained, "the ones who don't get it will crucify me. Of course, we could move the association display there."

"It's awfully far from the office," Alice protested. "Is there anyone who isn't in the Show at all at the moment, who might want to be added?" She cocked her head and appeared to consider her own question.

"Not that I know of," he pondered. "Unless . . . Alice, what about you?"

"Me?"

"Sure, why not? You've been out on the garage-sale circuit since March; surely you've got enough stock?"

"Oh, I've got enough," she agreed. "I've got a garage full, in fact. It's mostly boxed up, too. Only . . ."

"Only what? It doesn't have to be great stuff, as long as it's identified properly. And you've been working your tail off here for no pay; no one will dare object."

"I'll need help," Alice warned. "Ennis is out of town—not that he'd help anyway, but I can't do the loading and unloading all by myself."

"Go down and get one of the workmen, and tell him I've authorized him to help you." Michael scribbled a quick note and handed it to Alice, his brilliant blue eyes snapping with excitement and, Anneke thought, mischief.

"All right, that sounds like it would work," Alice said composedly. "You're sure about this?"

"Positive," Michael declared. "You'll be doing me a favor, I promise you."

"If you say so. I'll have to get started right away, though." She looked meaningfully at the pile of papers on the table.

"Lydia can finish that," Michael said impatiently. "Get going." Alice picked up her purse and departed. Anneke thought her face looked curiously triumphant behind its reserved façade. So did Michael's; in fact, he looked positively gleeful. Martha's death certainly had been beneficial for both of them.

"Now," Michael said, rubbing his hands together with satisfaction, "what can I do for you?"

"I just wanted to do some research."

"Oh? Anything in particular?" She looked at him, considering. He was certainly one of the suspects, but he was also the

most knowledgeable expert she had available. If he were guilty, she wouldn't be telling him anything he didn't already know.

"Tell me," she said, throwing caution to the winds, "do the initials 'J.A.P.' mean anything to you?"

"J.A.P.," he repeated. "Not immediately. What is it—pottery, silver?"

"I don't know," she confessed, hoping he wouldn't press her for specifics. "It's just something I came across."

"Hmm. J.A.P." He stared into space. "Seems familiar somehow."

"Jewish-American Princess." The offering came, with a cascade of giggles, from Lydia Frazier, looking up from her desultory tapping on the typewriter. "Well, I didn't make it up," she said defensively in the face of Michael's scathing look.

"I don't think that's what was meant," Anneke said hastily. But as Michael returned to his pondering, she contemplated the repulsive phrase. Was it any less likely a term for Joanna to use than "Jap" for a Japanese woman? Except that, as far as Anneke knew, there were no Jewish women among the suspects. There was, of course, a Jewish man. Anneke regarded Michael's classic features in profile. Jewish-American Prince? No, that didn't make sense. The contemptuous, and contemptible, reference was never applied to men. At least, not that she'd ever heard . . .

"What about glass?" Michael asked. "Or jewelry?"

"I don't know," Anneke said again, spreading her hands. "Is there a J.A.P. among any of them?"

"Well, there are some things we can check." He went to the big bookcase and scanned the shelves before reaching up and removing three heavy volumes. "Let's start with these," he suggested, clearing a space on the conference table and setting the books down. *Miller's Antiques Price Guide,* read the title of the topmost book.

"It covers the top of the field, and it's got a pretty good index," Michael explained. "This one"—he held up a volume

entitled *Kovels' Antiques and Collectibles Price List*—"isn't quite as upscale, but it's very comprehensive, especially on medium-value collectibles."

"I think I'll concentrate on the high end," Anneke said.

"All right." Michael regarded her sharply but made no further comment. "I'll take a quick look through some of the more specialized references."

At the end of an hour they had about half a dozen possibilities and a severe case of eyestrain.

"Who's J. A. Patterson?" Anneke asked.

"Clockmaker," Michael replied, paging through a thick reference book. "The piece referred to in here is a longcase clock, valued anywhere from two to four thousand dollars."

"Are the initials J.A.P. on it?"

"I don't think so. Clockmakers usually signed their pieces in full."

"It isn't really valuable enough anyway," Anneke shook her head. "Besides, it's too damn big."

"Isn't valuable enough for what?"

"Just an idea I had," Anneke said vaguely. "Never mind. But thanks anyway, Michael."

"Are you coming to the Show tomorrow?" he asked as she prepared to leave.

"Yes, I suppose. so." She actually hadn't given it much thought.

"Monte Enright has a batch of good new stuff," he coaxed her, referring to a young chemistry student who supplemented his student loans as a part-time dealer in Art Deco.

"Does he? That S.O.B." Anneke laughed. "He usually calls me when he gets anything good. All right, you talked me into it. Providing," she warned, "the weather is good." He rolled his eyes in mock horror as she left.

Outside on the pavement she stood irresolute for a while. It was past five o'clock, and she knew without thinking about it that her refrigerator contained nothing one could make dinner

out of. For the first time in a long while it occurred to her that spending Saturday night alone with a computer and a television set was perhaps not the ideal way of life. Although after Dennis, it had seemed so; for a long time she'd been grateful for the emotional privacy, the sheer peace of being alone. Somehow, tonight it seemed more sterile than peaceful.

Making a face at empty air, she crossed the street to the little gourmet take-out shop, bought a chicken pie and, as an afterthought, three triple-chocolate cookies. On the way home she stopped at a nearby video store and, after long contemplation of the latest movies, rented two tapes of football bloopers.

NINETEEN

She didn't notice the car parked in front of her house until she'd passed it pulling into the driveway. For one ugly second she thought, "Dennis," but then realized Dennis wouldn't be caught dead in a Ford Escort. As she alighted from the Alfa, Ellen Nakamura and Ted Burns emerged from the Escort and hastened up the driveway toward her.

"Anneke, can we talk to you? Please?" Ellen was clutching a large brown-paper grocery bag and sounded slightly breathless. Ted stood next to her, his face pale and drawn in the late-afternoon sunlight.

Her instant impulse was to refuse, to put them off at least until morning. She wanted to go inside, put her feet up, listen to mindless television, and analyze her own thoughts. But there was no way to reject the appeal on Ellen's face. Besides, she thought caustically, I probably overanalyze everything anyway.

"Come on in," she sighed, pushing open the door. She considered making a pot of coffee, then changed her mind. No;

she'd had enough herself, and she didn't want to make this a social occasion.

But when she took a closer look at her unwanted guests, her self-absorption dissolved. Ellen and Ted sat stiffly together on the edge of the sofa, sitting erect and forward with their feet flat on the floor. Their faces were twin masks of tension, making them look oddly alike. Ellen still clutched the paper bag in her lap with one hand, her other hand in Ted's.

Silently Anneke set down her parcels and went to the liquor cabinet, where she poured three glasses of sherry and carried them on a tray to the coffee table.

"Thank you." It was Ted who spoke, although he made no move to reach for the sherry. Ellen took a glass and drank off half the pale amber liquid at a gulp.

"It doesn't really make me feel any better," she smiled dimly, "but it'll make talking easier." She put down the glass and her hand returned reflexively to the paper bag.

"Now, what did you want to talk to me about?" Anneke asked, trying for a brisk tone. Ellen and Ted exchanged glances, and finally Ellen shrugged, opened the paper bag and carefully withdrew a newspaper-wrapped bundle. She peeled away the newspaper and set her burden, a pale green vase, on the coffee table in front of her.

"That's the vase Ted brought to you at the shop last weekend, isn't it?" Anneke recalled.

"Yes." Ted looked grim. "If she'd told me the truth at once we wouldn't be in this mess."

"What mess?" Anneke prompted. For the first time she recalled that these anguished children were involved in a murder case.

"That piece of porcelain," Ellen said, her voice wavering slightly as she jerked her head toward the vase, "is a Song dynasty piece worth somewhere between thirty and fifty thousand dollars. I bought it last Saturday morning for twenty-five dollars."

"Wow." Anneke regarded the vase, which to her eyes looked ordinary and rather dull. "At a garage sale? How great for you."

"No, you don't understand." Ellen shook her head.

"You're afraid the police will think you killed Joanna and stole the vase from her," Anneke said, light, she thought, dawning at last. "Look, I can see that this would qualify as a Big Score, but surely you can tell them where you bought it. The seller will probably remember you."

"No, you still don't understand," Ted repeated Ellen's words. "She didn't buy it at a garage sale."

"You're right, I don't understand," Anneke said helplessly. Surely Ellen wasn't about to confess to the murder?

"See, I was at this sale, on Westwood." Ellen looked down at her hands. "I was buying a set of Japanese rice bowls, and this woman came up to me and said she had a Chinese vase, and it just occurred to her that she might want to sell it. She was the next-door neighbor," Ellen said confusedly.

"You mean she lived next door to the woman having the garage sale," Anneke untangled the sentences.

"Yes. Anyway, she asked me if I'd like to see it—everyone gets that sometime or other, but I do especially because I'm Asian. I went next door with her, expecting some piece of Hong Kong junk, of course, but you always have to look." Ellen's voice was firmer now, more controlled.

"And then she brought out . . . that. I almost fell over when I saw it; in fact, I can still hardly believe it. I asked her what she wanted for it, and of course the stupid woman said she didn't know, and what did I think it was worth? In the end we finally agreed on twenty-five dollars." Ellen sighed and reached for the sherry again.

"I still don't see the problem," Anneke confessed when it was clear that Ellen was finished speaking.

"Ellen is a dealer," Ted came to the rescue, grasping his wife's hand once more. "There's a risk that what she did could be construed as fraud."

"It *is* fraud," Ellen said tiredly. "There've been all sorts of court cases in the last few years against dealers who've done what I did."

"But if you pay what the seller asks . . ." Anneke protested.

"That's probably okay at garage sales," Ellen said bitterly, emphasizing the word "probably." "There the seller has a preset price, and the dealer is in the same position as everyone else. But in this case, the damn woman specifically invited me to look at the vase. She even asked me what I thought it was worth. That definitely makes me liable for civil penalties and might even qualify as criminal fraud."

"I see." Anneke thought over Ellen's story. "At least, I see the situation. But I still don't see why it was a problem as long as nobody knew about it."

"In other words, why are we telling you all this?" Ted asked with a flash of humor, squeezing Ellen's hand. "Because, unfortunately, Ellen and I managed to behave like a bad sitcom script, and now somebody else does know about it."

"Steve Olewski saw Ted bring it to the shop," Ellen picked up the thread of narrative, "and I guess he recognized it was something special by the way I acted. Anyway, he researched it"—so that's what he was using the association library for, Anneke realized—"and he hit me with it a couple of days ago."

"Blackmail, you mean?" Anneke wrinkled her nose in disgust.

"Actually, he's convinced I did kill Joanna for it." Ellen managed a weak smile, looking peaceful for the first time since she'd arrived.

"And he's blackmailing you for the profits?"

"Oh no, nothing so crass." Ted made a face that was part disgust, part humor. "He isn't out to share the proceeds; he's out to share Ellen."

"Even though he thinks I'm a murderer. Can you imagine?" Ellen shuddered delicately. "What a toad."

"I did warn you he was on the make for you," Ted reminded her mildly.

"I know, I know." Ellen sighed. Husband and wife shared a moment of silence. So Ted had not been oblivious, Anneke reflected, merely unconcerned. Unconcerned, almost unbelievably free of jealousy, and yet obviously, palpably in love with his wife. So men like that actually existed.

"I still don't know," she said, putting aside this unprofitable psychosocial analysis, "why you've come to me."

"Because we know we have to go to the police," Ellen said, "and we were hoping you'd talk to them about it first. You know, sort of pave the way for us?" The tension was back in her face.

"You see," Ted continued before Anneke could protest, "I'm not very good with the police. I tend to get kind of strung out by authority figures—I blew my cool when they first questioned Ellen, and I'm afraid . . . well, it would be much easier if they already knew the basic facts before we had to talk to them."

"But you'll have to see them anyway," Anneke argued, discovering a vast reluctance to approach Karl again.

"Please, Anneke. It really would help." Ellen's voice was close to pleading, and she gripped Ted's hands so hard her knuckles were white. She's doing this to spare him, not herself, Anneke understood; she'd never plead for herself.

"All right, I'll tell the police what you've just told me," she capitulated unhappily. "But you'd better be prepared for a long session with them."

"We know that." Ted correctly inferred that Anneke's warning was aimed at him. "I'll behave, even when confronted by the Mountain That Walks Like a Man."

"And I assume you'll have to return the vase," Anneke continued repressively, wondering how often Karl had to put up with similar gibes. For the first time it occurred to her that size and strength in a man were not, perhaps, a wholly unmixed blessing.

"I know," Ellen said forlornly, reaching out a hand to stroke the vase.

"Well, next time you'll tell me when you make a score like that," Ted told her severely.

"Next time!" Ellen exclaimed. "Do you think anyone can make two finds like this in a lifetime?"

"Sure." Ted patted her hand. "You can." He rose to his feet. "Thank you, Anneke. Please tell the police we'll be waiting for their call." He looked dignified and serious and, Anneke thought, quite absurdly young for the responsibilities of being in love.

When they left, clutching the vase in its wrapping and holding hands like children, Anneke sat where she was for several minutes. Then with a quick gesture she picked up Ted's untouched glass, downed the contents at a gulp, and strode to the telephone as quickly as she could, before she lost her nerve.

Karl was still in his office; he'd probably be there most of the night, Anneke realized with an unwanted pang of sympathy. But his voice on the phone was as calmly pleasant as always.

"What can I do for you?"

"I've been asked to talk to you," she said carefully. "By Ellen Nakamura and her husband."

"Oh?" She could hear his quickening interest.

"It's rather complicated, I'm afraid," she began, ordering her thoughts.

"I assume it's not . . . Will you excuse me for a moment, please?" The click of the hold button dropped her into silence, and it was several minutes before he came back on the line. "I'm sorry to have cut you off," he said, sounding for the first time somewhat harassed. In the background Anneke could hear multiple voices. "This place is a madhouse, as you can imagine. Look," he continued, "it's impossible to talk here. I'll be leaving in about an hour; may I stop by your house on my way home instead?"

"Yes, I . . . yes, of course, if you prefer," she said, taken aback, unable to think, quickly enough, of a better alternative.

"Thank you. I'll see you later, then." Only after he hung up did she realize she hadn't given him her address.

Well, he's a cop, she thought, grimly amused; presumably he can find it even though my phone is unlisted. She did a quick check of the house, jeering at herself as she carefully stowed the used sherry glasses in the dishwasher and folded and stacked newspapers. Then she ran the pot pie quickly through the microwave and ate it in front of the television, watching mindless sitcoms while she waited.

It was nearly nine o'clock when he arrived, and he accepted her offer of brandy rather than coffee with obvious gratitude.

"Rough day?" she asked, her sympathy engaged despite herself.

"Not one of the great ones. I think I spent more time dealing with the press than with the evidence. Such as it is."

"I never thought about that part of police work," Anneke commented.

"Three murders in one week produces a certain amount of agitation," he observed wryly. "It also brings in the out-of-town press, which tends to upset the politicians." He leaned back against the sofa, looking around the room with interest but no apparent appreciation.

"You don't like it much, do you?" she asked after a moment.

"That depends on what you mean by 'like,'" he replied thoughtfully. At least, she approved, he didn't back off with facile protests of admiration. "It's undeniably beautiful, especially that piece"—he nodded at the liquor cabinet—"but I've always found Art Deco a bit sterile. I think they often carried their dislike of ornamentation too far."

"It wasn't precisely dislike of ornamentation," she protested. "It was a reaction to the excesses of Art Nouveau and all its pseudo-romanticism. They preferred to concentrate on the beauty of pure, stylized lines. Like this piece . . ." She leaned forward to pick up the Preiss statuette from the coffee table, and as her arm brushed his knee she felt once more that overwhelm-

ing physical awareness. She touched the statue and retreated hastily, moving farther on the sofa. "Well," she said carefully, "this isn't why you're here, after all."

"No," he responded mildly. "You said Ellen Nakamura asked you to talk to me."

"Yes. She and Ted were waiting out front for me when I got home last night." Economically, Anneke reported their conversation, glad to return to business. When she concluded, she asked: "Is Ellen really in any trouble?"

"They really are a couple of young idiots, aren't they?" Karl shook his head. "Not from me, at least," he answered her question, "assuming her story checks out."

"It seems to clear her of the murder, anyway," Anneke offered.

"Why do you say that?"

"Well, if she bought the vase as she said she did, then she obviously didn't kill Joanna for it."

"But we don't know what Joanna was killed for," he pointed out.

"Maybe not, but we know Ellen had already made a Big Score," Anneke persisted. "I decline absolutely to believe that she was so greedy she'd kill for a second Big Score."

"How do you know," he asked gently, "which one came first?"

"Oh, damn." She mulled over his words, and finally asked: "Does Steve's blackmail attempt mean he's not the murderer?"

"Not in particular. Apparently he knew there was some secret about the vase, and he may simply have decided to use it to get what he wanted. He could hope Ellen would be afraid the vase would be used against her even if she was innocent."

"Can he be arrested for blackmail?" Anneke asked hopefully.

"Probably not, I'm afraid," he replied regretfully. "Unless Ellen has hard evidence, which I doubt. Or she's willing to string him along to get evidence, which I not only doubt but wouldn't even recommend."

"So you're just going to let the son of a bitch walk," she said more angrily than she'd intended. After all, it wasn't his fault. Although he *was* a cop, dammit; there had to be something he could do.

"That isn't exactly what I said," he replied, unoffended.

"What do you mean?"

"Let's just say that some people are going to be investigating Steve Olewski's business practices very closely in the next few weeks. People like the fraud squad, and the IRS, and the state treasury department."

"Oh. Well, good," Anneke said awkwardly, feeling embarrassed and resenting it. Damn the man; why did he always make her feel like apologizing?

That was when he kissed her, without warning but without haste, as if it were the most natural thing in the world. He gave her no opportunity to question, or consider, or analyze; her body responded before her mind could protest, pure white-light sensation washing over her with such intensity that, for once in her life, her damnably analytic mind was forced into background mode.

Only when he finally released her did her mental processes kick back in. At least, she thought chaotically, all that physical magnetism wasn't just a product of my own overheated imagination. The question is, is physical attraction all it is? And if so, is that the way I want it? She felt his hand playing with tendrils of hair at the back of her neck, sending bright curlicues of sensation through her, making it difficult to order her thoughts. Intense physical desire, equally intense fear of emotional entanglement—beyond that, there were too many unknowns. . . .

"Well?" He was gazing down at her quite patiently, the corners of his mouth twitching in a faint grin. "Does it compute?"

"Insufficient data," she blurted, and felt her face flame as he burst into laughter. "I suppose you're another one who's going to tell me I think too much," she said caustically.

"God forbid." He ran a finger along the side of her face. "I'll happily provide you with all the data input you need." He kissed her again, for a long time, his hands moving over her body; somehow, too, they were standing up, her arms around his neck and their bodies pressed together. "It seems to me," he said, looking down at her with the flicker of a smile, "that you really need to run a program before you can evaluate it, don't you?"

"Oh, absolutely." Her voice sounded breathless in her own ears, but her mind was suddenly, perfectly clear. "A beta-test version, at least." After all, she told herself as they kissed again, when faced with an emotional conflict, why choose the less attractive alternative? And spared a derisive inward grimace for her traitorously Jesuitical powers of argumentation as she led him toward the bedroom.

TWENTY

She woke Sunday morning in a state of euphoria so complete that for a moment it was pure feeling, referent-free. Her body's recall was better than her mind's; she felt the shards of memory before she could process them, so that at first she seemed to remember the entire evening as a single gestalt.

He'd made love the way he seemed to do everything else, smoothly and skillfully, with controlled passion and, thank God, a leavening of humor. He had an athlete's body still, lean and hard; the scars of past football injuries added substance to the remembered sensation, so strong that when she turned over in bed she was momentarily surprised to find herself alone.

She sat up with a sigh, mentally shaking herself back to reality. Great sex, after all, was merely that—great sex. One didn't dare allow it any further encroachment into one's real life.

Traffic was already pouring into town when she turned her car onto Packard at ten A.M. She had the top down on the Alfa, but wished for once that the little car had air-conditioning; the weather had turned abruptly from balmy spring to hot,

muggy summer, and the sky had a dangerously hazy look to it.

The State Street–South University Avenue intersection was a three-way-stop corner, one of those places where people seemed to forget how to drive. Here, where town and gown rammed together between the central campus and the Michigan Union, traffic was already hopelessly backed up, and Anneke was forced to work her way around via Thompson to the Maynard parking structure, snarling under her breath at a Volvo-load of tightly coiffed matrons sightseeing at fifteen miles an hour. She pulled her car into the permit section of the structure and got out with a sigh of relief, her clothing already clinging stickily to her body.

She had dressed more carefully than usual that morning, jeering at herself as she did so—considering and rejecting two or three casual outfits before settling on pale blue silk pants and matching shirt, with big gold-and-amethyst earrings and an amethyst ring so big it reached nearly to her knuckle.

Her office, as usual on Sunday, was nearly full, as student programmers scrambled to finish tasks interrupted during the week by classes, papers, and other less cerebral elements of campus life. Carol Rosenthal worked furiously at the Compaq, a spreading coffee stain on the printouts next to her. Aston was at one terminal, and Jackie Franklin at another. Ken Scheede was hunched over the Macintosh, pounding on the keyboard and muttering to himself.

"Morning, Ms. Haagen," he said, looking up.

"Hi, Ken. Looks like we have a full house."

"Sundays." He grimaced. "Everyone's playing catch-up. Wow." He whistled, pointing to her hand. "That's some rock."

"I know." She glanced down at the amethyst ring, feeling something between embarrassment and defiance. "I guess every now and then vulgarity is good for the soul." Ken himself, she noted, was wearing a red T-shirt whose white lettering said: "Welcome to Ann Arbor. Now go home."

"For the antique show." He said, following her gaze.

"I wouldn't mind one myself," she agreed. "The traffic is already awful."

"Not going to the show?" he asked.

"Oh, I probably will. As long as it's screwing up the city, I may as well get some benefit from it."

She took a cup of coffee to her desk and looked briefly at the Sunday newspaper. Martha's murder had gotten bigger coverage than Joanna's—upper right-hand corner, complete with a picture of the "death car," as the caption called it. Where Joanna's murder had seemed an isolated incident, the paper now talked about the second in a series of "Garage Sale Murders." An anonymous city official was quoted as suggesting that the city might move to prohibit garage sales until the killer was apprehended. There was, she noted, no reference in the story to gilt paint on the victim's shoe.

Martha's obituary, on page two, ran nearly a full column. Anneke was reluctantly impressed with the woman's academic career, which had been long and successful, beginning at a time when a woman Ph.D. was virtually a freak. It explained a little, at least, her supercilious attitude, not uncommon among successful women of her generation. Not even entirely unknown, she admitted to herself, among today's Superwomen.

She worked for most of the morning before heading over to the Show. But when she emerged from her air-conditioned office into weather like a boiler room, she almost headed straight back inside. Only the thought of Monte Enright's Art Deco turned her steps toward Liberty. Well, that and the urge to see what effect, if any, this third murder had had on the local antiques world.

And, she admitted as she walked the four blocks to Main Street, the stream of tourists was almost as good as a floor show. By the time she reached the first row of dealers' booths, she concluded that her fourteen-carat amethyst wasn't even a contender in the vulgarity sweepstakes.

There was the woman with poisonously gold hair wearing five large diamond rings and diamond earrings. There was a man in white Bermuda shorts and high white socks, accessorized with leopardskin shoes, belt, watchband, and tie. There was the woman tightly encased in a glittering silver jumpsuit and high-heeled silver sandals, teetering along on the arm of a man wearing a gold-nugget watch and ring and three heavy neck chains.

She was about to award the Vulgarity Oscar to this last couple when she saw the woman in black embroidered linen. The clothes, while far too dressy for the occasion, were at least beautifully cut and elegantly designed. But she seemed to be in the grip of a gold fixation which had to qualify as a terminal Midas complex, if there was such a thing. She wore heavy gold earrings, a multitude of chains and bangles, several bracelets on each hand, and three or four rings. And—and here Anneke fell apart laughing—all ten of the woman's fingers were topped with long, solid gold fingernails.

She shared a grin and mutual eye-rolling horror with a young couple who did a double-take as the woman passed. Compared to the conspicuous-consumption suburbanites, the local kids in their vaguely punkish attire seemed fresh and amusing, cool in both senses of the word. Anneke plowed through the crowd, sidestepping a balding man in lime-green shirt, pants, and shoes, and stood on the corner momentarily to get her bearings.

Main Street looked as though someone had kicked over a human anthill. Street, sidewalks, and shop doorways were clogged with people; the wooden booths, running down the center of the blockaded street, were nearly invisible, engulfed by the torrent of humanity. All of them seemed to be shouting, gesticulating, eating, or all three at once; all the Main Street restaurants had takeout stands set up in front of their doors, and all seemed to be jammed with hungry Show-goers.

South down Main Street first, Anneke decided; she'd browse the booths down toward William, then work her way back north

and end up at her favorite gourmet shop. Taking a deep breath, she plunged forward into the maelstrom.

She fetched up at the first booth to find an eclectic, not to say motley, collection of items—old kitchenware, advertising signs, baskets, glass, and bits and pieces in uneasy coexistence. Still, some attempt had been made to arrange the various items into coherent groups, and the displays were neat and even imaginative.

"It was the best I could do at such short notice." Alice Cowan smiled and spread her hands apologetically. She didn't look particularly apologetic, though; she looked almost exultant.

"You've done wonders," Anneke congratulated her.

"Thank you." Alice darted away. "That's real monkey fur," she explained to a thin, nearly anorexic woman fingering a large muff.

"It seems to be going well," Anneke remarked after the sale of the muff had been completed.

"It's been fantastic," Alice said, her eyes shining. "They're buying everything that isn't nailed down. And this stuff is just junk, really; next year I'll have time to prepare. I'll be able to buy some big-ticket items now that I have an outlet for them."

So Alice was grabbing her big break and running with it. Well, good for her, Anneke figured. Alice even looked better, in a navy-and-white batik shirt and lightweight navy-blue pants that did far more for her short, stocky figure than the preppy skirts ever had. Watching her negotiate with an Ann Arbor couple (blue jeans, T-shirts, and a baseball cap), Anneke decided that Alice, at least, had benefited tremendously from Martha's death.

Nonsense, she thought, shaking her head. There were easier ways of getting a spot in an antique show than murder. But Alice certainly did seem changed, even in the short time Anneke had known her.

The next booth was devoted entirely to vintage clothing, and the one after that to American Primitive, neither of which held any interest for her. Beyond those were several booths of mixed collectibles, a booth full of dolls, and another of clocks and

watches. She reached the corner of William without having bought or even considered anything, and found Ellen and Ted in the last booth, under a hand-carved sign reading "Kiku Antiques" and a stylized rendering of a chrysanthemum.

Ellen was sweating and disheveled, but her face lit up when she saw Anneke.

"I was hoping you'd come by," she said. "I have something for you." She reached under a cloth-covered table and withdrew a small object, which she placed in Anneke's hand.

"For me?" Anneke examined the tiny netsuke, a beautifully carved figure of a monkey barely two inches across. It felt warm and smooth in her hand, almost alive.

"It's ivory," Ellen explained. "This one is a symbol of cleverness. Ted and I wanted you to have it."

"Ellen, it's beautiful." She scrutinized the figure more closely, marveling at the expressiveness of the tiny face.

"Please take it," Ellen insisted, forestalling any protest Anneke could make—although, in truth, she hadn't intended to protest. The little figure was wonderful. "It's important for us to thank you."

"I'll accept it with great pleasure," Anneke replied, understanding that Ellen meant exactly what she said. For both Ellen and Ted, it was important to pay one's debts, real or imagined. Anneke might not feel she'd done them any great service, but it was their feelings that mattered.

A small wave of customers invaded the booth, and for a little while Ellen and Ted were both busy explaining and negotiating. A beefy man in a painfully bright patterned shirt insisted that a bowl labeled Chinese export was actually Japanese, and after a few words Ted withdrew from the discussion and discreetly let Ellen take over.

"They don't argue as much with her," he said under his breath to Anneke, mopping perspiration from his face. "And if they do, she just goes all inscrutable on them." They both laughed.

"I take it you've sorted out the problem of the vase?" Anneke asked.

"Yes, finally. The police caught up with us this morning, before the show. After they got through questioning us about Martha's murder, they took us, with the vase, back to the woman we bought it from, and she confirmed the whole thing."

"What about the other issue?"

"All fixed up." He smiled broadly. "After the cops left, we told the woman we were dealers and explained what the vase was really worth. She was so impressed with our honesty"—his voice held a note of self-mockery—"that she asked us to broker it for her, for the standard twenty-five percent fee."

So that's all right, at least, Anneke thought, taking her leave with the little netsuke in a cloth bag tucked carefully into her purse. They were off the hook. Except . . . There was still the matter of Joanna's last words.

Anneke worked her way back up the street toward Liberty, through the ever denser crowds, trying to will herself not to sweat. The air was even hotter and thicker than before, without a trace of breeze but with an ominous haze that turned the sun into a baleful, translucent disk.

She had just crossed Liberty when she saw the massive male figure in front of her, nearly filling a booth already crammed with dark, glossy wood furniture. He was wearing a casual beige linen sport shirt, open at the neck, and she realized that, out of business attire, he looked even larger than before. As she hesitated, Karl turned and greeted her with an easy, unsurprised smile.

"Anneke, come and give me your opinion." He took her hand to draw her into the booth, and she felt a series of small, bright tremors, the physical attraction between them so strong it seemed to cast visible lines of force. "What do you think of this?" he asked, indicating a large brass-bound campaign chest in highly polished mahogany, whose four-figure price tag gave her a start.

"It's beautiful," she said, forcing herself to match his casual, unself-conscious tone. She lifted the lid, which slid smoothly and silently open to reveal a velvet-lined interior fitted as a liquor cabinet, complete with crystal decanters wearing identifying medallions in polished sterling silver. "Oh, wonderful," she exclaimed, entranced.

"If you'll come down ten percent I'll take it," Karl said at once to the hovering dealer, a tall, thin man with a lugubrious face. "That is, if you can deliver it."

"Sure, if you can wait till tomorrow," the dealer assented. Karl agreed and wrote out a check as Anneke waited, still awed by the price. It was not the sort of purchase normally available to someone living on a policeman's salary; but then, neither were Thunderbirds and camel's-hair jackets. American culture clearly valued football players more than policemen, she thought acidly—which was hardly Karl's fault, she reminded herself.

They left the booth together and fell into step by unspoken consent, working their way up Main Street through the crowds. With Karl next to her, Anneke realized with amusement, it was much easier going; crowds seemed to part at his approach.

Going with the flow, she thought as they slowed for a small knot of teenagers, and why not? Why the hell can't I just relax and do the same, without overanalyzing everything?

"I wouldn't have expected you to be interested in antiques," she commented, determined to enjoy herself without thinking too much.

"You mean because I'm not a collector?" He smiled. "It's possible to appreciate beautiful things without becoming obsessed with them, you know." Anneke looked at him sharply, but his expression was blandly casual. "Have you bought anything?" he asked.

"Not yet, but there's supposed to be a good Art Deco collection somewhere around." She peered into the nearest booth. "Not here, though."

"No." They looked with equal disfavor at a display of ungainly Mission oak and moved quickly on.

"Is it true that people are being asked not to have garage sales until the murders are cleared up?" she asked, feeling pretty sure of the answer but wondering what his reaction would be.

"There's a good deal of anxiety among city officials," he said, in a tone that would have been sarcasm if his voice had been less even.

"I assume there was no evidence of theft in Martha's murder," Anneke ventured.

"No. In fact, there seems to be some question whether she'd been going to sales at all yesterday morning."

"Alice said she hadn't seen Martha all morning." Anneke had a sudden, vivid recollection of the backseat of Martha's car, the platter and the fireplace tools alone on the seat. "An appointment, you mean?"

"Possibly."

"She knew something, didn't she?" Anneke said, revelation striking. "I overheard her at Peter's party. She was talking to Alice, and she said something. . . ."

"What did she say? Can you remember it exactly?" Karl had stopped walking and stood looking at her, heedless of the flow of pedestrians around them.

"I think it was just something vague and general." Anneke tried desperately to recall Martha's words. "I can't repeat it exactly, but it was about figuring out the type of thing that would have been stolen. I'm absolutely sure, though, that she didn't mention anyone specifically."

"It makes sense." Karl resumed his leisurely stroll up Main Street. "She saw or heard or figured out something that told her who killed Joanna, and she either let it slip or was foolish enough to try for a piece of the action herself."

"If she hadn't gone to any sales," Anneke contended, "then she must have been meeting someone. And she wouldn't set out to meet a probable murderer unless she was setting something up herself."

"Yes, I think that's probably the most likely scenario," he agreed. "Unfortunately, it doesn't really help much."

"Well, at least you know you're not looking for a maniac serial killer with a hatred of garage sales."

They continued up Main Street, browsing companionably past several more booths. One of them was Joyce's, but she was so inundated with customers that she could only spare Anneke a harassed wave and, when Karl's back was turned, a broad (and irritating) wink.

Michael was not so rushed. In fact, he confided, he hadn't been doing as well as he'd hoped.

"Well, it may pick up," Anneke comforted him. "The Show runs until eight tonight, doesn't it?"

"Yes, if the weather holds," Michael said gloomily, looking skyward. Anneke, born and bred a Midwesterner, instinctively glanced to the southwest. Overhead the sun still threw shimmering heat, but the horizon was a dark smudge.

"Maybe it'll hold off long enough for one more wave of Bloomfield Hillbillies," Michael said acidly. "That's an original Cropsey, by the way," he told Karl, who was studying a muddy landscape painting with every appearance of interest. "Hudson River School, and priced at about half what it would go for in a New York gallery."

"Very nice," Karl said noncommittally, taking a closer look. But not at the painting itself, Anneke realized; he was actually scrutinizing the gaudy gilt frame surrounding the canvas, especially one spot where an elaborate curlicue had quite obviously been repaired. And regilded.

"I don't think there's a dealer anywhere who hasn't repaired a picture frame occasionally," she declared when they'd left Michael's booth.

"I'm sure you're right," he agreed, in a flat tone that left Anneke feeling vaguely rebuffed.

TWENTY-ONE

Even though they'd been discussing murder she hadn't really thought of him before as a policeman. But that's what he was—a cop, never entirely off-duty. What must it be like, she wondered, to be perpetually suspicious of everyone, to view every person as a potential suspect, capable of the most horrendous crimes, so that even the teenage daughter of a murder victim must be viewed first as a possible murderer before she could be seen as a grieving child?

"Shall we go this way?" he asked, touching her elbow. "Steve Olewski's booth is just down the block."

Did people stop being people? she wondered. Did they become merely categories—victims, suspects, perpetrators, witnesses? And also, perhaps, useful investigative tools, like herself?

Around her, crowds pressed closely, bustling and noisy, children sticky with food, adults laden with the spoils of their shopping forays. Suddenly, as though a switch inside her clicked off, she had had enough. The sheer mass of antiques, of heavy

wood and twisted shapes and glutted booths, seemed to close in on her, looming in the sticky heat. The brightly colored throngs of people all seemed to have a single face, and its expression was sweating, voracious greed.

"I think not, if you don't mind," she said shakily. "I'm happy to help with your investigations, but I don't think I'd be much use to you for the moment. I seem to have OD'd on *things*. If you'll excuse me, I need to find a place to detox." She left him quickly, not waiting for him to offer to join her, not wanting to find out, here and now, if he would offer or not.

She thought about simply going home, but her car seemed impossibly far away. Instead, she went a block west on Washington and fell gasping into the air-conditioned darkness of a small neighborhood bar too dingy-looking from the outside to attract much of the tourist crowd.

She drank two glasses of water in quick succession and then wolfed down a large hamburger and a plate of fried zucchini. The food was filling but not soothing; when she was finished she felt physically better but no happier than before.

She sat for a while toying with a large glass of Pepsi, letting the cool air wash over her, thinking again about what it meant to be a cop. Was constant wariness a prerequisite, constant suspicion the norm? Was it inevitable that people became objects for manipulation? Or was she overreacting? What she had defined was virtually paranoia, yet Karl seemed the sanest man she had ever met.

Still, such a mindset would explain a lot—too much. For instance, why he had shared all that confidential information with her, making her virtually an undercover accomplice in his investigation. Not that she'd objected, of course; she was too honest to pretend even to herself that her curiosity wasn't engaged.

Nor could she honestly complain about last night—or want to, for that matter. She could hardly claim to be a seduced innocent, for God's sake. All that had happened was that they'd

shared one night of great sex, she told herself brutally; and after all, wasn't she the one who wanted to avoid any emotional entanglements?

"May I join you for a moment?" She looked up, startled, trying to compose her face into lines of impersonal calm. Karl waited for her nod before sliding into the booth across from her, nearly filling it. His movements in the confined space were graceful and economical, with no waste motion.

"I'm sorry I left so abruptly," she said formally. "The heat must have gotten to me."

"I think there's been a misunderstanding." He brushed her apology aside. "I hope you don't think I've been using you to spy on your friends."

"No, that's all right." She shook her head, determined not to appear more foolish than she could help. "There's someone out there who's killed three people, and if involving me will help you get him off the streets I'd be an idiot to object. Only"—she paused, choosing her words carefully—"since I'm not accustomed to it, the situation does make me uncomfortable at times."

"Oh, damn. I should have seen this coming," he said almost to himself. "Look"—he leaned forward only slightly, but the table between them was so tiny that it brought his face only inches from hers—"you think I've been involving you in this case because you can help me get close to the suspects, don't you?"

"I told you, it's all right," she insisted, drawing back slightly, physical awareness of him so strong she felt it must be a visible thing, like a Kirlian photograph.

"No, it's not all right," he said in a whisper that managed also to be a roar. "It's not all right because I will not have you thinking that I've merely been using you. In this or any other way." He dropped each word on the table like chunks of amber. "In fact, when I involved you in all of this I was paying you the compliment, I thought, of appealing to your intellect. And be-

cause I still respect that intellect"—he looked at her shrewdly while Anneke, dumbfounded, sought desperately for a response—"I'm not going to attempt to convince you that last night was more than an evening of recreation, because you already know damn well it was. Instead I'll put it to you in the terms you appreciate best: pure logic. Do you really believe," he declared as he slid out of the booth in a single smooth motion, "that I would go to this much *trouble* for a one-night stand?"

And he was gone, leaving Anneke with her mouth open in wild astonishment.

She paid the check and left the bar, feeling entirely happy but feeling also, to her surprise, no urgent need to catch up with him. There was time enough; first, she'd chase down that cache of Art Deco.

The heat outside struck like a physical blow, leaving her instantly drenched with perspiration. And overhead, she saw, the sky was luminous and heavy with impending rain. Humming to herself, she turned north into the one block of the show she hadn't yet covered, searching for Monte Enright's booth. But before she'd taken more than a few steps she was stopped by the sound of her name.

"Anneke? Over here." Steve Olewski waved to her from the edge of his booth, bringing her down from euphoria with a thud. Reluctantly she turned toward him, not sure how to react. Did he know she knew about his blackmail attempt? Did he even know that Ellen had blown the whistle on him? If not, the police might have good reasons for keeping him in the dark, and she had better be careful to act naturally. Not an easy task, she thought, feeling her lip curl in disgust.

"Hi, Steve." She greeted him as casually as she could manage, distracting herself from his face by reading his T-shirt. Today's was light blue with dark blue lettering that said: "Pardon me, but you've obviously mistaken me for someone who gives a shit." It was a funny line, and she would normally have laughed,

but it struck her that, for Steve, the words were more real than comic.

"Hang on a minute, I have something I think you'll like." He darted to the back of the booth and whispered something to a girl in a red tank top who was showing pieces of rhinestone jewelry to a pair of chattering teenagers. The girl gave Steve an arch look and giggled meaningfully.

"Sorry." Steve returned to Anneke. "Here, look at these." He reached into a small display case and extracted a pair of earrings, which he held out to her on the palm of his hand.

"Oh, beautiful!" Anneke exclaimed, taking them from him. They were large double circles of gold, enamelled in rich green and yellow. "But probably too expensive for me." She allowed regret to seep into her voice, falling automatically into the accepted pattern of negotiation.

"They're not as much as you'd think," Steve countered. "I can give you a good price on them—a lot less than you'd pay at a New York shop. And these are an investment."

"I'm sure they are," Anneke parried, "but . . ." The litany of bargaining went on; when they had reached a mutually agreeable figure Anneke took out her checkbook while Steve wrapped the earrings in white tissue. But as she wrote the check, delighted with what she knew was a true bargain, it struck her that the price was remarkably low. For the first time, recalling Ellen's tale, it occurred to her to wonder where, and under what circumstances, Steve had acquired the earrings. Was she buying fraudulently obtained property? And if so, she thought with a pang, would she have to give them up?

My God, I'm as bad as the rest of them, she thought sardonically, taking the tissue-wrapped bundle from Steve and depositing it in the depths of her purse. Maybe the police attitude is right; maybe everyone does have the soul of a crook.

"Ooh, how much are those?" a red-haired girl standing next to her exclaimed, pointing into the showcase.

"They run from twenty-five to fifty dollars apiece." Steve

reached in and withdrew a tray full of milky, jagged quartz crystals in varying shapes and dimensions, the largest nearly fist-sized. "These are real crystals, the same ones you see advertised for healing, and for channeling, and all kinds of psychic operations." He winked at Anneke as the girl leaned over the tray.

"Wow, that's a lot of money." The girl pouted, poking at the crystals. "After all, they're just rocks."

"Not at all," Steve remonstrated. "These are natural gems, just like diamonds or rubies. And think what you can do with them." He held up one of the crystals and twirled it so that it caught the sun, prisms of light flashing through the booth. "Think of the power they hold"—flash—"and the beauty"—flash—"and the connection to the natural harmony of earth"—flash.

There was something she was trying to remember, Anneke thought, half hypnotized by the shards of light before her eyes. Something someone said earlier, something that was suddenly, vitally important . . .

And then she remembered. She knew the answer to one of her questions, had had it right in front of her all the time.

"Anneke? Is something the matter?" Steve touched her arm and she jumped and drew back.

"No, nothing." She hoped he didn't notice the quiver in her voice. "I think the heat's getting to me. I'd better be going. Thanks for the earrings," she babbled, backing out of the booth.

She looked around wildly, searching idiotically for Karl in the teeming crowd. Ridiculous; she shook her head, forcing herself to calmness. You'll never find him by standing around staring at the mobs. There was an Antiques Association booth, she recalled; maybe they'd have a paging service.

But the big, rawboned woman at the information table shook her gray head apologetically. "Wouldn't be possible in this swarm." She gestured at the crowds.

"Well, I'm looking for a man," Anneke said desperately.

"Mid-forties, dark hair, six foot six or seven, about two hundred fifty pounds."

"Hell, honey"—the woman cocked her head and smirked—"who isn't?"

"Oh, please," Anneke didn't know whether to laugh or throw something. "It's really urgent. His name is Karl Genesko. If you see him, will you tell him Anneke Haagen needs to find him? Please."

"Sure will." The woman grinned amiably. "At least I won't have any trouble recognizing him."

No, she wouldn't. In fact, even in this throng he ought to be visible. Unless he'd left, Anneke thought suddenly. He might have gone home, or back to City Hall; should she try to call? Not yet, she decided; she'd make one circuit of the show first.

And then she did spot him, half a block away, walking easily through the crowd. She raced down the street, her flimsy sandals slipping on her sweaty feet, caroming off angry tourists and craning her neck desperately to keep him in view. She reached him finally in a booth full of Art Deco that she didn't even notice.

"I thought I'd never find you," she gasped. "It's the rock." The personal matters between them would have to wait.

"What about it?" he asked, understanding her instantly.

"I think I know why you couldn't find the rock that Joanna was killed with," she said, struggling to catch her breath. "Because it wasn't really a rock."

"When is a rock not a rock?" he asked with every appearance of seriousness.

She told him. He stared at her for a single long moment, then took her arm and strode out of the booth, turning south toward William. He gave no appearance of hurry, but Anneke found herself half running to keep up with him.

"You're going the wrong way," she said, panting.

"Telephone," he said briefly, pointing to the public phone at the corner. He leaned forward into the surrounding plastic cone

so that his huge back muffled his words. Anneke heard the word "warrant" and one or two other snatches that told her nothing. Finally he turned sideways and said, "I'll be waiting in front," as he hung up the receiver.

"Can't you just go and get it?" she asked as they hurried back the way they'd come. "I'm afraid it'll be sold. I mean, this is a public event—you don't need a warrant for that, do you?"

"Safer to have it," he said, looking grim. "I don't want this one to get away." He led her at breakneck pace back up Main Street, but when they reached the corner of Washington he paused and looked at her.

"I think you'd better stay here," he told her.

"Not a chance," she declared. "Not after getting in this deep—and at your instigation, if you recall. Besides," she added, "you need me to identify it."

"All right, point taken. Anyway"—he smiled brilliantly and took a firm grip on her arm—"I can use you for protective coloration while we wait for the warrant. Come on, let's wander up and down the street like tourists."

It seemed to Anneke that hours went by before Brad Weinmann, with a uniformed patrolman in tow and brandishing a large envelope, finally caught up with them.

"The judge wasn't thrilled, but he signed it," Brad said, looking at Anneke curiously but making no comment.

"He'd be a damn sight less thrilled if we lost the guy," Karl declared. "Let's go."

And then they all trooped up the worn stairs under the gaily decorated banner announcing "Artists' Open House" and into the big, color-filled frame shop, where Anneke pointed to the amethyst geode and Karl proffered the search warrant to a stunned Peter Casaday.

TWENTY-TWO

"Hullo, I see the cops are back on the job." Peter recovered quickly. He was apparently back to his old self, cheerful and flip, whatever trauma remained from Lesley's death pushed well into the background. He was dressed for the Show in full sixties regalia, beautifully embroidered bell-bottomed blue jeans and a white linen Nehru jacket, of all things, with two or three medallions around his neck. And as before, he looked astonishingly handsome.

"We have a warrant to conduct a complete search of the premises, Mr. Casaday. Would you like to see it?" Karl held out the stiff paper. Peter's expression didn't change, but his smile seemed frozen on his face.

"No, I believe you." He waved the paper away. "But look, what about . . ." He gestured around the room, where a dozen or so people wandered, gazing at the various artworks. An occasional thump overhead indicated the presence of more people in the studio above. "Can't you wait until after the

Show? No, I suppose you can't," he answered his own question. "You're one of those real anal-retentives, aren't you? Oh well, it's more or less winding down anyway."

"If you'll just take a seat, please," Karl said politely, "we'll clear the premises as quietly as possible." Peter shrugged and moved to the front of the room, where he arranged himself elegantly in one of the beanbag chairs. Being rather too agreeable, Anneke decided.

Shortly a small stream of people began moving reluctantly toward the door and disappearing down the stairs to the street. Anneke moved out of their way, positioning herself near one of the tall front windows where a portable air conditioner worked fruitlessly against the heat.

"Ms. Haagen, can you identify this object?" Brad Weinmann approached her with self-conscious formality, holding the amethyst geode in a sealed plastic bag. Anneke examined it with equal formality. Like all geodes, it had begun as a round, featureless rock, growing its crystals secretly inward, toward the center. This was a good-sized one—as a full sphere, it would have been nearly six inches in diameter. And it had been broken open rather than cut, so that what remained was close to two-thirds of its original size, the jagged crystals inside shading from dark lavender to nearly clear. It was unmistakable.

"That is the geode I saw Peter Casaday buy at a garage sale last Saturday," she stated, "at approximately nine-thirty A.M."

"Thank you," Mike replied.

"Well, the pretty lady has a good eye," Peter drawled. "What's the story on the geode, anyway?"

"We believe that this is the weapon used to murder Joanna Westlake," Karl informed him.

"Amazing. And are you arresting me?"

"No, sir," Karl answered. The words "not yet" seemed to hang in the air. "The geode will be sent to the state police lab for testing."

"Testing?" For the first time Peter dropped his uninterested

pose. "For what? It's just a rock, after all." Yes, just a rock, Anneke thought. How stupid that it had taken her so long to realize it. She might not have done so yet, if not for Ken Scheede's comment about her ring, and the girl's comment about Steve's crystals.

"They'll test it for several things," Karl explained matter-of-factly to Peter, as if he were answering a reporter's question. "Whether its shape fits the wound on her head, for one thing. Whether the chips found in the wound match its composition. And of course, spectroscopic analysis will show up microscopic bloodstains, if this was the weapon. Human blood is the devil to remove entirely," he added conversationally.

Peter said nothing, but his eyes darted back and forth across the room. He sank into the beanbag chair and stretched his legs out in front of him, trying unsuccessfully to look casual. His façade was finally cracking, Anneke decided. She glanced at him out of the corner of her eye, seeing his handsome face in profile and knowing it for the first time as the face of a murderer.

"What exactly are we looking for?" Brad asked Karl.

"Anything that looks exceptionally valuable, if you can recognize it"—he shrugged—"or anything that looks as if it's been hidden."

They fanned out through the room, and Anneke took up a perch on the spiral staircase, keeping out of their way but watching with fascination as the search team poked and probed—moving furniture, examining the bottoms of drawers, looking in places it would never occur to her to use for concealment. She cast her eyes around, noting the empty shelf of the étagère where the geode had stood.

"Lieutenant, I'm not sure how to define 'anything hidden,'" a young officer said quietly to Karl.

"What've you got?" he asked.

"Well, there's a lot of stuff crammed into these cabinets over there, but it looks more like storage than concealment."

"Anything that looks valuable?"

"Not really. It's just . . . stuff. Things like dishes and mugs, household junk, lamps, stuff like that. A lot of things with peace symbols on them."

"It does sound more like storage," Karl nodded. "Let it go for now."

"I think we're through down here," Mike announced.

"All right, let's start upstairs." Anneke moved quickly away from the staircase and stood aside while the search team ascended. One man, she noted, stayed behind, standing casually at the foot of the steps but keeping a careful eye on Peter. It hardly seemed necessary; he appeared deep in introspective thought, oblivious to the activity around him.

When she was sure the police were clear of the stairs she followed them partway up, stopping two steps below the surface to be sure she remained out of their way. She expected at any moment to be politely escorted out to the street; she had served her purpose, after all, once she'd identified the geode. But she didn't want to leave; the search process fascinated her, and her curiosity drove her.

From her vantage point near floor level, the big studio had a queer, foreshortened look. The odd furniture seemed even odder, and Lesley's painting, still in its place on the wall, looked hostile and angry in its black frame. What had Karen called it? "Fractured Unicorn."

Even the shag rug covering the bedroom half of the floor looked different at eye level. Dirtier, for one thing—she could see flecks of dirt, smears of paint, and various bits of detritus trapped among its long strands. And one corner was twisted slightly; there seemed to be something stuck under it.

One of the searchers spotted it, too. He reached down and lifted the corner of the rug, plucking something carefully from under it with a pair of long tweezers. He dropped the object into a plastic bag, which he carried directly to Karl.

"Now that's something we've been looking for. Good work,

Joe," Karl congratulated him. "Let's go see what Mr. Casaday has to say about it."

The young officer's face flushed with pleasure as Karl motioned toward the staircase. Anneke backed down the stairs hastily as they descended, and returned to her position by the étagère.

"Mr. Casaday, a question, if you don't mind." Karl said as he approached Peter.

"Oh? About the meaning of life, no doubt?" Peter looked up, his eyes glittering.

"We found this upstairs, under the rug." Karl held out the plastic bag. "Is it yours?"

"What is it? Oh, it's a tube of gilt. And what of that?"

"Is it yours?"

"I've no idea in the world. I assume that if you found it in my studio it's mine. I use it to repair picture frames. It's amazing how many old frames look like they've been chewed by the family dog."

"Please notice that it's been squashed, and that the tube has broken at the bottom. Do you have any idea when or how that happened?"

"Nope." Peter seemed to have lost interest.

"I must tell you that smears of gilt like that from this tube were found on the shoes of both Lesley Shea and Martha Penrose when their bodies were discovered," Karl informed him. "Can you suggest any explanation for that?"

"Explanation? No." Peter crossed his ankles and appeared to contemplate his own shoes. "If it was found on their shoes, I can only guess they stepped in it."

"That's certainly the most plausible explanation," Karl agreed. "And of course Miss Shea was a frequent visitor to your studio. But did Martha Penrose also visit you often?"

"Martha? God, no." Peter smirked offensively. "I don't believe I'd ever be that hard up. She was here for the party, though. Earlier this week. *She* was here," he pointed to Anneke,

seeming to notice her presence for the first time. "I guess old Martha stepped in the gilt then."

"That's certainly possible," Karl said agreeably.

He disappeared back up the staircase, and Peter watched him go with an expression of casual interest that Anneke thought seemed strained. For the first time, he looked his age; not aging yet, but no longer a kid. Like it or not, time had turned him into an adult.

She had the sure conviction that he didn't like it. She recalled him at the party, needling Michael about being the "grand old man." From her vantage point, Peter had been firmly part of the younger generation that evening, unquestionably one of the kids; but she also recalled Steve's crack about Lesley preferring "someone her own age." Perhaps in their eyes—and in his own—Peter was already no longer "one of the kids."

Everything had seemed different at the party, she thought, remembering. The room had been happy, filled with chattering, brightly dressed guests; she had a quick mental image of Martha, in her flowered silk dress, holding forth didactically by the étagère. . . .

And suddenly, finally, it all fell into place.

She stood perfectly still while she ran it through once in her mind, sorting and analyzing her conclusions. Too much induction, not enough deduction, but that didn't invalidate her conclusion. There was simply no other way events could have happened, no other hypothesis that explained everything.

Rapidly she ascended the staircase, ignoring the men examining walls and probing cushions, and went straight to Karl.

"Martha couldn't have gotten gilt on her shoe at the party," she told him at once.

"You were there, weren't you?" He gave her only part of his attention, keeping one eye on the continuing search. "Did you have her in view all the time?"

"I didn't need to." Anneke shook her head. "She was wearing a flowered silk dress." He looked at her more attentively now,

waiting for her to continue. "The gilt you found was on a pair of running shoes," she explained. "That's what a lot of dealers wear for garage sales. I didn't notice what shoes Martha wore to the party, but I certainly would have noticed if she'd been wearing running shoes with a silk dress."

"I see." She had his complete attention now. "So Martha must have been here on some other occasion."

"Yes, and at the same time as Lesley," Anneke pointed out. "And presumably at a time when Peter wasn't here, or he'd have picked up the squashed tube. Don't you see," she burst out, "there's only one way Martha and Lesley could both have stepped on that tube of gilt here, in this studio? Martha had to be the one who made that phone call that decoyed Peter to Birmingham. Martha broke in here while he was gone, to search for whatever he stole from Joanna. Martha killed Lesley."

"It fits the facts, I'll admit that," he agreed without any obvious enthusiasm.

"You said yourself it could have been an accident," Anneke persisted. "Look, Lesley was in and out of the studio all the time, and besides, she was helping to set up the exhibit for the Show. Assume Lesley came to the studio and surprised Martha in the act of searching. There was a struggle, and Martha pushed her so that she fell and hit her head on something. Maybe that." She gestured toward the sheet-metal sculpture, which suddenly seemed a menacing presence in the room. "It's about the right height," she reasoned aloud.

"It's possible," Karl agreed. "But if it happened that way, why would Martha move the body?"

"She wouldn't, but Peter would. Remember, he's already a suspect in one murder. And he's hidden something that he desperately doesn't want anyone to find. He's got to know that if he calls the police and reports finding Lesley's body, they'll go over this place with a microscope, and he can't afford to have that happen."

"So far"—Karl quirked his lips, watching the search—"it

doesn't seem that he had anything to worry about. Besides, how did Martha know that Peter killed Joanna?" They were accepting that as a given, Anneke noted.

"I think maybe I can guess," she said slowly, knowing this was the weakest link in her deductive chain. "Did you find a weird-looking lamp hidden somewhere? A thing like a vacuum-cleaner hose filled with Christmas-tree lights?"

"It wasn't mentioned. Why?"

"Because it was there at the party, right next to the geode in fact, and now it's gone." Martha was vivid in her mind, switching the peculiar lamp on and off, commenting on "other people around who like peculiar modern things." Joanna was known among the regulars for buying contemporary pieces. "I think that lamp was one of Martha's clues."

" 'One of?' "

"She said something else, too." Anneke dug into her memory. "About 'the sort of thing it would have been'—the thing Joanna found. The thing is, Joanna bought mostly contemporary pieces. And if it was contemporary, Peter would have been the person she'd ask about it."

"Could the lamp possibly be valuable enough to kill for?" Karl asked dubiously.

"God knows. I doubt it." Anneke spread her hands. "But I'm sure it means something."

Karl turned away and spoke briefly to Mike, and then to one of the searchers.

"It may be in that storage cabinet downstairs," he said to Anneke, motioning her toward the staircase.

Downstairs, he waited while the young policeman knelt and scrabbled inside the cabinet, emerging finally with a coiled plastic tube which he held carefully between two fingers.

"Is this what you wanted, Lieutenant?" he asked doubtfully. "I thought it was a piece of ductwork."

"Hey, be careful with that," Peter called. "It's a valuable collector's item."

"Is this what you meant?" Karl asked Anneke. When she nodded, he turned toward Peter. "How valuable would you say it is, Mr. Casaday?"

"Not valuable enough to kill for, if that's what you mean." Peter grinned wolfishly. "It's called a Boalum. By Castiglioni— worth maybe a couple of hundred."

"May I ask where you got it?" Karl asked, while Anneke stared in amazement at the preposterous lamp. Not valuable enough to kill for, perhaps, but valuable enough to covet.

"You're the cop," Peter answered. "You can ask anything you want and get away with it, can't you? Oh, hell, I'd better tell you." Peter ran his hands through his curly blond hair and essayed a boyish smile. "As a matter of fact, I bought it from Joanna last Saturday."

"I see," Karl said neutrally. "How much did you pay her for it?"

"Twenty dollars." Peter held his hands out, palms up. "Well, that's all she asked for it."

"You didn't mention this when we questioned you after her murder." Karl made it a statement rather than a question.

"Well, would you have?" Peter asked reasonably. "It didn't have anything to do with the murder, after all, and I knew you guys would get all bent out of shape about it. You certainly don't think I'd kill someone for a two-hundred-dollar lamp, do you? I mean, it's not like it's the only one in the world; if I wanted one that badly I could just grit my teeth and buy one from a dealer." So that was his story, and he was going to tough it out.

"Where and when did you buy it from Joanna?" Karl asked.

"Pretty early in the morning, I think, but I'm damned if I remember where." Peter furrowed his brow in ostentatious thought. "Somewhere on the west side, I know that."

"We'll hold this as evidence." Karl didn't pretend to take Peter's answer seriously. "Is there anything else you haven't told us?"

"Not a thing," Peter's expression was bland.

"The trouble is," Anneke said when they had returned to the studio upstairs, "it's too plausible. The regulars often do buy things from each other on the run like that."

"I know." Karl nodded, his lips compressed. "And I assume he's telling the truth about its value—it's easy enough to check. It's not something a person—even a dedicated collector—would normally kill for."

"We're not on the wrong track, are we?" She used the plural unconsciously.

"Oh, no," Karl said grimly. "He did it, all right. But unless we find what he did it *for* we may never get a conviction."

"You don't think"—Anneke was stricken by a sudden thought—"that Martha actually found this ... whatever-it-is, do you? That it's not even here anymore?"

"If we're assuming that Peter killed Martha, either because she was blackmailing him or because she'd found and stolen the thing, we can also assume it's here," he reassured her. "Even if she did find it, he wouldn't have killed her until he'd gotten it back."

"Then where the hell is it? And *what* the hell is it?" Anneke glared around the studio, her eyes made weary by the sensory overload of color and pattern and twisting shapes. Lesley's painting seemed to loom over her in its heavy black frame.

"Wait a minute. There's something ..."

"What is it?" Karl asked quietly. "Something that's different from the night of the party?"

"Yes. The painting. It's Lesley's; I noticed it then. Only ... I'm pretty sure it wasn't framed."

They both stared for a long moment at the clashing abstraction of "Fractured Unicorn." Then Karl strode across the room, plucked the painting from the wall, and turned it over. The back of the canvas was sealed in brown paper.

"Oil paintings aren't usually paper-sealed," Anneke said. Karl appeared not to hear her. He pulled a penknife from his pocket

and Anneke held her breath as he sliced through the paper from corner to corner in two swift motions and folded the pieces open to reveal the cavity inside.

It was empty.

Anneke's sensation of disappointment was so intense that for a moment she felt physically ill. She dropped to her knees next to the painting and stared inside, as if she could will something to appear. Maybe it was caught under the edge of the stretcher, she thought, digging her fingers under the rough wood.

"Wait a minute." She clawed at the ends of the paper and yanked it free of the stretcher. "Look at this."

Karl dropped to his knees next to her and looked where her finger pointed. Along the edge of the stretcher they could see the ragged edges of not one but two canvases, one on top of the other.

"There's another painting underneath," she said unnecessarily, her voice shaking slightly as she watched Karl wedge his knife under the first of the staples holding canvas to stretcher. Then she remained silent, hardly daring to breathe as he worked his way carefully around from corner to corner, turned the canvas over, and gently lifted "Fractured Unicorn" away.

They stared at the painting underneath. It was a set of broad concentric circles, like an archery target, heavy on black and red and in a rough, almost ragged style.

"Not my sort of thing." Anneke said shakily.

"Nor mine," Karl agreed, "but I've never seen a painting I enjoyed more." They both stared at the lower right-hand corner of the big canvas, where the artist had signed his work with the three letters "JAP."

"Is this it?" Anneke asked, feeling breathless and foolish in equal portions. "This? What the hell is it?"

"I have no idea." Karl shook his head. "But I know who does. Shall we?" He picked up the painting, holding the sheet of stiff canvas carefully, and headed for the staircase, pausing to let her go ahead of him. So that her body shielded the painting as they

descended, she realized. Only when they reached the bottom did he hold up the canvas for Peter to see.

"Mr. Casaday, can you identify this for us?" he asked quietly.

Peter looked up from his intent perusal of his hands, and his face went ashen. He struggled up from the beanbag chair and stood glaring at the painting for a moment, swaying slightly.

And then he bolted.

Anneke was never sure of the exact sequence of succeeding events. Peter dashed for the doorway, Karl shouted a warning, and the officer who had been assigned to watch Peter made a futile swipe as he dove past. Then, shockingly, there was an explosive crack of sound that seemed to rock the studio, and Peter fell forward with a high-pitched scream and lay, sobbing, on the floor by the door. Anneke looked around, stunned, searching for the source of the noise, wondering which policeman had fired the shot, wondering why Karl looked disgusted rather than concerned as he strode forward to where Peter lay in a huddle.

"Get up, you idiot," he said, standing over Peter but making no attempt to help him. "It's only thunder."

Outside, Anneke saw through the streaming front window, the rains had come at last.

TWENTY-THREE

· · · · · ·

"A Jasper Johns painting," Ellen said Monday afternoon. Her voice was awestruck. "From a garage sale—awesome. And all this time I was trying like hell to figure out what 'Jap' meant if it didn't mean me, I never even thought of Johns. Some art expert I turned out to be."

"I thought only Old Masters went for really huge sums," Carmela said. "It's hard to believe that something by a living artist could be that valuable."

"There was a Johns painting at Sotheby's a couple of years ago that went for more than three million dollars," Ellen pointed out.

"The Big Score to end all Big Scores," Joyce murmured.

"What's the biggest you ever hit?" Alice Cowan asked. They fell to reminiscing, sitting around the big, scarred table in the workroom of Remains to Be Seen. Anneke sat at the computer and listened with half her attention while she expunged Steve Olewski's files from the system.

"He may not be guilty of murder," Joyce had told her, "but he's probably guilty of fraud and he's certainly guilty of sexual harassment." At Michael Rappaport's urging, they had offered Steve's space to Alice and she had accepted.

"Of course the signature 'Jap' wouldn't have meant anything to Joanna," Ellen said.

"And of course, being Joanna," Carmela commented acidly, "she didn't bother to research it herself. She just tried to pick someone else's brains."

"Yes, and when you think about it," Anneke pointed out, "even without knowing what it was she'd found, Peter should have been the most likely suspect."

"Why Peter?" Carmela asked.

"Because Joanna bought mostly contemporary things. Look, Peter kept insisting that he didn't have any competition on the garage-sale circuit, but in fact a lot of sixties pieces are indistinguishable from good contemporary still being made—bright, clean design, lots of chrome, that sort of thing. Unfortunately, the only one who made the connection was Martha."

"I still don't understand how Martha comes into it," Alice confessed.

"I assume she figured out that Peter killed Joanna and tried to blackmail him," Joyce said. She turned to Anneke. "Wasn't that it?"

"Not exactly." Anneke swiveled from the computer. "She figured out that Peter had done it, all right. But what she did was more devious even than blackmail. She called Peter and set up a spurious appointment to get him out of town, so she could search his studio and appropriate whatever it was he'd killed for."

"But how did she know what it was?"

"She *didn't* know what it was." Anneke recalled Peter's angry outburst. Once they'd gotten him up off the floor and convinced him he hadn't been shot, he collapsed like a pricked balloon, ignoring Karl's clearly stated Miranda warning and babbling on

and on into near hysteria. "But she was an expert with a high opinion of her own expertise. She was sure that if she had a chance to search the studio, she'd find Joanna's Big Score and recognize it. I don't think she would have, actually, even if she hadn't been interrupted."

"Interrupted?" Alice asked.

"By Lesley." Their faces remained puzzled. "Of course, you don't know the connection. Do you remember that art student whose body was found on the jogging path?" They nodded vaguely. "She was Peter's girlfriend. She showed up at the studio while Martha was searching; there was a struggle, and Lesley hit her head on a big metal sculpture."

That, at least, was the way Peter had reported Martha's version of the events. Anneke found it particularly hard to forgive Peter for Lesley, despite his babbled protestations of undying love. He'd returned from his successful conquest in Birmingham to find Lesley—already dead, he swore—in a heap on the studio floor. Terrified that he'd be blamed, and equally terrified of a police search, he'd bundled Lesley's body into his van and driven around until he found a safe place to dump it. He'd never noticed the squashed tube of gilt or the smear on Lesley's shoe.

"Anyway," Anneke continued, "the next day Martha called Peter and announced that she intended to share the proceeds of his Big Score." For all her intelligence, Anneke thought, Martha had been sadly lacking in that commodity known as street smarts.

"So he killed her." Alice shuddered.

"Yes. They agreed to meet on the road. Martha thought she was being smart, being out in the open like that, but she forgot how deserted residential streets can be early Saturday morning."

"She probably didn't think of it as early," Joyce commented. "Nine o'clock Saturday is midday to us, after all."

"I still don't understand," Carmela said insistently, "how

Martha knew in the first place that Peter was the one who murdered Joanna."

"There was a lamp," Anneke replied. "A unique modern piece that Martha saw Joanna buy that morning. And then she recognized it in Peter's shop the night of the party."

"But that's crazy," Ellen protested. "You mean he stole a million-dollar painting and went to all that trouble to hide it, and at the same time he stole a lousy lamp and set it out in plain sight?"

"The lamp was an afterthought." Anneke laughed at Ellen's outraged reaction to illogic. "He saw it in the back of her car after he'd hit her, and he just couldn't resist; it's some sort of important sixties collectible. But it isn't hugely valuable, and it just never occurred to him to hide it until it was too late. He added a frame to the painting after that, too, just to be extra safe. As it turned out, I think if he'd left it alone he'd have gotten away with it."

"It's still hard to believe," Joyce remarked. "I mean, I know we're all awfully fixated by *things* in this business, but still . . ." She made a face. "How many times have we said we'd kill to have something or other? Do we really mean it?"

"Peter did not kill for love of an object," Carmela declared, "he killed for plain, ordinary greed. For money." She sounded disgusted.

"And I think probably for ego as well," Alice suggested. "He wasn't very successful, after all, and he wasn't as young as he tried to think he was," she added incisively.

"And there was all that sixties crap of his, too," Ellen said sternly. "All that self-indulgent, do-your-own-thing nonsense, and screw the rest of the world."

"No!" Anneke said explosively. "I mean, yes, that's the way Peter saw the sixties," she added more temperately, "but that's not the way they were." She thought back 25 years, recalling the feelings of optimism, of endless possibility.

"Look," she went on, "you've gotten it the wrong way round,

and not entirely by accident—all you've heard over the last couple of decades is the counterrevolutionary, 1980s rewriting of what the sixties was really all about. Don't you see that protests, political action, commitment to social change are the very opposite of self-indulgence? Which is more self-indulgent, after all—joining the Peace Corps or joining Bank of America?"

"Yes, but what about the drugs, and the dropping out, and the general irresponsibility?" Ellen insisted.

"Of course some of it was wrongheaded," Anneke acknowledged. "But even the most foolish excesses were part of the context, the attempt to define a whole new way of living and relating. What Peter got hold of were the actions without the context—he never understood what the sixties were really about. Look at the decor of his studio, for instance."

"*You* look at it." Joyce wrinkled her nose.

"That's the point," Anneke declared. "Not the actual style, but the way it fit together—or didn't fit together." She visualized the studio once more. "He had some good things, some real quality. That purple lounger, for instance." She laughed at the look on Joyce's face. "All right, not your style, but you know quality when you see it. But he had a few things like that mixed in with beanbag chairs and bead curtains and Lava Lamps. As if he couldn't discriminate between what was good and what was junk." She paused thoughtfully. "I think he had the same problem with the philosophy of the sixties that he had with its furniture."

"They will be able to convict him, won't they?" Carmela asked. "This is the sort of thing that gives all dealers a bad name."

"I don't think that's going to be a problem," Anneke assured her. "Even if his confession isn't admitted"—as Karl had worried even while Peter babbled on—"there's plenty of evidence, now that they know where to look. The sellers identified both the painting and the lamp, and both are sure they sold the things to a woman, even if they can't identify Joanna specifically."

"Suppose he says he bought them from Joanna," Alice suggested. "After all, we all buy from each other from time to time."

"In fact, he said he did try to buy it," Anneke replied, "but she wouldn't sell it to him." She heard again Peter's outraged squawk as he recounted the event to Karl:

"She said she wanted to keep it because it matched the color scheme in her family room!"

"And anyway, how could he explain hiding it away like that, and not saying anything about it? No jury would buy that. And besides," Anneke pointed out, "there's still the geode. He'd soaked it in soap and water, but they still found microscopic traces of blood on it. Not enough to get a blood-type match, but with the other evidence it should be enough."

"Soap and water?" Joyce sneered. "Men. Didn't he know about Mr. Clean?"

"One question." Ellen interrupted before they could reopen the never-ending debate over cleaning solutions. "What happens to the painting?"

"The Johns? Nobody's sure," Anneke replied. "For the moment the police are holding it for evidence. Both Joanna's husband and the woman who sold it have claimed it, but they've apparently already discussed selling it and splitting the proceeds equally."

"Good," Carmela declared. "Otherwise the only ones who will get rich will be the lawyers."

When Anneke got home, there was an Express Mail parcel tucked inside her screen door, its label in an instantly recognizable hand that made her stomach lurch.

She carried the thing inside, suppressing the urge to burn it unopened, and poured herself a large brandy and soda before sitting down at the dining room table with the parcel in front of her. Inside the mailer was a thick, lumpy eleven-by-fourteen manila envelope addressed in Dennis's neat, almost architec-

tural handwriting. She took a long gulp of brandy before tearing open the flap and shaking out the contents.

There was the antique silver compact she thought she'd lost; a paperback copy of a Sarah Shankman novel; and a red silk scarf, which she'd left, long ago, in Dennis's Bloomfield Hills condo. There were two three-and-a-half-inch computer disks with her name on them in Dennis's handwriting. And there was a two-page, typewritten letter, on yellow lined legal paper, signed "Dennis Grantham" in thick, angry letters.

Reading it through, Anneke marveled at the unimaginative quality of his obscenities, even as the ugliness made her skin crawl. Still, it meant that at least he'd finally given up. But the best came at the last.

"Also unloading your crummy game. Stupid bitch, did you really think this crap was worth anything? You aren't any better at programming than you are at fucking, you repulsive old cunt." The letter tailed off into further obscenities, but even as Anneke shuddered reading them, she also exulted.

She had Whitehart Station back! However loathsome the letter, it constituted a legal quitclaim on the program, returning all rights to her. If necessary, she'd be willing to produce the unspeakable document in open court—probably more willing than Dennis, if it came to the point.

Still holding the precious letter, she picked up the discs and took them into her den, where she inserted one into the drive and switched on the Compaq. And laughed aloud when the screen displayed nothing but gibberish. So he'd taken a magnet to them as a final act of spite. Going to her filing cabinet, she lifted out a plastic box and took from it the two safe copies of her program.

She looked at the letter for several moments before slipping it into an envelope for transfer to her safe-deposit box. It was impossible not to feel brutalized by the torrent of obscenities, yet at the same time an overwhelming sense of release made her

almost giddy. As if she'd just won the lottery. Or inherited a castle. Something worth celebrating, anyway.

Except, for too long there had been no one to celebrate with. No one in her life, in fact, to share anything with, bar the superficialities of everyday living. It was time she dealt with this last vestige of the hash Dennis had made of her life. Firmly, she picked up the phone and dialed, and when the deep voice answered she spoke quickly, not giving herself time to think.

"Just how much trouble *are* you willing to go to, Lieutenant?"

If you enjoyed *Something to Kill For*, read on for an excerpt of *Curly Smoke*, the next mystery by Susan Holtzer featuring Anneke Haagen...

Mackinac Court in pale December daylight had a tentative look, as if it were not sure whether to come into full focus. The sun was a watery orange disk riding low in the southern sky, partially screened by tangles of naked tree branches, adding no perceptible warmth to the frigid air.

Anneke wheeled her chocolate brown Alfa-Romeo into the court's communal parking area and levered herself carefully out of the driver's seat, trying not to destabilize the young mountain of packages surrounding her. She'd wakened energized, finally, after four days of emotional narcolepsy, and when Hudson's opened at ten o'clock she'd gone through the store like a tornado, heedless of cost.

She hadn't even bothered to check in with her office. She knew Ken Scheede, her office manager, could cope; besides, during Christmas break Ann Arbor came to a near standstill, even those elements that had no direct University of Michigan

connection. Refusing to feel guilty (which meant, she admitted to herself, that she felt exactly that), she stood next to the Alfa for a moment, puffing out patterns of frosty breath and savoring the bitterly cold air on her face.

It had been an odd winter all around—if there was such a thing as a "normal" Michigan winter. A seemingly endless succession of Alberta clippers had kept the temperature hovering near zero for weeks, yet there had been little snow. Only a light frosting of rime dusted lawns and shrubbery.

The cold, of course, had compounded the effects of the fire. Anneke tried not to think about the ruins of her house, buried under a fantastic edifice of ice where the water from the fire hoses had frozen, it seemed, almost in midair.

It didn't do to think about the house. Instead, she concentrated on Mackinac Court, taking in her new home for the first time. She'd seen the cottage, rented it, and moved in, all in one evening, paying little attention to its surroundings. But now, looking at the court with some interest, she recognized it as a true oddity.

It had been carved out of the center of a block that was now an agglomeration of commercial and University buildings, but towering oaks and looming hedgerows made the residences inside wholly invisible from Division Street. Standing in the parking area, Anneke saw a ragged semicircle of five houses and two tiny cottages, in a mismatched assortment of periods and architectural styles.

Two of the houses were massive Victorian structures, one at the edge of the entry, the other taking pride of place at the center of the semicircle. The other three full-sized houses had clearly come later—what Anneke referred to mentally as elderly McKinleys. A pair of them, on either side of the small parking area, took up the north arm of the court. The third was on the other side of the court, with two tiny cottages squeezed in beside it.

The two Victorians—mansions now, to contemporary eyes—still dominated, but they had a harassed look, like Great Danes surrounded by yapping terriers. Anneke, pleased by the image, plucked several parcels from her car at random and headed across the court toward her cottage.

As she fished for her key, she heard the clangor of Burton Tower, just a few blocks away—first the full four sections of the Westminster chimes, then twelve long, sonorous strokes, and finally the boisterous cascade of sound that signaled an infrequent carillon concert.

And then, as if on cue, the empty courtyard was abruptly populated, as the glossy red front door of the adjacent house burst open and small bodies seemed to come boiling out.

The smallest of them reached her first, tumbling down the wooden steps and skidding on the icy turf in his haste. He reached to just above Anneke's waist, and she guessed his age somewhat doubtfully at five or six. Close behind him was another boy, two or three years older, and finally, bringing up the rear with a certain self-consciousness, a pair of girls on the edge of their teen years.

"You're the new lady, aren't you? We wanted to come say hello, but Mommy said not to bother you till you came outside, so we've been waiting to see you—and now you're here, so we can come say hello." He paused for a prodigiously deep breath. "Do you like your cottage? Are you going to stay for a long time? Did your house really burn down?"

"Cashin!" One of the girls nudged the child sharply, and he subsided, looking sheepish. "I'm sorry, Miss Haagen," she said. "He gets carried away sometimes."

"That's all right." Anneke smiled at the girl. "He was just being enthusiastic."

"We did want to welcome you to Mackinac Court." The other girl, serene in a pink down-filled parka and fur-trimmed boots, moved forward gracefully, as if to distance herself from the younger children. "I'm Victoria Roper, and this is

Marcella Smith, and that's Cashin Smith, and that's Ross Barlow." She indicated each child with a small, leather-gloved hand.

"All right, you lot, leave Miss Haagen alone. She's got enough problems without havin' a batch of kids around." Barbara Smith, Anneke's new landlord, descended the porch steps behind the children and made shooing motions with her hands. She was tall and angular-looking in an olive green parka and brown pants tucked into short, no-nonsense winter boots. "Are you moved in okay?" she asked Anneke. "It's a pretty good place for an Ann Arbor rental, if I do say so myself, but of course it's hard to keep a place looking nice when there's tenants, you wouldn't believe what some of them get up to when it's someone else's property. I know you didn't have much to bring with you, so if you need anything, just come next door to me, I'm the only one who's usually around all the time anyway."

"Thank you." Anneke wedged the words in as Barbara paused for breath. Obviously this was Cashin's mother. "I think I'm starting to pull myself together. And I've spent the morning buying out the stores." She indicated her packages.

"So I see." Barbara's sharp eyes, under her tightly curled hair, took in Anneke's full-length red shearling coat and high fawn-colored suede boots. The coat had been an insane extravagance, far too elegant for the hypercasual Ann Arbor culture, but just now Anneke didn't give a damn. As soon as she'd tried it on, she knew she had to have it.

She was aware that she looked overdressed, especially with the big gold earrings that had been a last-minute purchase. But then, she admitted, she usually did. She had realized, when she'd reached the age of forty, that she was simply one of those women who looked either dowdy or elegant, no middle ground.

Besides, Karl would appreciate the coat.

"It's going to take me forever just to carry everything inside." Anneke laughed, refusing to be apologetic. "And some of it weighs the earth—I never realized how heavy sheets and pillowcases are."

"Can I help?" The newcomer appeared out of nowhere so abruptly that Anneke started visibly. "Sorry." He grinned and extended his gloved hand. "Cleve Marshall. I live next door." He motioned with his chin toward the second cottage, an apparent twin to Anneke's.

"I'm Anneke Haagen." She turned toward him, juggling packages to accept his handshake. He was medium height, with a narrow, rather British face and razor-cut, straw-colored hair. Almost, but not quite, too young to be interesting—say, early thirties, with a good deal of intelligence underlying his bland expression. Still, he lacked the force of Karl's personality, she thought, and then laughed at herself—had she really reached the point of comparing every man she met with Karl Genesko?

"Have you lived here long?" she asked politely, making sure her voice held no hint of personal interest. The last thing she wanted was an emotional complication with someone living next door.

"Just since September. I'm here on sabbatical."

"Oh? What are you in?"

"History. UC Berkeley." Cleve responded to the academic's usage of the word *in*. "And you?"

"Not faculty. Computer consulting."

"With the U?" His face held a combination of surprise and reevaluation, the mixture as usual.

"Independent," Anneke answered automatically. She had long ago decided that *freelance* was too casual, the phrase "my own company" too pretentious. "Some academic work, some government, some business."

"Sounds interesting." He didn't sound interested; humani-

ties types, Anneke knew from frequent experience, often made a point of disdain for "electronic gadgetry."

"Barbara, I wanted to catch you anyway." Cleve lowered his voice. "When is the funeral?"

"There's not gonna be a funeral," she replied. "Rosa always said she didn't want one, she'd arranged ahead of time to be cremated. And anyway, they figured it'd be too hard on Ross." Barbara glanced meaningfully out into the courtyard, where the children were involved in some complicated activity. The older of the two boys was standing slightly aside, with the group but not of it. His small face looked pinched and withdrawn.

"Damn it, they're wrong," Cleve said angrily. "Ross adored his grandmother—he was named after her, for God's sake. He needs a chance to mourn her properly."

"He needs to forget about it." Barbara's thin lips tightened. "He'd only get all upset, dwellin' on it."

"But you can't pretend it didn't happen," Cleve argued. "My God, she only died last night, and you're behaving like she never existed."

"Was that what the ambulance was all about?" Anneke asked, suddenly remembering.

"Yeah," Barbara answered. "She lived over there"—she jerked her head toward the big Victorian house at the edge of the court—"with her son Harvey and his boy Ross. Harvey found her when he got home last night. She'd been sittin' up watching television when she went."

"Where was Ross?" Cleve asked sharply.

"Upstairs asleep. He slept right through it all, don't worry."

"What did she die of?" Cleve pursued. "Do they know yet?"

"Hell, she died of being seventy-eight years old, I guess," Barbara responded irritably.

"But she was a perfectly healthy woman," Cleve insisted.

"Oh, let it be, Cleve," Barbara snapped. "She's gone and

that's the end of it, and I'll never know what you saw in her anyway, an old woman like that, and a nasty one too, for a fact."

"Your definition of *nasty*, of course, is anyone who stands in your way," he said poisonously. "Good ol' T.G. probably broke out the champagne when the ambulance drove away."

"If you think I'm gonna say I'm sorry she's gone, you're mistaken," Barbara retorted, unmoved by his anger. "Anyway, I can't stand around talkin' all day, I'm not one of those spoiled college types who gets to sit around for a month and do nothing just 'cause it's Christmas break."

"What on earth was that all about?" Anneke asked as Barbara stalked away.

"Just that, with Rosa dead, there's nothing standing in the way of the project," Cleve said bitterly. But before Anneke could ask what project he meant, an errant football caught him neatly on the shin, followed by a tumble of breathless children.

"Hey, do I look like a goalpost?" He laughed.

"Sorry, Professor Marshall," Marcella gasped.

"*De nada.*" He patted her head, all signs of anger smoothed away. "How about you folks helping me unload Ms. Haagen's car. She seems to have succumbed to terminal white-sale fever."

"I can help!" Cashin shouted, racing toward the Alfa. "My daddy says I'm real strong!"

"We'll all help," Marcella said, following him.

"Be careful of the car!" Anneke called out anxiously. Thank God the cherished Alfa had been parked at the curb the night of the fire. She'd bought it, as a kind of defiance, after her husband left town with his twenty-three-year-old graduate assistant, fully aware of what a cliché the purchase was. But even as she told herself that "it's only a car," she acknowledged that sometimes things have symbolic importance even when the

symbol is a cliché—and that sometimes a thing becomes a cliché because of its underlying truth. Besides, she reasoned, at this point it was about the only personal possession she had left.

"Be careful, gang," Cleve echoed her. "You get the door"— he grinned at Anneke—"and I'll deploy the troops, okay?"

"Ready when you are," she capitulated.

By the time she deposited her own parcels on the table and shed her coat, the others arrived in procession, Cleve bringing up the rear with two bags of groceries.

"You know what?" Cashin said, depositing his burdens on the floor and eyeing the grocery bags. "We haven't had any cookies all day!"

"Well," Anneke said amid general laughter, "I just bought two big boxes, and they'll only make me fat if I eat them myself."

"All riiight!" Cashin crowed. "Cookies!"

"Are you sure we're not bothering you, Ms. Haagen?" Marcella asked anxiously.

"Not a bit," she replied, discovering somewhat to her surprise that it was true. The cottage felt better with people in it—more like a home. "I'll even make some hot chocolate."

While she heated milk in the microwave and arranged Pepperidge Farm cookies on a plate, she looked around the cottage, really seeing it for the first time. It was charming in its way, she admitted reluctantly, with a bright, airy quality despite its small size. In the kitchenette, a double casement window over the sink flooded the area with light; other casement windows next to the door opened toward the courtyard. On the north and south walls, under the beamed ceiling, light filtered through clerestory windows and brightened the surprisingly spacious main room. There were expanses of soft matte-finished wood that Anneke tentatively identified as birch, warming without overpowering.

Most of the furniture was inoffensive but uninspired, leaning to brown tweed and white Formica. But along the south wall, a built-in banquette surrounded by cantilevered bookshelves, also of birch, seemed to spring almost organically from the paneling. And for a wonder there was a comfortably spacious Formica-topped desk, with enough room for a computer and its associated peripherals. There was even an actual, full-size file cabinet.

In the bedroom, she knew, the architect had skimped on space. The double bed, which nearly filled the room, was set on a semidiagonal in one corner, flanked by a triangular night table of the same wood used throughout the cottage. There was also a small Formica-topped dresser. The far wall was all doors—one to the small bathroom, another to the closet. In this room, too, there were clerestory windows, along with the single casement over the night table.

"Do you always shop in job lots?" Cleve asked, taking a cookie from the plate and arranging himself on the floor.

"Only when I'm reduced to borrowing underwear," she retorted. Then, in response to his quizzical look: "My house burned to the ground Sunday night."

"My God." His eyes widened. "Totaled?"

"Completely. I got out with nothing but a bathrobe and slippers." She felt her throat close at the memory of the heat and flames, the terror-filled struggle with the recalcitrant bedroom window, the hysterical flight across the frozen lawn to the house next door.

"Can they salvage anything?" Cleve asked.

"They don't know yet." She spread her hands, pushing back memory. "The insurance company is sending someone in, but right now it's all under a couple of tons of ice."

"Well, at least you're insured," he said consolingly. "And you've found a decent place to live, too. Considering the Ann Arbor rental market, you were lucky to find this place."

"I suppose so," Anneke said grudgingly. For the last four days people had been telling her how lucky she was—to be alive, to be insured, to have found a new place. She thought if she heard the word one more time she would definitely scream. "It'll do for a while at least." She was still unwilling to concede the cottage's virtues. As if I'm being disloyal to the memory of my dead house, she jeered at herself.

Coming from St. Martin's Press in October 1995.

Build yourself a library of paperback mysteries to die for—DEAD LETTER

NINE LIVES TO MURDER by Marian Babson
When actor Winstanley Fortescue takes a nasty fall—or was he pushed?—he finds himself trapped in the body of Monty, the backstage cat.

_____ 95580-4 ($4.99 U.S.)

THE BRIDLED GROOM by J. S. Borthwick
While planning their wedding, Sarah and Alex—a Nick and Nora Charles of the 90's—must solve a mystery at the High Hope horse farm.

_____ 95505-7 ($4.99 U.S./$5.99 Can.)

THE FAMOUS DAR MURDER MYSTERY
by Graham Landrum
The search for the grave of a Revolutionary War soldier takes a bizarre turn when the ladies of the DAR stumble on a modern-day corpse.

_____ 95568-5 ($4.50 U.S./$5.50 Can.)

COYOTE WIND by Peter Bowen
Gabriel Du Pré, a French-Indian fiddle player and part-time deputy, investigates a murder in the state of mind called Montana.

_____ 95601-0 ($4.50 U.S./$5.50 Can.)

As storm clouds gather over Europe and FDR receives such guests as Albert Einstein, Joe Kennedy and crime buster Eliot Ness, Eleanor is thrust into danger much closer to home. One of the President's staff has been found dead, poisoned by cyanide mixed in his evening bourbon. Even worse, the accused killer is another White house aide, diminutive beauty Thérèse Rolland.

Although the police are determined to pin the crime on Thérèse, Eleanor is immediately convinced she is innocent. Calmly, but firmly, the First Lady uncovers a web of lies and secrets swirling around the Louisiana political machine...until another shocking murder is discovered. Suddenly, the investigation is taking Eleanor Roosevelt places no proper First Lady would ever go—to the darkest underside of society, and toward a shattering truth that lies within the White House itself!

An Eleanor Roosevelt Mystery

"Compelling!" —*Kirkus*

In prison, they call her the Sculptress for the strange figurines she carves—symbols of the day she hacked her mother and sister to pieces and reassembled them in a blood-drenched jigsaw. Sullen, menacing, grotesquely fat, Olive Martin is burned-out journalist Rosalind Leigh's only hope of getting a new book published.

But as she interviews Olive in her cell, Roz finds flaws in the Sculptress's confession. Is she really guilty as she insists? Drawn into Olive's world of obsessional lies and love, nothing can stop Roz's pursuit of the chilling, convoluted truth. Not the tidy suburbanites who'd rather forget the murders, not a volatile ex-policeman and her own erotic response to him, not an attack on her life.

MINETTE WALTERS
THE SCULPTRESS

"Creepy but compulsive...The assured British stylist doesn't let up on her sensitive probing of two tortured souls...Hard to put down."
—*The New York Times Book Review*